The Boy Next Door

CARRIE JACOBS

for Austin
my most favorite former teenager

Chapter One

Thump!

The familiar sound of a heavy package being unceremoniously dropped onto the front porch startled Kim Donahue, causing her to click the wrong button on the video she was recording. "Crap." That would need to be fixed.

Kim stood and stretched, pressing her hands to her aching lower back. It was time for a break anyway. As much as she loved her office – a converted sunroom off the kitchen – she'd been sitting at the computer too long.

On her way through the kitchen, she paused to scratch Sadie, her sweet calico cat, who sprawled in the middle of the island.

"What do you think the UPS man left us?"

Sadie ignored her, opting to lift her leg and groom herself in a most unladylike display.

Kim opened the door to see the UPS driver wave as he pulled his big brown truck away from the curb. She waved back, then picked up the box he'd left on the porch. It was slightly larger than a shoebox, heavy for its size, and from a big warehouse store, so there was no telling what might be inside. Carrying it back into the house, she set it on the kitchen island next to the cat.

A box? Now Sadie's interest was piqued. She sniffed the box and rubbed her cheek against the corner of the cardboard, marking it as hers.

"I don't think I ordered anything," Kim said, frowning. She got the scissors out of the drawer, but before she slit the tape, she realized the name on the label wasn't hers. "Nate Sanders? Who's that? And why's he using my address?" So weird.

Sadie rubbed the box again but didn't answer.

Kim inspected the label more closely. "Oh. Duh. I guess he's not. 168 Meadow Drive. Not 166. They must have finally sold the house next door." What an ordeal – when the previous owner passed away four years earlier, the family had literally come to blows in the front yard over the estate and then fought bitterly in court, all while airing the details of everyone's dirty laundry on social media, of course. Kim had felt bad about watching, but not bad enough to stop following the drama, which had finally died down months ago. She pulled on a hoodie. "I guess we'll find out."

She picked up the box. Sadie meowed and swiped her paw out, protesting the injustice of her box being taken away. "It's not ours."

Sadie flounced across the island and jumped to the floor, insulted.

"Yes, I know, Your Highness. Everything in the mortal realm belongs to you." Kim watched Sadie leave the kitchen, her tail winding around the door frame as she exited.

Her most-worn shoes waited neatly beside the front door. The day was reasonably warm for March, so she slipped on her flip flops and walked across the front porch and through the lawn to the house next door. The pretty blue vinyl siding was in good shape but could use a power wash after several years of neglect. The empty front porch needed a fresh coat of bright white paint and some decorations. Kim's mind churned with ideas. A rocking chair over here, a wooden welcome sign over there, perhaps a braided rug, and some hanging baskets or wrought iron lanterns would make the porch cozy and welcoming.

Kim climbed the three steps to the porch, then crossed to the front door, a fading dark blue that matched the shutters and complemented the light blue siding. A nice spring wreath would make a world of difference for the porch's curb appeal. She lifted her fist and knocked on the door.

Music played inside the house. She couldn't make out anything but the rhythmic drumbeats. She waited a full minute, then knocked again, louder. The music stopped and footsteps clomped from the back of the house. The door jerked open a crack.

"What!" a man demanded, his voice gruff and hostile.

Kim couldn't see much through the six-inch opening, other than to note that he was tall. "Hi. Are you Nate Sanders?"

"No." He slammed the door shut.

What the…? Kim stood with her mouth hanging open. She considered setting the package down next to the door and leaving, but nope. His reaction was uncalled for. Irritated, she rapped her knuckles against the door until it jerked open again.

An unfriendly scowl greeted her. "Go away."

What an ass.

Kim held up the box and shook it. "This package for Nate Sanders, 168 Meadow Drive, was delivered to my house."

His eyes shifted down to the box in her hands, narrowing suspiciously.

"I'm 166." She pointed to the cute yellow house across the lawns. "Is it yours or not?"

He didn't answer.

Exasperated, Kim rolled her eyes and turned to go. "You don't have to be a jerk. I'll just have UPS pick it back up."

"Wait." His voice wasn't exactly *friendly*, but it had lost the hostile edge. The door opened wider. "I'm Nate." She got her first good look at him. He definitely fit the bill for classic tall, dark, and handsome. Unfortunately, he also seemed to fit the bill for paranoid, weird, and unstable.

She pushed the box in his direction. "Kim."

He took the box, holding it gingerly as if it might bite him.

So much for being neighborly and friendly to the new guy. If any more of his packages landed on her doorstep, she'd just send them back. Since it would be pointless to waste another word on this jerk, she simply spun on her heels, went down the steps, and crossed the lawn back to her own house. She half-wondered if the package contained bomb parts or something. Wouldn't that be grand? Finally get a new neighbor, and he's the next Unabomber.

She slipped out of her flip flops, hung her hoodie up, and went to the bathroom to retouch her makeup and fluff her short blonde hair. What an odd interaction. Shaking her head, she put it out of her mind and went back to recording her *Fifteen Minutes to Fabulous* segment.

Chapter Two

Unsettled by the interruption, Nate locked the door. He peeked through the blinds, watching Kim – if that was her real name – as she crossed the yard and went into the house next door. When he was satisfied she wasn't coming back, he turned and eyed the package suspiciously. It wouldn't be the first time a fan had shown up at his house with a gift.

He double-checked the lock and went back to the kitchen to finish unpacking his plates and silverware. As he placed the spoons in the drawer, the tightness faded from his shoulders and the blood stopped thumping behind his ears. She hadn't seemed to recognize him, and she *did* walk over to the house next door and go inside. The last spoon in place, he finally remembered ordering the battery pack and parts for his ancient computer. He shook his head at himself. Way to be paranoid. And now his new neighbor definitely thought he was a lunatic. She was probably already on the phone, gossiping about him. Way to stay inconspicuous.

He used a butter knife to split the tape on the box. No lingerie or suggestive notes or flowers or books of romantic poems from a stranger who thought she was in love with him.

Nothing but the computer parts he'd ordered last week and had shipped to his new address.

Wasn't the whole point of moving to a small town in the middle of nowhere so he could live a normal life? Normal didn't mean behaving as though everyone he met was a crazed fan. How arrogant was that, anyway? Odds were good that there were at least a handful of people in Hickory Hollow who had never even heard of *Daystar Rising*. And if they had, odds were even better they wouldn't recognize him out of his alien makeup and prosthetic body parts. He needed to relax.

The thought of apologizing flitted through his mind, but he disregarded it. If she was actually his neighbor, he'd surely run into her again. And when he did, he'd act like a normal human being. That would be enough. Resolved, he finished unpacking the silverware and went to find the boxes that held his computer equipment.

He was standing in what would be an office, trying to decide which box to start unpacking, when his phone dinged with an incoming text.

Pick me up at 8.

Miranda. He shuddered. No, nope, huh-uh. He thought he'd heard the last of her. His fingers hesitated over the keyboard, then he typed out:

I'm out of town.

She immediately returned:

Srsly? On my BIRTHDAY?????

followed by a string of middle finger emojis and an angry face.

Typical. Nate shoved his phone back into his pocket. He'd been fool enough to think their on-set romance would last. Miranda was made for the spotlight, loving the red carpets and parties and interviews. He, not so much. Every ounce of chemistry between them had been scripted. On her end, at least. He'd thought there was a bit more to it, but thankfully he hadn't gotten up the nerve to actually tell her he'd been developing feelings for her. Even more thankfully, the feelings he had were mostly superficial and evaporated rather quickly.

After she decided producers would help her career more than fellow actors, their relationship existed only on camera, which suited him fine. Truth be told, he'd been a bit star-struck by her, and was probably attracted to the idea of her just as much, if not more, than to her as a person. Not that he'd ever gotten to know the real person under the façade. He doubted if anyone ever had. Or would.

Nate pushed the thoughts from his head. It didn't matter. She didn't matter. Right now, the only thing that mattered was getting the rest of the boxes unpacked. He'd moved in four days ago, and was sick and tired of the sea of brown cardboard. He emptied a box and tossed it to the far corner of the room.

A few hours later, his office, such as it was, was set up and his computer connected to the internet. An hour after that, the kitchen was mostly finished, all the cups and bowls and coffee pods had homes. He'd deal with the small appliances later.

He tackled the bedroom last, putting away extra sheets and pillowcases – things he hadn't thought of, but his mother had. He smiled. Some things never changed. She was always looking out for him, making sure he had his head on straight. She treated him the same whether he was a gopher handing out cups of coffee or a filthy rich superstar. He didn't consider himself a mama's boy, but Hickory Hollow's close proximity to his mom – a short fifteen minute drive – was a huge factor when he'd bought the house. Close… but not *too* close.

As if she heard him thinking of her, his phone rang. "Hey, Ma."

"Are you unpacked? Settled in?"

"Working on it. I'm putting away towels as we speak."

"Good. How's the town? Have you gotten out any?"

He hesitated, knowing she'd see right through any untruth. "No. I've been too busy unpacking and getting the house in order."

"Nathaniel. Don't become a hermit." No matter how old he was, that stern tone of hers never changed.

"I'm not." He hated the mildly defensive tone in his own voice. He might as well stamp his feet and declare that he was a grown man, dammit.

"I mean it. You need to get out and meet people and make some friends."

He snorted. "Friends. I've had enough friends to last a lifetime."

"*Real* ones."

"I can't seem to tell the difference." He sighed, not wanting to have a deep conversation with her.

Her voice turned soft. "Honey. Take people for how they are, not how you want them to be."

He knew exactly what she meant. He had a bad habit of listening to what people said and ignoring what they did. Until he had a cheating girlfriend and a stalker. Then the pendulum swung too far in the other direction and he stopped trusting everyone. Except his mother.

"You should get a dog."

He snapped out of his unpleasant walk down memory

lane. "What? Why would I get a dog? I'm never in one place long enough. It wouldn't be fair."

"You're not renting anymore. You're not acting anymore. You're looking to settle down and stay in one place. So get a dog."

It wasn't the worst suggestion. "Maybe I'll get a cat."

She went with it. "Or get a cat."

"Or a fish."

"There you go."

He kind of liked the idea. "I could get one of those big tropical tanks that takes up half the room."

"Maybe you should go to For Pet's Sake and ask them about setting up an aquarium."

"'For Pet's Sake?'" He liked a good pun as much as anyone, but that was really cheesy.

"Midge and Stan Foster own it. Ron used to play golf with Stan."

"Golf?" He couldn't imagine his stepdad playing golf without being bored.

She chuckled. "I'm pretty sure they spent most of their time in the clubhouse."

"Ah. That makes more sense."

"I think his clubs are still in the attic." She paused. "Anyway. That's your homework. Go out in public and talk to someone."

"Homework." It felt a little silly, but it was the same advice his therapist had given him months ago. He probably should have listened then.

"Yup." He could tell from her tone she thought he was going to argue.

"Okay." *You're not the boss of me.* His inner child knew darn well he'd do as she said. Not because she said it, mind you, but because she just happened to be right.

"Good. Next time we talk, I want to hear all about the town and a new friend or two or ten. Okay?"

"Town? Yes. Friends? Don't hold your breath."

"Hmm. I'll take it. For now. Love you."

"Love you, too." Nate tapped the phone to disconnect the call. Life would be simpler if he could just have everyone he met talk to his mother. She had some kind of built-in radar that detected decency – or lack thereof. It was unsettling when she'd instantly take a dislike to someone, because he'd never known her to be wrong. He wished he had that gift. It would have saved him a lot of trouble.

Chapter Three

Satisfied with the final edits, Kim pushed the button to send her video live. The newest episode of *Fifteen Minutes to Fabulous* would soon be on the computers, tablets, and phones of her nine and a half million followers. Soon to be ten million. The "little" video series everyone said would go nowhere was making her a very nice living.

She glanced at her watch. "Okay, Sadie, I need to go shopping before Jared gets home from school. You hold down the fort, okay?"

Kim grabbed her oversized purse and dropped her phone into it, then fished out her keys. In her car, she set the GPS for an antique shop she'd recently found. She'd been there two or three times in the past month, but it would take a while to memorize all the twists and turns on back roads it took to get there.

An old three-story sewing factory had been renovated into an antique and craft shop with all manner of home décor, from antique hand-carved rocking horses to wooden barrels to candles to soda crates to reclaimed fixtures and hardware from demolished properties.

As she followed the GPS's instructions, she thought through some of the painting ideas she had for outdoor spring decorations.

Fifteen Minutes to Fabulous was Kim's web channel. She posted new content every Monday and Thursday. Magic Mondays were all about transformation. She reviewed beauty and fashion products, demonstrated makeup techniques, and gave tips for updating and repurposing wardrobe items. Thrifty Thursdays were all about the home. Decorating, crafting, and cooking, all on a tight budget with occasional splurges. Her biggest draw was that everything she demonstrated could be done in fifteen minutes, which her time-crunched fans appreciated.

Pulling into a parking space, Kim tossed her sunglasses into her purse. She made her way inside and smiled at Fern. The friendly older woman stood behind the counter, a huge wooden and glass case that had been rescued from an old general store that was falling down near the Poconos. "Can I help you find anything?"

"I'm hoping you can. I'm looking for some windowpanes. Preferably smaller, with four panels." She held her hands about eighteen inches apart. "About this big, maybe a little bigger."

Fern nodded. "Second floor, left-hand side, about three-quarters of the way down the aisle."

"How do you know where everything is? Half the time, I can't even find a pen when I need one." Kim was impressed. Fern knew her shop inside and out.

Fern laughed. "I can never find a pen, either. I may have cheated a little on the windows. Ted brought a new load in just this morning from a house they tore down last week. How do you like the glassware you bought the other day?"

"Love it. The blue bottles are perfect on my kitchen windowsill."

"We got some red ones that would go nicely with them up on the third floor." Fern pointed toward the ceiling.

"I'll take a look. Thanks."

A customer came through the door, so Kim took the opportunity to walk away while Fern was distracted. A nugget of an idea popped into her mind. She should invite Fern to be a guest on her show. Maybe they could even record it on location. Suddenly, the idea of a whole new day of content formed. She could invite local crafters and bakers and decorators to share their own tips. She pulled out her phone and sent herself a message. This wasn't an idea she wanted to forget.

She browsed through aisles of antique toys, books, and housewares. The entire building smelled of scented candles and history. On the second floor, she found the windows and selected two. Both were framed with solid wood featuring peeling white paint. Perfect.

Kim looked to make sure there was nothing breakable behind her, then slung her purse over her shoulder so she could grip the two windows and maneuver them down the narrow stairs. She carried them to the first floor and leaned them against the counter. "Is it okay if I leave these here?"

"Of course." Fern sat on a stool, reading a magazine.

"I won't be long."

"Take your time. They'll be fine right there."

"Thank you." Kim trotted back up the stairs and turned the corner to the next set of stairs that would take her to the third floor. There, she walked through the aisles of dishes and glassware. She found the red bottles Fern had mentioned. She held one up to catch the light from the window. It glinted brightly, just like the blue glass had. She selected two bottles and moved to the next display.

The wooden floor creaked behind her. She glanced back and saw a vaguely familiar, tall man studying an antique typewriter at the far side of the aisle. He looked up and caught her gaze, then immediately turned away, looking as though he'd been caught doing something wrong.

Kim raised an eyebrow, trying to place him, but her mind was more focused on the new idea for hosting guests on the channel. The stairs creaked as the man left her alone on the third floor. She finished browsing the shelf of glassware and went down to the main floor to pay for her items. Fern handed Kim her change, then wrapped the glass bottles with thick paper and carefully put them in a bag, which Kim put into her purse. She got a firm hold on the window frames and walked to the door.

"Here, let me get that for you," the tall man said, pushing the door open and stepping through to hold it for her.

That voice. Definitely the package jerk from next door. *Great.* "Thanks." She caught his face in profile as she stepped past him. He wasn't half bad looking. "You're my new neighbor."

He fidgeted with his hoodie zipper and looked around at everything but her. "Yeah," he said slowly, "I thought you looked familiar. Hello." His eyes fixed on the ground, he was clearly awkward and uncomfortable.

Okay, this is weird. Maybe he just doesn't like people. Kim said, "Well, have a good day." She walked down the stairs to the parking lot, then carefully leaned the windows against the side of her SUV while she located her keys. She popped the hatch open and loaded the windows. From the corner of her eye, she subtly watched Nate get into his car. He was definitely odd. Oh, well. At least he wasn't hostile this time.

Chapter Four

Nate shook his head at himself. Instead of disabusing her of the notion he was some kind of weirdo, he'd reinforced it by being shifty and tongue-tied. He missed the days when he was confident. Or at least normal. Back before going out in public filled him with dread – and fear. Back before *Daystar Rising* exploded into an international phenomenon almost overnight, spawning conventions and theme cruises and rabid fans with no concept of boundaries. Back before he was Qaaxag, alien warrior and savior of Planet Earth.

Back when he was Just Nate. Wannabe actor, production assistant, glorified coffee gopher, waiting tables on the side, enjoying life but struggling to make ends almost meet. Now he struggled with everything *but* money.

The GPS directed him back to Meadow Drive, a road that was starting to feel familiar. The four houses on this street were spaced a good distance apart, each sitting on a two-acre lot, giving them plenty of space. He'd bought the property because it backed up against conservation woodland, so there would never be any more houses on this street than there were right now.

He pushed the button to open his garage door, then pulled his car – a two-year-old gray Chevy Malibu – in. The garage door closed, and he let out a deep breath. Releasing the steering wheel, he frowned and stretched out his fingers, the joints groaning in protest. He hadn't realized he'd been gripping it so tightly. So much for not being anxious about going out in public.

Leaning back, he tried reasoning with himself. He'd gone out and nothing bad had happened. No one followed him. No one ambushed him in the antique shop. He'd survived an unexpected meeting with Kim. No one drove their car up over the sidewalk and nearly killed him.

Nothing bad happened.

He repeated that over and over until his pounding heart slowed, then went into the house. He couldn't keep from checking over his shoulder and locking the garage door behind him, then doing a quick walk-through of the house to make sure nothing was out of place. It was better, though. Now, he could just glance into a room. He didn't have the overwhelming compulsion to check the closets and cupboards and under the bed, before he could relax. It was progress.

Maybe later, he'd venture back out and try the grocery store. For now, though, he turned on the radio and unpacked more boxes, considering that his mother might be right about finding a new therapist. Or getting a cat. It would be nice to have a cat to talk to while unpacking the endless boxes.

A dog barked somewhere on the block. Nate pulled back the curtain and looked around. The neighbor was pulling into her garage. Kim. He wondered what she thought of him, then immediately wondered why he cared. She'd probably completely written him off after his strange behavior. Who could blame her?

At least he knew he was acting strange. That was progress,

right? After he'd gotten out of the hospital, he had a lot of trouble differentiating between healthy skepticism and rampant paranoia.

While he looked out the window, a school bus stopped at the end of their street. A tall, lanky teenage boy got off the bus, slung his backpack over his shoulder, and walked past the first two houses. Nate wondered for a second if the boy was heading to *his* house, then chastised himself for being ridiculous when the kid went into Kim's without so much as a glance in Nate's direction.

He let the blinds fall back into place. No more messing around. He had to get himself together.

Chapter Five

From her office, Kim heard the front door open and close. "Jared? That you?" It was a dumb question – who else would it be?

"Yeah," he mumbled. The unmistakable *whump* of his backpack dropping onto the floor sounded right before his footsteps tromped into the kitchen.

Kim checked the clock. Quarter after four. He'd had gym class in the afternoon, so he'd no doubt be starving. "There's chicken parmesan ready in the crockpot if you're hungry. Extra mozzarella's in the fridge."

"Okay."

She heard rummaging in the plate cupboard and walked out to the kitchen to talk to him. She leaned her hip against the island and watched him spoon chicken onto his plate. "How was your day?"

"Fine." He put the lid back on the crockpot as he gave her the one-word answers that were typical for any fourteen-year-old boy.

"What'd you do in gym class?"

He made a disgusted noise. "Volleyball." He grabbed the

package of shredded mozzarella out of the fridge and piled a handful on his chicken.

"Did you turn in your essay for English?"

"Yeah."

"How was your science test?"

"Okay."

"And?"

He shrugged.

"Was it graded yet?" She pulled open the silverware drawer and handed him a fork.

"Yeah."

"What did you get?" It was like pulling teeth to get details.

"B."

"That's great."

He shrugged again.

"I'm really proud of you."

His eyes flicked upward through the curly dark hair hanging in his face, and the tiniest ghost of a smile curved his lips for a split second. He held up his plate and gave her a nod. "Thanks for dinner."

She smiled and watched her nephew retreat from the kitchen, grab his backpack, and head up to his room on the second floor. The kid had been through so much, and he'd come such a long way in the year he'd been with her. A year filled with so much misery and pain. She was glad it was over.

She heard the floorboards above her creak and knew Jared was settling in front of his computer, where he'd stay until the middle of the night, chatting with his friends.

It was a compromise she'd made. He could have unlimited time on the computer, as long as he kept his grades up and stayed out of trouble in school, and he always gave her his passwords. So far, he'd lived up to his end of the bargain. She wasn't thrilled with the amount of time he spent online, but it wasn't a hill she was willing to die on.

She fixed herself a plate and ate at the kitchen table with her iPad, scrolling through trending topics so she could plan her next few video segments. Most days, she still couldn't believe she was earning a living – a nice one at that – doing videos. It was way too much fun to be considered work. Even the editing, which was tedious at times, challenged her in a good way. She looked at her show as a great stepping stone to the ultimate dream career: her own show on the Home Network.

When she'd put her plate in the dishwasher, she returned to her office to finish editing the video she'd be posting the following Thursday. It was dark outside when she finally closed the laptop and clicked off her lamp.

Upstairs, she knocked on Jared's door. He immediately said, "Come in."

Pushing the door open, she leaned in and was surprised to find him sitting on his bed instead of at the computer. "Hey. I'm heading to bed."

His curls were a curtain over the top half of his face. He flicked his head to the side, exposing an eye. "Night."

"Everything okay?"

He shrugged.

"I figured you'd be online."

He held up a book. "I have to finish reading this for Lit."

"*Jane Eyre*. I loved that book. Do you like it?"

"It's okay, I guess. I liked *Animal Farm* better."

Kim scrunched her eyebrows together. "I haven't read that one in years and years, so I don't remember much about it."

He didn't volunteer anything.

"You sure you're okay?"

He nodded, but a second later he sniffled and swiped his hand across his face.

Kim hesitated, then walked across the room and sat on the edge of his bed. "Hey. You can talk to me."

A tear trickled down his cheek.

She felt his breath change, like he was gathering the courage to speak. She sat still, waiting. The minutes ticked by.

His voice was a whisper. "I miss my mom."

"Oh, honey, so do I." It was mostly true. She missed the woman her sister had been before her very essence was stolen away by drug addiction. She missed the woman her sister could – and should – have been. The wasted body she'd last seen in a satin-lined casket a year earlier had belonged to Danielle, but in truth, her sister had been gone for years.

"Don't be mad." His voice was small, and it was a sharp reminder that even though he was tall and even had a stray hair or two on his upper lip, he was still a child.

"Why would I be mad?" She reached out and put her hand on the worn knee of his black jeans.

His shoulders rounded, making him seem to sink further into himself. "Because you do stuff for me, but I still want my mom." His words broke off into a sob that crushed her heart like a vice.

Kim scooted up toward him and wrapped her arms around his bony shoulders. "Jared. I do stuff for you because I love you. Of course, you miss your mom. I... I'm not trying to ever take her place. I want you to talk about your mom. Jared, she loved you more than anything else in this world, and she tried so hard to do right by you." She left out her own judgmental opinion about how Danielle had failed spectacularly. "I love you. You're safe with me. And that means anything you want to talk about, I'm here for you. Okay?"

He let himself be pulled into her embrace and nodded against her shoulder. As the minutes passed, the stiffness in his body relaxed. He didn't pull away, so she sat and simply held him, consciously curbing her natural inclination to babble and fill the silence. After a while, he relaxed and leaned back against his headboard. Kim grabbed a few tissues from the box on his desk for him. A framed picture of his mother smiled at her. She wished Danielle was here right now so she could force her to see what she'd done to her son. What she'd done to the entire family.

"Thanks," he mumbled as he wiped his eyes and his nose.

"Do you want to talk any more?"

He shook his head. His dark curls, so like his mother's, swished across his face and brushed his shoulders. "No thanks. I gotta finish this." He held up the book.

"Okay." She pushed his hair away from his face and kissed his forehead. "Good night. I love you."

He gave her a half-hearted but genuine smile. "Night, Aunt Kim."

She stood and left his room, pulling the door shut gently behind her. In her bedroom, she let out a long breath and pressed her forehead to the wall. She loved her sister, but she hated her, too. More importantly, she loved Jared with all her heart, but he shouldn't be here. He should be living at home with his parents, being a regular kid with regular problems, not grieving and traumatized, and living in the shadow of what they'd done.

Sadie sat on the bed, fastidiously cleaning her paws. She stopped mid-lick and stared at Kim.

"I think I need to get him back into therapy. Poor kid needs to talk to somebody, and I don't think I'm the right person."

Sadie slowly put her leg down and flicked her tail, her gaze still locked on Kim.

"I'll call first thing in the morning and make him an appointment."

The tail flicked again.

"I know he's not going to like it. But it helped him a lot, and I think it'll be good for him."

Sadie stared.

"Don't give me that. Okay, fine. Maybe I should make an appointment for myself, too."

Stretching, Sadie finally turned her attention away from Kim, then curled up in the middle of Kim's pillow.

"Yeah, don't tell me animals don't understand exactly what's going on," Kim muttered.

Chapter Six

Nate got up, determined to do something his mother would approve of. Namely, get out of the house. It had been two weeks since he'd ventured out to the antique store, and since then he hadn't been anywhere except two late-night quick trips to the grocery store.

He finished shaving and grimaced at his face in the mirror. He'd always been – and would always be – pale, but his face hadn't seen actual sunlight in too long. Maybe now that the weather was turning warmer, he could convince himself to start running again. Maybe even rejoin a gym. He flossed and stared hard into his own blue eyes.

"Today is Opposite Day. We're gonna ignore those instincts and pretend to be a normal human being." He high fived the mirror.

It was early, so he decided the perfect thing would be to find a place to have breakfast. For some reason, he imagined the breakfast crowd was milder and less likely to be overwhelming than the dinner rush.

His hands trembled, but only a little, as he buttoned his shirt and tucked it into his jeans. He checked and double checked that he had his wallet, phone, and keys. "Quit stalling or we'll miss breakfast," he muttered.

He backed his car out of the garage and hit the button to close the garage door. The two best breakfast options were Sonny's diner, just a few minutes away, or the Cracker Barrel that was a fifteen-minute drive. His first impulse was to stay close, so he made a left and headed to Cracker Barrel.

The busy parking lot made him anxious, but he pulled into a space and took a deep breath. It was breakfast. Just breakfast. His stomach rumbled at the vision his mind conjured of pancakes soaked with warm syrup. Just inside those doors.

On the way to the entrance, he almost lost his nerve, but the doors flew open and a family came out. A grinning little girl held the door open for him.

Nate managed a smile. "Thanks," he said as he accepted the gesture and walked through. The general store lobby smelled of coziness and breakfast food. His anxiety noted that there were plenty of places to duck and hide if he needed to. So far, so good.

He glanced over the spring decorations for sale on his way to the hostess stand.

A chipper hostess said, "Good morning, sir. How many in your party?"

"Uh, just one."

She tapped at something behind the counter he couldn't see then smiled up at him. "It'll be about a twenty minute wait."

"Okay." His mouth went dry. The cluttered area felt like it was closing in. Before he could tell her to scratch his name off the list, she moved away and called out, "Donahue?"

He turned around ran into a woman. "*OhI'msosorry.*" He took a step back and his hip knocked into a rack of audiobooks. Every head in the crowded room spun to look right at him. "Sorry. I... sorry." Blood pounded behind his ears as his embarrassment multiplied. He couldn't have just run into a stranger. Of course not. He'd run smack dab into Kim.

Her hand steadied the rack of audiobooks. "Sorry, I took the corner too fast. Are you okay?"

"Yeah, yes, fine, my fault." He swallowed hard and stepped aside to let her pass so he could get out of here and go back home. He could get pancakes another time.

She walked past him, then abruptly turned back. "Do you want to share a table, Nate?"

No immediately sprang to his lips, but he hesitated. Opposite Day. Instead of an answer, he said, "Why?"

Her eyebrows rose.

He expected her to decide it was too much trouble and walk away, but instead, she challenged him. "Why not?"

His throat constricted a little. "Um." He couldn't think of a good reason. "Okay."

She smiled. "Great."

The hostess was already erasing his name from the waiting list. She grabbed a second menu and said, "Right this way." She wound her way through the crowded restaurant to a table for two along the windows. "Your server will be right with you."

His legs were shaky. They itched to run out of the building, away from everyone who had witnessed his humiliation. He forced his breathing to slow and managed to thank the hostess. He waited for Kim to pick her seat, then sank gratefully into the chair across from her.

The words on his paper menu swam together. The voices from the crowd felt unnaturally loud. He wanted to crawl under the table. But it was Opposite Day, so he made himself glance around. He was glad he did. Nobody was pointing or laughing. In fact, nobody was looking in their direction at all. He relaxed a fraction, then turned his attention back to his menu.

Kim asked, "What are you getting?"

"Pancakes. And sausage. You?" As his stomach calmed, his appetite increased, helped along by the delicious smells of syrup and coffee filling the air.

"French toast and bacon."

"Sounds good."

The waiter came and took their orders, then returned with their drinks – coffee and ice water for Kim, orange juice and ice water for Nate – just as the silence between them started to feel unbearably awkward.

Nate focused on spooning ice out of his water and into his orange juice. He could feel Kim watching and suddenly felt the need to explain. "If I order my orange juice with ice they put too much in and then it gets watered down and you don't get nearly as much juice..." Opposite Day. He snapped his mouth shut, fighting the impulse to keep rambling.

She nodded like she understood. "I like ice in my juice, too. I don't know how people drink it room temperature."

Nate wasn't sure what to say, so he took a sip and said nothing.

Kim stirred one creamer into her coffee, then another. "So, what do you do, Nate?"

His eyes darted up to meet hers, a fleeting second of panic slicing through him. "Oh, um, I, uh… nothing right now. I was in uh, an accident, and had to leave my old job – career – so I'm figuring things out right now." There. It was the truth, and it didn't kill him to say it.

"I'm sorry you had an accident. Life has a funny way of crapping all over our plans, doesn't it?"

A small but genuine laugh escaped him. "It sure does. How about you?"

"Believe it or not, I –"

"Oh my gosh!" Two women hurried over to their table. "I

was just saying to my friend that I know you. Well, I mean, we've never met," she gushed, "but I feel like I know you. I watch you all the time."

Fear spiked through his chest. His fingers clenched the edge of the table and tensed to shove his chair back. Just as he was about to bolt, the waiter appeared with their food, blocking his exit. He frantically wondered if he could dive through the glass.

"We used your video for my daughter's prom hair. The one with the updo and spiral curls. It turned out beautifully. I have a picture." She tapped at her phone.

Wait, what?

The waiter cleared his throat. The women moved to the side enough for him to reach around them and set the food down.

The adrenaline pumping through his veins slowed enough for him to finally realize the women were fawning over Kim. They had exactly zero interest in him. He loosened his grip on the edge of the table and tried to understand what was happening.

Kim said, "I'm so glad it worked out for her." She shot him an apologetic look.

"Here's a picture." The woman shoved her phone toward Kim's face.

"She's beautiful. Her hair turned out perfectly."

"Here's the back," the woman said, swiping across her phone. "And we got her dress on that formalwear thrift website you linked a while back. It was only thirty dollars!"

"Gorgeous."

The second woman cleared her throat and touched her enthusiastic friend's arm. "Sorry to interrupt your breakfast." She jerked her head toward the exit.

The first woman waved her off. "Oh, yes, so sorry to disturb you."

Nate didn't think she seemed all that sorry.

"No problem." Kim smiled patiently.

"Would you mind taking a picture with us?"

"I'd be delighted."

The woman shoved her phone at Nate. His hands trembled a little as he snapped a few pictures of the women crowding behind Kim.

"Thank you so much," the woman gushed as she grabbed her phone back and immediately checked the pictures.

"No problem," Kim repeated. "You ladies have a wonderful day. Thanks so much for watching."

"I'll be sure to tag you on Insta."

The second woman finally pulled the first away.

Nate sipped at his water, trying to combat his dry mouth.

Kim didn't seem bothered, even though she was apologetic. "Sorry about that. I don't get recognized very often. It always seems to be when I'm eating though." She poured syrup on her French toast. "I guess that kind of answers your question, doesn't it? I have a video channel. I do hair, makeup, and fashion videos on Mondays, and on Thursdays I do videos for the home. Crafts and cooking and stuff."

"Huh." His hammering heart was returning to normal and he forced his breathing to be steady. "That... interesting."

"It is." She sounded a little defensive. "It's a lot of fun, and the best part is that I make my own schedule. It's been a life-saver since Jared came to live with me."

The constricting of his throat had released, and he felt mostly back to normal. "Jared?" He'd no more than asked when he remembered the boy getting off the school bus.

"My nephew. He's been living with me almost a year now."

She paused as though she was carefully considering her next words. "His parents died."

"I'm sorry." The words were automatic, but they were true. He couldn't imagine losing his parents at such a young age.

"His mom was my sister. The father's family isn't in the picture."

He caught the disgust when she said 'father.' "You didn't like Jared's dad?"

"Jared's dad murdered my sister and then killed himself."

Nate's fork froze mid-way to his mouth. "Oh." He felt like he should say something more, but what?

Her cheeks reddened. "I'm sorry, I shouldn't have just blurted that out." She managed a smile. "Wow, look at me oversharing."

"I shouldn't have pried. Sorry."

Kim raised an eyebrow. "You weren't. Not at all." She fidgeted with her napkin. "Your turn. Tell me something about your family."

Nate thought about his family. "Mine's pretty boring."

"Boring is good."

"My mom and stepdad live about twenty minutes from here. My biological father left when I was a kid." He didn't mention that he had shown up, supposedly wanting a relationship, after he'd learned about Nate's fame with *Daystar Rising*. Or that he periodically showed up on Nate's credit report, trying to open new cards and lines of credit in his name.

"Sorry to hear that."

He shrugged. "Water under the bridge. My stepdad's been around since I was three, so he's always been my dad anyway."

"Is that what brought you to Hickory Hollow? So you could be close to family?"

"Partly." He had no obligation to share anything with her,

but he didn't want to alienate her, either. He had a feeling they could be friends, and that was something he sorely needed. His words were halting. "After the… accident, I needed to… not be where I was anymore."

"Too many memories?"

"Yeah. And too many people in my business. I couldn't breathe." He hadn't meant to add that last part.

Kim nodded. "I get it. I mean, I know it's not the same, but after my sister died, I couldn't even go to the grocery store without people walking up to me asking what happened and offering their opinions on her life and her choices. Like we didn't know. It got worse when my husband walked out and word about *that* got around."

"Right after your sister died?"

"Yup."

"Nice guy." It wasn't that hard to imagine, though. He'd met plenty of people who had zero empathy and took narcissism to epic levels.

She shook her head. "Ick. Enough about that. Are you getting settled in to your new house? You've been here, what, a month?"

"Almost six weeks. I'm settled in for the most part." He ate the last bite of sausage. "I got so sick of seeing cardboard everywhere. I started just putting stuff wherever it would go, so I probably won't be able to find anything when I need it." He was finally relaxed enough to take in the details about Kim. Her short blonde hair, perfectly subtle makeup, warm brown eyes, and two tiny pearl earrings in each earlobe that matched a pearl dangling from a delicate silver chain around her neck. She was quite pretty.

Those brown eyes glanced up and met his. The corners crinkled with amusement. "That's what Walmart's for. Midnight runs for towels and silverware. Or phone chargers."

"That sounds like the voice of experience." His heart rate was finally back to normal. The sweat he'd felt beading on his face had dried. "Did you move in recently?"

"About six years ago, but I'm still traumatized. And I know I have a set of expensive towels in a box somewhere in the purgatory that is my attic. Moving is the worst."

Nate nodded in agreement. "I don't plan to do it again for a very long time."

"Same." Kim laughed. "If I do, I'll sell the house furnished and just start over from scratch. It'd be easier." With a jolt, Nate realized he'd been focused on Kim and hadn't been scanning the room for possible threats since the two overzealous women had left their table. It felt strange to have a moment of normalcy, and then it felt twice as bad when it came crashing back over him.

The waiter came around with drink refills and laid their check on the table.

"Crap. I didn't ask him to split the check." Kim craned her neck, looking for the server.

Nate picked up the slip of paper. "Let me. Please. I'd probably still be in the lobby if you hadn't taken pity on me."

"You don't have to do that."

"I'd like to. Really." He meant it. There weren't words to express to Kim how appreciative he was of this bit of normalcy.

"I'll leave the tip," she conceded.

"Great." He waited while she fished in her massive purse and put a generous tip on the table, then stood and followed her through the maze of tables to the general store, where the row of cash registers was. After he paid the check, they walked outside.

Kim poked her thumb over her shoulder. "I'm parked over there. Thanks for breakfast."

"Thanks for sharing your table. And you're welcome."

She slipped a pair of large sunglasses on and said, "It was fun. We should do it again sometime."

Nate's eyebrows rose and his tongue froze in his mouth. He managed to nod and choke out, "Yeah."

"See you." Kim turned and walked to her car.

Nate watched her walk away, trying not to read too much into her comment, but he couldn't ignore the brand new flutter in his belly.

It felt a lot like hope.

Chapter Seven

Kim jammed the key in the ignition and stuck her tongue out at her reflection in the visor mirror. "Gaaaah, really? Let's do this again. How freaking lame can you be? Don't answer that."

Okay. So Nate wasn't a complete weirdo. She didn't know what made her invite him to share her table, other than the pang of sympathy she'd felt because he'd looked so miserable and out of place, but she was glad she had. And glad he'd accepted. They had more in common than she'd thought from their previous interactions.

She drove home and set up to record her next video. She showed how to make faux etched-glass using the windows she'd picked up at the antique shop, and showed examples she'd premade of glassware and picture frames. "These are perfect for gifts," she said to the camera. "I especially like to personalize wine glasses for wedding gifts."

As she always did, she pretended the camera was a good friend she was teaching. She made lots of direct eye contact, spoke clearly, and made sure to walk through each step, leaving out no details. A couple of times she had to redo a line or fix a mistake that would be edited out. An hour later, she was done shooting and after a bathroom break, she was ready to start editing. She'd just sat down at the computer when her phone rang.

She glanced at the screen and realized it was the school. She answered, curious and concerned.

"Ms. Donahue, this is Owen Dupek. There was an incident with Jared, and we're going to need you to come down to the school."

Kim was shoving her feet into her shoes and closing the laptop before he finished the sentence. She asked the principal, "Is he okay?"

"He's fine." His tone was brusque.

"What happened?"

"We'll discuss it when you get here, if you don't mind."

She did mind, but said, "I'll be there in ten minutes."

"Thank you."

She itched to text Jared's phone, but assumed he was in the office and wouldn't be able to see it anyway, let alone respond. Driving a little faster than she should, she turned into the parking lot of the middle school and jerked to a stop in a space along the sidewalk. She practically ran to the huge doors and rang the buzzer.

A bored voice droned, "Can we help you?"

"Kim Donahue. I'm here to see Mr. Dupek."

"For what purpose?"

Kim glared into the little glass eye of the camera. "He's expecting me."

"Do you have an appointment?"

"Sure."

"Are you a parent?"

Seething, Kim gripped the handles of her purse. The school secretary was a thousand years old and had been a snotty bitch even back when Kim was a student here. She knew exactly who Kim was and she knew perfectly well she wasn't techni-cally a parent. "He asked me to come in immediately. Shall I call and let him know I'm here, or are you letting me in?" Anxiety and worry for Jared, combined with her annoyance, had left her with zero patience.

After a long silence, the door mechanism clicked loudly. She grabbed the handle and yanked it open.

Kim used the walk down the long hallway to take some deep breaths. It wouldn't do any good to get into a confronta-tion with the secretary, no matter how many generations of teenagers would cheer her on.

She pushed open the door to the office.

The gatekeeper scowled. "Can I help you?"

Kim bit back the sarcastic comment that leapt to her tongue. She was saved from responding by Mr. Dupek's appearance in the doorway. The first thing she noticed was his stupid tie with wild cartoon bunnies all over it.

"Ms. Donahue. Come in, please."

Kim followed him through the door and gasped. Jared sat in a poorly padded chair in front of Mr. Dupek's desk. His lip was split open and he had the beginnings of a black eye. She hunkered down in front of him, putting her finger under his chin to lift his face so she could get a better look. "Jared, what happened?"

Jared shrugged, his gaze locked on the floor.

"Ms. Donahue, Jared was involved in an altercation." He walked around to his chair but remained standing, his hands resting on his hips, his stupid tie askew.

Kim turned away from Jared and faced the principal. "I can see that. What happened?"

"Please have a seat."

Kim stood, unwilling to let him have the textbook upper hand in the seated/standing powerplay he was attempting.

Her father was a cop, and had taught her how to stand her ground in any situation. Even though she knew he wouldn't – or couldn't – tell her, she asked, "Where's the other kid?"

He surprised her with an answer. "Back in class." But it sure wasn't the answer she'd expected.

"Why? How is he being punished?"

"He's not. Jared was the aggressor."

Kim blinked rapidly, struck stupid by words that made no sense. "You'd better start at the beginning."

The principal finally sat down, so she sank into the chair beside Jared, perching on the edge, her back straight, her hand protectively resting on the armrest between her and Jared. He was hunched down into his hoodie, staring at the floor, his curls covering most of his face. She glanced down and saw angry red scrapes across Jared's knuckles.

Mr. Dupek cleared his throat. "It began with an unfortunate exchange on social media. Some students were posting inappropriate comments about and to Jared."

Kim swung her gaze to him. "And what was his response to these posts?"

"He didn't respond, as far as we could see."

Kim gritted her teeth. "Then it's hardly an *exchange*, is it? What did these posts say?"

"We're looking into it."

Oh, no, she was not going to accept some stupid canned generic response. "If you know he didn't respond, you obviously know exactly what the posts said. You called me down here, and I expect to leave here knowing the whole story." Every nerve ending jittered with frustrated energy that had no outlet.

He shifted uncomfortably. "The posts seemed to mostly be in reference to… Jared's unfortunate situation with his parents."

She'd always thought "seeing red" was a just figure of speech. It wasn't. Dark red spots danced at the edges of her vision. Her fingers clenched the armrest. "Go on." The words felt like venom as they left her mouth.

"The exchange happened last evening. This morning, presumably when Jared was made aware of the posts, he took matters into his own hands. Instead of reporting the incident, he got into a fight. It was a completely inappropriate response, and we have a zero-tolerance policy for fighting."

"What is the punishment for the other students involved?" The red haze still clung, blocking the periphery of the room from her sight.

"Jared is the only one being punished at this time."

Kim's legs tensed, itching to leap to her feet and grab the principal by his stupid crooked bunny tie. "Excuse me? What about your zero-tolerance policy on bullying?"

Mr. Dupek leaned back in his chair and tented his fingers. "Unfortunately, that happened off school property, so it's outside our purview… our *reach*," he clarified.

"I'm aware of the definition of 'purview,' Mr. Dupek."

"That's not true," Jared finally spoke. "They were snapchatting all morning in class."

"If that's true, we'll look into it."

Kim felt Jared trembling through his hoodie. "If? So, you're saying Jared just walked in and started hitting people for no reason."

"Well, not exactly."

"Then what, *exactly*?"

The principal gave her a smile he'd probably learned at a seminar on how to soothe irate parents, given by some HR specialist who'd never actually seen an irate parent. "It seems that some of the students made some comments to Jared about the social media exchange, and it was after one of these comments that he assaulted one of the students."

"What were the comments?"

"We're looking into that. Irregardless, the comments wouldn't excuse a physical assault."

Irregardless? Seriously? Kim's opinion of him sank even lower. "No, but the comments *would* constitute bullying, and that *did* happen on school property, so what are you planning to do about it?"

"Ms. Donahue," he began, sounding like he was addressing a petulant kindergartener. "We can't lose sight of the fact that Jared assaulted another student."

"He was also assaulted. Unless you think he slammed his own face into a locker?"

"The other student was reprimanded."

"In violation of your policy."

"Excuse me?"

"Your zero-tolerance policy on fighting. Which states that any students participating in a physical fight will be suspended, *regardless* of who started it."

"Every situation is handled on a case-by-case basis."

"Case by case? District policy is crystal clear. As is your policy on bullying. There is no room for interpretation."

"Please calm down."

Kim actually smiled. "Did you just tell me to calm down? Because I'm pointing out your inappropriate response to this situation? Your violation of your own policy – excuse me, multiple policies?"

"I see we won't be making any progress with this meeting. Jared is suspended for two days, plus the rest of today."

"Can he get his assignments before I take him home?"

"No, I don't want him disrupting classes."

Kim fought the urge to leap across the desk and strangle

him. "So not only are you unjustly punishing him, you also want him to fall behind in his classes."

"I realize his situation is difficult, but we have to ensure the safety of all our students."

"Except Jared."

"Ms. Donahue-"

"We're done here." Kim stood. "We'll be stopping at Jared's locker to get his books. Unless you're having us escorted off the property, of course."

"There's no need for sarcasm. We decided not to involve law enforcement. This time."

The only comment she could make would have made the situation worse, so she ignored him. She waited for Jared to stand, and put her hand on his back as she followed him out of the office and to the hallway his locker was in.

Jared's hands shook as he fumbled with the combination lock until the metal door swung open. He shoved his books and notebooks into his backpack.

The bell sounded, marking the end of the class period.

Jared froze, his eyes wide and darting up to the speaker.

"Let's go." Kim slammed his locker shut and led him to the closest exit, even though it was around the building from where she'd parked.

In the car, he fastened his seatbelt and stared at the floor.

Kim shoved the key in the ignition and tried not to scream. She bashed her palms against the steering wheel.

"I'm sorry, Aunt Kim." His voice was a whisper.

"No. Don't you dare apologize. I don't know who he thinks he is." She took a deep breath and took a good look at his face, taking a moment to let her anger cool. "Please tell me the other kid looks worse than you."

He glanced up at her. "Yeah."

"Good." She took a deep breath and backed out of the parking space. "Did you see the posts with your own eyes?"

There was a long silence. "Yeah."

"Tell me, Jared. Everything."

He shrunk back against the seat; his face hidden by the hood of his sweatshirt. "I don't want to talk about it," he mumbled.

"I know you don't. But we're going to." Kim hated feeling like a hardass, but she needed to know how bad the situation was.

The drive home was quiet, the silence broken only by the low radio. When she pulled into the garage, she turned and put her hand on Jared's arm. "I'm on your side."

His hood nodded.

"Let's go inside and talk." He got out of the car and trudged into the house like he was being marched to his execution.

Kim tossed her purse on the table inside the door and kicked her shoes off. "Iced tea?"

He shrugged but followed her into the kitchen. She poured two glasses of tea and set them on the island counter, then sat on one of the barstools. "Okay, kiddo, start at the beginning."

Jared sighed heavily but sat across from her. "It's no big deal."

"Nope, not doing that."

He stared into his glass.

Sadie came into the kitchen and jumped onto the island, then stepped down onto Jared's legs. She head-booped his chin, then curled up on his lap, purring.

"How long have these kids been messing with you?"

Shrug.

"Is it the same kids who were picking on you back before Christmas break?"

The barest of nods. The only perceptible movement was his hand rubbing Sadie.

She let out a long breath. "I need to know everything."

Jared's hands shook as he pet the cat. "There's like four or five of them that just run their mouths all the time. I try to ignore them but…" Kim waited for him to continue. He sucked in a big breath and blurted, "They got a picture of my mom off the internet and made a bunch of comments. They said my dad killed her and killed himself because they couldn't stand to be around me. Because I'm so ugly and stupid they didn't want to live anymore. Then they started saying I should kill myself."

Her hands were suddenly freezing and numb.

"Then they said you got stuck with me and you'll probably kill yourself to get away from me, too."

"What. The. Actual. Hell." Kim slid off her stool and put her arms around Jared. "Those are sick, sick individuals. Normal people don't talk like that – they don't even *think* like that."

Jared's phone dinged.

Kim looked down at the screen.

> Lololololol ur suspended loser tole u not 2
> mess w me

"Who is that?"

"I don't know. They put my number in the bathroom. I tried blocking them but there's… there's a lot." His voice cracked.

"Fine. We'll go today and get you a new number. Little assholes." Kim pulled her attention away from the phone and back to her nephew. "I need you to hear me, Jared. Your parents had a lot of problems. You know about the drugs and stuff. *None* of their problems had anything to do with you. Zero. They were messed up before you came along, and they were messed up after. They both tried getting clean, but addiction is a horrible thing. It's not something you can wish away or overcome without help. Your parents were sick, and it had nothing to do with you. And as much as I hate your father for what he did, I can say this. He loved you. Your mom loved you."

Jared sat perfectly still.

"And I love you. Your grandparents love you. You're an awesome kid, and I'm glad you're here."

His chin trembled. "I messed up everybody's life. William left because of me."

William. Her stupid, lousy ex-husband. Kim put her finger under Jared's chin and forced him to look at her. "No, Jared. Not because of you. William left because he's a selfish, narcissistic piece of crap. He couldn't handle the fact that I was giving him less attention because I was trying to grieve for my sister."

Jared's phone dinged again. And again. He ignored it. His bloodshot, bruised eyes bored into hers as if he was desperate to believe what she was saying.

"You're not responsible for your parents. You're not responsible for William. And you're certainly not responsible for these little assholes." She snatched his phone off the table.

> kill urslf losr

> i haaaaaaattttteeeeeeeeeeee u go die

So much for Principal Assface's insistence that the bullying took place outside of school hours and off school property. "How long has this been going on?"

He shrugged.

"Jared."

"A while."

Kim ran her hand down over her face. "I guess I should have been checking your phone, huh." The rule when she bought him the phone was that he had to give it to her at any time, and she had to have the unlock code.

Another shrug.

Kim tapped in the unlock code and spent a few minutes scrolling through pages and pages of hateful messages. There was no point in even trying to block the numbers because there were so many. It'd be easier to delete all the text threads and get a new number.

> r u ok call me l8r

She almost missed the message and scrolled back up to see it. She tapped the thread open and saw several unanswered messages that grew increasingly concerned at Jared's non-response throughout the morning. "Who's 'Izz'?"

"Isobel. She's not one of them." He jerked upright; his tone defensive.

Sadie lifted her head at the disturbance until Jared went back to scratching her head.

Kim relaxed her clenched jaw and took a deep breath. "Okay. Let's go get you a new number, and we'll go from there."

Her mind spun, trying to think of anything she knew about how to pull him out of school. Not much.

Jared picked Sadie off his lap and put her on the island. "I have to go to the bathroom."

"Okay."

She watched him walk out of the room and waited until she heard the upstairs bathroom door close before she leaned heavily on the counter, her legs threatening to give out under her. Hot tears stung the backs of her eyes. Impotent rage settled in her chest like a vice gripping her heart. They'd had a similar situation between the fall and Christmas breaks, where a pack of these hateful beasts went on a social media campaign against Jared and a few other boys. It had been bad, but nothing like this.

She heard the toilet flush and water run in the sink, so she pulled herself together. Wiping her eyes and straightening her spine, she picked up Jared's phone. It vibrated again, but she couldn't bear to even look down and read the newest message.

"Okay, let's go," she said as Jared came into the kitchen. His eyes were red and puffy on top of the bruises, the wet ends of his bangs evidence that he'd tried to wash away the tears.

Silently, he flipped his hood up and shoved his hands into his pockets.

Sadie wound around his ankles and meowed, bringing the first hint of a genuine smile to his face. He leaned down and scratched her head until she purred so loud the sound filled the entire kitchen.

Kim watched as Sadie bounded up from the floor to the chair to the island, then stretched out to head boop Jared, who leaned over to offer his forehead.

Thank God for cats.

Chapter Eight

Nate lifted his hand in a wave as Kim's car drove past his on their street. He glanced at the clock on his dash. It was barely noon, but the boy was in the car with her. For a second, he wondered why he wasn't in school, then rolled his eyes at himself. It was none of his business and he didn't care. So why was he wasting mental energy on it?

Because it was easier than spending mental energy on his own issues, probably. He pulled into his garage and hit the button to close the overhead door. He gave himself a mental pat on the back for only giving a cursory glance around the garage before getting out of the car.

In the house, he did a quick walkthrough before making a sandwich and then settling on the couch with the remote. His phone vibrated in his back pocket.

"Hey, Ma."

"Hey yourself. So? Any updates?" Her tone held a challenge.

Nate grinned. "Oh, ye of little faith. I bet you think I haven't left the house since we talked the other day."

There was a pause, then he could hear the smile in her

voice. "Okay, I admit that's exactly what I thought. But you went out?"

"I did." He deliberately waited, knowing the lack of information would make her want to come through the phone and strangle the story out of him.

"And?"

He put his sandwich back on the plate and set it on the coffee table. "And. I went out a few days ago and found an antique shop. I didn't get anything, but I plan to go back. You'll love it."

"That's great, honey. I'm so glad you got out and did something. I'm really proud of you."

"But wait, there's more," he said in his cheesiest infomercial voice.

"Do tell."

He paused for dramatic effect, knowing she was probably holding her breath, waiting to know what he'd done. "This morning I went out for breakfast."

"Out? To an actual restaurant?"

"Bingo."

"Nate, that's awesome."

"Not done yet."

She made a weird squawking noise that was part surprise, part skepticism, part anticipation. Or something like that.

He spoke slowly, drawing it out, knowing it was making her antsy. "My next-door neighbor was also there for breakfast, so we sat together and had a perfectly normal conversation like perfectly normal people do."

There was a long pause. "When did you meet your neighbor?"

"A few weeks ago. I ordered a package and it got delivered to her house by accident. She brought it over."

"*She*?"

"Slow your roll, Mom. She's like eighty."

"Oh." Disappointment oozed through the phone.

Nate laughed. "I'm messing with you. Her name's Kim. She looks to be about my age, and she's raising her nephew after her sister died."

"That's… really nice, Nate."

He knew his mom well, and it gave him some level of amusement to know she was reining her enthusiasm in, trying to keep it to a reasonable level. He knew she was chomping at the bit to interrogate him about every last detail. He let her stammer for a minute, then gave her some of the details she was undoubtedly wanting. "Yes, she's single. Yes, she's pretty. Yes, she's nice. No, it wasn't a date. No, we don't have plans to see each other again. No, I'm not interested in anything romantic. Her career is too public, and I'm not going down that road."

Nate could practically feel the wheels spinning in her head.

Pattie casually said, "What does she do?"

"She's a vlogger. That means she does –"

"Oh, for Pete's sake, I know what a vlogger is."

He raised an eyebrow. "Hey, sorry, I didn't realize you were up on all the hip new lingo."

Her laughter rang through the phone. "You make me feel like I'm a thousand years old sometimes."

"Well, if the shoe—"

"Nathaniel Sanders, if you finish that sentence… So help me, boy."

"Yeah, I know. Just because you personally witnessed the extinction of the dinosaurs doesn't mean you're *old*."

"I'm gonna witness another extinction pretty directly if you keep talking."

"Are you free tomorrow? You can come inspect the house

and make sure I put the towels away properly, then I can take you to that antique place I found."

"It's a date. I'll be there around ten, and you're buying me lunch."

"At ten? Bleh."

"Smartass."

"I learned from the best."

Nate hung up feeling hopeful. First, a nice normal breakfast with Kim. Then a nice normal stop at a convenience store to get gas. Then a nice normal conversation with his nice normal mother. Well, that might be stretching it. He chuckled at the thought. His amusement slid into gratitude. He truly didn't know what he'd do without his mom. She'd been his biggest cheerleader and fan from the time he was born, and his steadiest, most honest reality check when his head threatened to swell from attention and money.

On his first trip down a red carpet, his "date" had been his mom. He always thanked her first in every award speech he'd given. She'd dropped everything to get on a plane while he was in surgery to repair his shattered body, and she was the one holding his hand when he woke up.

Miranda had come to the hospital, shed a few crocodile tears, insisted she couldn't bear to see him that way, and left.

His mother had watched her leave and simply said, "Really, Nate?"

She'd been the one standing watch over him when the woman who'd run him down made it all the way to his room, pretending to be his wife. She was the one who turned into a superhero and literally held the woman on the ground until security arrived. She was the one who refused to let up until the actual police were on their way.

He shook the memories away, then stopped. His palms weren't sweating, and his heart wasn't pounding. He wasn't panting and struggling to breathe. He didn't feel trapped and claustrophobic. This must be what progress feels like.

The sandwich beckoned him, and he was surprised to find he was hungry. His stomach wasn't an iron pit of anxiety. He took a small bite as if testing his own body to see if it was going to start freaking out. It didn't.

It wasn't easy to eat his sandwich while grinning, but he managed. This was an excellent day.

Chapter Nine

While the kid at the counter worked on changing Jared's number, Kim poked around at the tablets on display. None of the preloaded demo games held her interest, so she gave up and walked over to where Jared was looking at phone cases.

"We should stop at the grocery store on the way home. What do you want for supper?"

"I don't care." He glanced at her, then back at the cases. "Can you make those pork chops with the gravy and the little potatoes?"

Kim grinned. "Heck, yeah. All I have to do is throw stuff in the crockpot for that. You can help me. You should learn how to do more than nuke ramen anyway."

He shrugged. "Sure."

"Okay, here's your phone." The guy behind the counter came over and handed Jared's phone to him. "Here's your new number."

Kim pulled out her phone. "Let me update my contacts right now, or I'll forget." She added the new phone number, then emailed herself a screenshot so she would remember to write it down. She didn't trust technology to not lose all her contacts, and she didn't want to be in a situation where she had no way of contacting anyone.

She quickly typed a text message and sent it to Jared's new number. When his phone dinged she rolled her eyes. "Duh, guess I didn't have to do that since your contacts will all be the same."

Jared smiled for the first time all day. "Yeah, well, you're old, soooo…"

Kim dropped her mouth open and planted her fist on her hip. "Watch it, mister." She shook her head as they walked out the door.

Pulling out of the parking lot, she muttered, "Old."

He laughed.

"Keep it up and we'll be having Metamucil for supper. And pudding. No more hard foods for you."

He feigned a shudder. "I should totally learn to cook then."

A few minutes later, they pulled into the grocery store parking lot. Kim got a mini-cart and pushed it through the sliding doors. "Remind me to get milk. And I think we're almost out of eggs."

They filled up the little cart. She looked through the items and snapped her fingers. "We need a packet of dry ranch dressing mix."

"Why?"

"It's the secret ingredient in the pork chops."

"Really? It sounds gross."

"It's not." She tossed the packets into the cart.

"How does that make the gravy?"

She held up a can of cream of chicken soup. "This makes the gravy. The ranch flavors it."

He made a face.

"You already know you like it."

"Yeah, but I didn't know that's how it was made."

"If this bothers you, you're in for a rude awakening when you find out where chicken wings come from." Kim laughed. "Ah, the magic of cooking." She pushed the cart to a self-checkout lane and scanned their groceries. She was almost done when the machine insisted there were unexpected items in the bagging area.

With a sigh, she waited for an employee to scan her badge and clear the error.

Kim thanked her and scanned the milk. The stupid machine once again claimed there was an unexpected item.

The employee came back and rolled her eyes. "These machines. I can't believe nobody's kicked one yet."

Kim laughed. "Me, either. It's very tempting."

The employee hovered nearby until Kim scanned her last item without the machine complaining. She paid for the groceries and Jared pushed the cart to the car. He was loading the bags in the back when he stopped and looked at her. "Thanks."

A little taken aback, Kim asked, "For what?"

His Adam's apple bobbed as he swallowed. "I didn't think you'd believe me."

Before she could respond, he pushed the cart toward the corral.

Fresh anger for her sister burned in her chest. Her sister, Jared's own mother, hadn't believed him when he told her about his father's relapse into drugs. He'd been eleven at the time and was in the car when Michael had driven into the bad part of town. He'd been watching as Michael handed over a wad of cash and accepted a plastic bag. He'd been right there when Michael slid a needle into his arm and he'd been there when the police pulled them over and took Michael away in handcuffs. Even when Danielle had to pick Jared up at the police station, she hadn't believed him. Somewhere, deep down, Kim thought Danielle had to have known the truth, but that was no comfort to the innocent little boy Jared had been.

Kim shook away the memory as Jared slid into the seat beside her. She started the car, but before she pulled out, she grabbed his hand and squeezed. "I've got your back, kiddo."

Not wanting to embarrass him or push him any more than he'd already been today, she let go and drove home. Jared fiddled with the radio. She watched him from the corner of her eye. He seemed to be in much better spirits. She, on the other hand, wanted to strangle the little punk who had put marks on Jared's face, and she wished she could grab her sister by the face and force her to see what she'd done to him. She also indulged in a mental image of doing physical violence to the smarmy principal with his bullshit zero-tolerance policies that only applied to certain people. Asshole.

They got home and carried the groceries to the kitchen.

"Okay, it's time for your grand cooking lesson. Grab the crockpot from the pantry."

She put the cold groceries in the fridge while Jared found the crockpot and set it on the counter. He plugged it in, then washed his hands.

"You'll need the pork chops, the can of soup, the potatoes, and the packet of ranch mix."

"Okay." Jared got the items from the grocery bags. "Now what?"

"Wash the potatoes and put them in a layer in the bottom of the crockpot."

When he was done, she said, "Now open the pork chops and layer them on top of the potatoes."

"They're gross."

"All raw meat is gross. Now dump the soup on top and sprinkle the ranch over that."

"This is kind of fun."

"Now wash your hands."

When he dried his hands, she had him put the lid on and set the heat level. "It's already one o'clock, so put it on high. I usually start it in the morning and let it cook on low all day."

Jared peered through the glass lid to the food inside. "That was easy."

"That's why I love my crockpot." She made them sandwiches for lunch while Jared opened a bag of chips.

"Can you teach me to make other stuff?" The question was so simple… but it wasn't.

Kim's heart squeezed, but she kept her voice light. "Of course. We'll work on a meal plan for the rest of the week later on. Okay?" She knew he couldn't possibly understand that his question meant he trusted her to be there for him.

"Yeah," he grunted and practically inhaled his lunch. "Can I get online?"

Kim raised an eyebrow. "Stay away from the trolls, Jared. And only give your new number to the people we talked about."

"Yup." He disappeared up the stairs. She heard his bedroom door close.

The situation currently under control, Kim finished her lunch and rinsed the dirty dishes. She scooped Sadie up and took her along to the office to work on her latest video.

Chapter Ten

The next day, Nate was putting dishes away when he heard his mother's car turning in the driveway. He shoved the last bowl into the cupboard and hurried to the front door. Grinning, he walked out onto the front porch, barefoot. The weathered wood was cool against his feet.

His mother wrestled with something from the back seat.

"Do you need help?"

"No, I've got it."

Once she said she had it, he knew it was pointless to try to help. He definitely inherited his stubborn streak from his mom. "What is it?"

"You'll see," she answered in a sing-song voice.

Leaning against the porch railing, arms crossed, Nate waited to see what she was up to. Finally, she stood straight, held two large paper bags aloft, and pushed the door shut with her hip.

Nate raised an eyebrow. He knew better than to ask again. She'd tell him when she was good and ready. He held the door open for her to walk into the house. She made a beeline for the kitchen, set the bags on the counter, then turned around and gave him a big hug.

"I've missed you," she said.

"You just saw me a week ago," he teased.

"What, I can't miss you? I've been worried about you." She patted his cheek. "You better not have been lying to me yesterday."

He held up his palms in surrender. "I would never, ever lie to you."

"Really? What are you getting me for my birthday?"

He mimed zipping his lips shut, then locking it and tossing the key over his shoulder.

She laughed. "Please. It's not for another month, so I know you haven't even thought about getting me anything yet. But speaking of gifts, I got you a few things."

"Such as?"

She grinned. "Come see."

As soon as he went into the kitchen, a movement through the window caught Nate's attention. He frowned and walked over and pulled the blind back. "What the heck?"

"What?"

The kid from next door was climbing out the second-story window, onto the porch roof. He inched toward the edge and peered down to the ground. His curly mop of hair hid his face.

Nate tensed. *What is he doing?* He pushed the curtain into place just as the boy snuck back to the house and climbed back in the window.

Pattie put her hand on his shoulder as she peeked out the side of the blinds. "You think he's okay?"

"I'm not sure."

A second later, the side door opened, and the kid stepped out, slowly pulling the door shut behind him. He held a back-pack in one hand. He stood still for a moment, then peeked around the corner and looked up and down the street. Then, he darted across the yard, toward the woods.

Frowning, Nate looked down at his mother. "I'm going to see if Kim's home. I'll be right back."

Concern was on her face as she nodded. "Go."

He shoved his feet into his sneakers and jogged across the yard. His knee protested by the time he got to Kim's front porch. He rang the doorbell. There was no answer, so he knocked and rang it again. Nothing. There was no movement from inside the house.

Something wasn't right.

Nate looked back over at his house. His mother was standing in the window. He pointed toward the woods and she nodded.

He touched his back pocket to make sure he had his phone. The GPS might come in handy since he hadn't been a Boy Scout for decades and would probably end up lost if Jared went too far. Too bad he didn't have Kim's phone number. That would have been handy.

Not quite limping by the time he reached the tree line, Nate tried to remember those Boy Scout days. The ground was still soft from a recent rain, so Nate was able to make out a few footprints. He followed them and stopped to listen. Branches cracked ahead, so he pushed forward, only to find squirrels making the racket. He considered turning back. Whatever the kid was doing was none of his business.

But something just didn't feel right. He pushed ahead, hoping he was on the right track. Spring was well underway, so the leaves were mostly full, effectively blocking his view. He stopped and tapped at his phone to find a satellite image of the area. Not too far ahead, there appeared to be some sort of lake or pond. Nate supposed that if he were sneaking out, he might head there.

Two more footprints reassured him he was on the right track, so he pushed onward. Briars grabbed onto his clothes and little twigs snapped around, stinging his exposed arms and face.

He shoved through the last bit of brush and found himself on a muddy sandy bank of a pond that was about the size of the inside of a baseball diamond. He looked down and saw more footprints. Following them with his eyes, he finally saw the kid, who hadn't yet seen him.

Great. Now what? Nate didn't want to scare him.

Jared sat on a big, flat rock, his legs pulled up, his arms wrapped around them, his forehead resting on his knees. His hoodie covered his head and shielded his face from view. His backpack lay beside him.

Nate took a deep breath and walked cautiously toward the boy. When he was about twenty feet away, he stopped. "Hey, uh, Jared?"

Jared's head snapped up, his face a mask of shock and fear. He tensed and grabbed his backpack, looking like he was ready to run.

Nate held his hands up and took a step backward. "I just moved in next door."

The boy's eyes darted around, no doubt searching for escape. His eyes were red and puffy as if he'd been crying.

"I talked to your aunt Kim yesterday at breakfast." The words sounded stupid to his ears, but he had no idea what else to say that might not make the kid bolt. "So, um, is there good fishing in here?" He gestured to the pond.

Jared rose to his feet and inched to the far side of the rock.

Nate kept talking, hoping Jared wouldn't take off. "I was just curious. Not that I'm much of a fisherman, but this is a pretty nice spot. Seems like a good place to come clear your head." When Jared's eyes met his, he continued. "It's good to have a place to go and think."

Jared's eyes flicked out over the water, then back to Nate's. He nodded.

A little pang of relief warmed Nate's chest. At least he'd gotten a response. "It's good to talk, too. If you need to get something off your chest, I'm happy to listen."

Jared's gaze shot downward. He shook his head.

As his hair swung, Nate saw the bruises, and for a moment, he was afraid he'd pushed too far. "I don't think I introduced myself. I'm Nate. Sanders. I just moved in next door." He repeated himself, unable to think of anything else to say, but wanting to keep talking.

Jared's eyes darted back up to his face. A second later, his eyes widened. "Nate Sanders."

"Yup."

"Holy cow. You're Qaaxag."

Chapter Eleven

Kim walked into the house and tossed her purse on the couch. "Jared?" She went upstairs and knocked on his bedroom door. "I'm coming in, so make sure you're decent." She waited a beat, then turned the knob and pushed the door open.

His desk was tidy. His bed was made. His dirty clothes were in his hamper, not on his floor. An icy tentacle of dread climbed up her spine.

She walked over and rapped on his closet door. "Jared?" It made no sense, but she pushed the door open. Nothing looked out of place. She pulled the door shut and walked over to his desk.

Sadie jumped up onto the bed and scratched at Jared's pillow.

Something felt off, but Kim couldn't put her finger on it. She lifted the lid on his laptop and the screen came to life. There was nothing unusual there.

She pushed out a deep breath and turned around, scanning the room. A sheet of folded paper lay on his nightstand. She nearly threw up at the sight of it. Forcing herself to cross the room on legs that didn't want to move, she drew closer to the paper. Her hand shook violently as she reached for it. She could barely feel her fingers as she lifted the paper.

Swallowing hard against the bile that threatened to spill out before she'd even read a word, she unfolded the page.

Dear Aunt Kim,

I'm sorry for all the trouble I've caused. I found my grandparents, so I'm going to Boston to be with them.

Thanks for everything.

Love you,

Jared

Kim's knees buckled with relief and she toppled gracelessly to the edge of the bed. Running away, she could handle. She shoved the paper into her back pocket and ran back downstairs. She grabbed her purse and ran outside to her car, but she had no idea what to actually *do*.

She stared stupidly at her phone. Should she call the police? She slapped her forehead and dialed her dad's number. He picked up immediately.

"Daddy, Jared ran away. I need help."

She could hear him getting to his feet. His voice automatically went into cop mode. "When did you see him last?"

"About an hour ago. He was in his room when I left to run some errands."

"Are you sure he was in his room?"

"Yes. I saw him when I told him I was leaving."

"We're on our way over."

"Dad, what do I do?" Her voice rose an octave by the time she finished the sentence.

"Just hang tight." She heard rustling. "Jared's run off," she heard him saying to her mother.

Her mother's gasp sent a spike of fear through her. Her mother was always the calm in any storm, constant and steady, no matter what the crisis.

"Kimmy? We're on our way." Her mother came on the line. "We'll be there in a few minutes."

"Okay." Kim's knuckles were white as she clenched the phone.

She could hear the car doors opening and closing.

"It might cut you off when the phone connects to the car," her dad warned. A moment later, there was static and clicking, but it connected without dropping the call.

"You still there?"

Kim nodded, not quite able to speak. She forced herself to say, "Yup, I'm here."

Her dad began asking questions. "If you saw him an hour ago, we can assume he left immediately after you did. How much money does he have? Could he have gotten a ride?"

A sob was the only response she could manage.

Her mother cut in. "He can't have gotten far."

"He left a note. It said he found his grandparents in Boston and he's going there." She wracked her brain, trying to remember Jared's grandparents' names. She'd never had much to do with Jared's father, so she couldn't remember any occasion where they'd talked about his parents. Hopefully, there would be information in Jared's computer or in his room that would help her find them, if that's where he was really going. "Do you even know their names?"

Kim could imagine the looks going back and forth between her parents, an unspoken conversation like they had done for years. She stood on the front porch, looking around, searching for clues. Preferably a glowing map with a red arrow pointing to Jared's location. None appeared.

Since there was nothing else she could do, she just focused on breathing. In and out, for the ten minutes it took her parents to arrive. Her dad parked haphazardly across the driveway, the only indication of his fear. He stepped out of the car, looking every bit the retired, no-nonsense cop he was.

Kim waited until he stepped onto the porch, then launched herself into his arms. He squeezed her, then grabbed her upper arms and gently pushed her back.

"Where's the note?" He took it from her, his eyes narrowing as he scrutinized it. "I called Martin. He's on the way with a dog." His former partner was still on the force. He put his finger under Kim's chin. "Hold it together."

She nodded and wiped her face.

<h1 style="text-align:center">Chapter Twelve</h1>

Nate nodded. "Yep, I played Qaaxag for six seasons." Instead of dread at being recognized, he was glad it gave him a connection to Jared, however tenuous.

Jared's eyes were huge and curious, surrounded by fresh, angry bruises. "What are you doing *here*?"

"Talking to you."

"No, I mean here, in Hickory Hollow."

"I live here now."

Jared's voice was all impatience. "*Why*? Why would you leave Hollywood and come to a place like this? Did you get fired? Is that why Qaaxag was killed offscreen? What's Katrina like in real life? Did you get to keep any of the costumes or props or anything?"

Nate held up a hand. "Whoa. Wow, that's a lot of questions." He was still about fifteen feet away from Jared. He didn't think Jared was going to take off anymore, but he didn't want to take a chance.

"Can we take a selfie?" Jared fumbled and pulled his phone out of his pocket.

"Later." At Jared's crestfallen expression, he added, "I promise. And I will answer all your questions about the show. But I need to know that you're not in the middle of doing something you'll regret."

The boy's expression changed, becoming guarded. "Whatever." His entire posture changed, seeming to shrink into himself.

"Look, I get that this is none of my business, but I had a bad feeling when I saw you heading into the woods. Maybe I'm wrong and this is all legit, but I kinda have to know."

Jared's shoulders slumped. "You're going to drag me back home, aren't you?"

Nate's mind battled between taking a firm stance or trying to be the kid's nice new friend. He shot for some sort of middle ground. "I'd rather not have to. Bad knee." He tapped his leg and gave what he hoped was a friendly, joking smile.

Jared sighed heavily. "Aunt Kim's going to hate me." He sat back down on the rock and covered his face with his hands.

Nate took the chance and sat down beside Jared. "I'm new to the neighborhood. I've only had one real conversation with your aunt. But that's all it took to know how much she loves you."

Jared hugged his knees and picked at a loose thread on his jeans. Wanting to be gentle, Nate said, "I know you've been through some stuff, and I won't pretend to know what's going on now, but I'm not sure this is the best way to handle it." He held his breath, hoping his words didn't cause Jared to put up another wall and stop talking to him.

"I can't go back to school. But if you miss too many days, your parents get a fine. I don't want to cost Aunt Kim more money than I already do."

Nate crossed his legs and picked up a pebble. Rolling it around his fingers, he nodded. The kid didn't want to be a burden. "What's your plan?"

"My dad's parents live in Boston. I'm going to go live with them. They totally want me to." His chin jutted defiantly as he stumbled over the obvious lie.

Not wanting to call the boy out, Nate said, "I'm guessing that since you're sitting in the woods behind your house and not on a bus to Massachusetts, maybe you're not totally sold on that plan."

Jared shrugged and looked down, his curls cascading over his forehead.

"Why don't we head back, and I bet your aunt will help you figure stuff out." Nate had no business inserting himself into their issues, but he couldn't help himself. Maybe because Jared reminded him of himself as a kid. Tall and skinny and wanting nothing more than to be invisible.

"She's going to be mad at me for leaving." Jared's voice was soft, scared.

Nate felt the shift in Jared's resolve and knew it wouldn't take much to convince him to go back home. "I'd bet she's way more mad at whoever did that to your face."

"Yeah, she was pretty mad about that."

"She's just going to be happy to see that you're safe. Let's get you home before she calls the cops."

Jared groaned loudly into his palms.

"What?"

"My grandpa's a retired cop. Oh, man, I'm in so much trouble." His eyes filled with tears.

Nate flicked the pebble away. "Then let's go before it gets any worse." He got to his feet and waited for Jared to make his final decision.

Glancing back every so often, Nate almost smiled at Jared's reluctant trudging behind him. They reached the edge of the woods and Jared mumbled, "I'm so dead."

There was a flurry of activity on Kim's porch. Two police

cars, complete with swirling lights, were parked in the driveway. Uniformed officers with a K-9 stood on the front porch, along with Kim, an older couple Nate guessed were her parents, and Nate's mom.

Nudging the boy forward, Nate walked a step behind him across the lawn, his hands shoved deep in his pockets. He had enough of his own drama. He'd tell them what he knew, which was next to nothing, and he'd go back home.

Kim spotted them first. "Jared!" Her voice was pure relief. She jumped down the porch steps and ran across the lawn full speed, slamming Jared into her arms, knocking his backpack off his shoulder and to the ground. "Where have you been? I've been worried sick." She pulled back and put her hands on either side of his face. "Are you okay? You can't do that again, Jared, you can't just leave." Tears streamed down her face and she grabbed him in another fierce hug. "We can go to Boston and see your grandparents, but you can't just take off like that."

The force of her hug sent Jared stepping backward. His foot bumped his backpack and Nate's heart nearly stopped. Pill bottles spilled out through the broken zipper and onto the grass. His stomach churned. How far would Jared have gone if Nate hadn't followed him into the woods?

Kim pulled back, gripping his shoulders, and squeezed him again. "Don't do that again. We'll figure this all out, Jared. We're in this together."

Jared nodded.

Kim turned to Nate. "Your mother came over. She said you saw him leaving and followed him. Thank you."

He shrugged uncomfortably. "You guys have a lot to talk about." His eyes darted down to the backpack, and Kim's gaze followed.

She hunkered down and picked the bottle off the ground.

Nate watched the color drain from Jared's face. Even his lips turned chalky. The only color was the bruising. For a second, he thought the kid was going to pass out.

"Jared?" She opened his backpack and pulled out four bottles of over the counter pain reliever, a box of cold medicine, and two bottles of water.

Nate could see her hands shake. She whispered, "No. Oh, Jared, no," then looked back up at Jared. "You didn't find them, did you? Your grandparents?"

Sobs exploded from Jared and he dropped to his knees. "I'm sorry, I'm so sorry," he wailed, the words barely understandable. "I didn't want you to worry about me anymore. I can't go back. I'm sorry. I can't."

Kim dropped the bottles and grabbed Jared, clutching him to her, muffling his words and his sobs. Nate wondered that the kid could breathe. He felt like a voyeur, intruding on a moment that was none of his business.

He took a step back, debating whether to walk to the porch or retreat back to his house. The uniformed officers and K-9 were leaving, apparently satisfied since Jared was back home. With a sigh and a feeling of dread, he left Kim and Jared alone and walked to the porch, where his mother grabbed his arm. "Is he okay? Are you okay?"

Nate gave a curt nod. "I'm fine. He's got a lot on his plate."

The burly man in front of him stuck out his hand. "Keith Donahue. Kim's dad. Jared's grandfather." His handshake was designed to crush Nate's fingers.

"Nate Sanders. Next door neighbor."

"MaryAnn. I'm Kim's mother." She held out her hand, forcing Keith to release his grip.

"Nice to meet you." Nate shook her hand as well.

She patted his arm. "We appreciate you going after Jared."

Keith jumped in, crossing his arms across his broad chest. "Why was that, exactly?"

Even if Jared hadn't mentioned that his grandfather was a retired cop, Nate would have figured it out quickly. "Why was what?"

"Why'd you follow him into the woods? You have some kind of sixth sense?"

"Keith!" MaryAnn scolded.

Nate met his gaze directly. "I saw him climb out his window and sneak into the woods. I had a bad feeling. Nothing more, nothing less."

Keith narrowed his eyes and grunted as Kim and Jared came up the porch steps. Kim ushered the boy inside, then turned to thank Pattie and Nate again.

Nate shook his head. "No problem. Call if you need anything." He immediately realized she didn't have his number, but it didn't seem like the time to give it to her.

She nodded and went inside. MaryAnn followed her, while Keith hung back.

"I'd hate to find out you're involved in this, son."

Nate interrupted him. "You're wasting your time. The kid needs help." He matched Keith's stare, unwilling to be either intimidated or combative.

Keith seemed to respond favorably to Nate's tactic. He reached out and shook his hand again, with much less force. "I appreciate you going after him."

Nate gave a nod, then turned and let his mother go down the steps in front of him, then walked home beside her. She waited until they were back inside his house before turning to face him. "What happened?"

"He's got some big problems. I don't even know the whole story. His parents are dead, and he lives with Kim. Apparently, he's having some problems at school. He's got a black eye and scraped up knuckles, and right now he's got the weight of the world on his shoulders."

"Poor kid." She waited a beat. "What about you?"

"What *about* me? My life's a cakewalk."

She eyed him for a long moment. "How about that lunch you promised me?"

Nate grabbed his mom in a hug. "I'm glad you're here." He pushed back. "Now let's get you fed before you get mean."

"Mean? Me?"

"When you're hungry, you start breathing fire. You get kind of mean."

"You exaggerate."

He touched her ear. "There's smoke coming out."

Pattie laughed. "Then let's go."

Chapter Thirteen

Looking at the faces around her kitchen table, Kim was at a loss. "I'm calling Dr. Everly."

Jared slumped down. "Dr. Everly is a joke. She doesn't listen."

MaryAnn said, "Maybe he should talk to Sawyer."

"Who's that?" Kim felt completely lost.

"He's the youth pastor at our church. He's also a counselor. That's what he does. The kids seem to really respond well to him."

"But we don't go to church."

"It doesn't matter." She held up a hand. "I promise this isn't a way to hound you into going back to church. I honestly think Sawyer would be really good for Jared to talk with."

Kim leaned back in her chair. She knew her mother wanted her to go back to church, especially since she was raising Jared, but she believed her that this wasn't a ploy to get them back into the flock. "Okay. Jared?"

Jared grumbled, "Is he going to be some kind of weirdo, just spouting Bible verses at me that will change my life?"

Keith answered, "He's a really good counselor, and your

grandma wouldn't have suggested him if she didn't think he was the right man for the job."

"Okay. Fine."

MaryAnn got up and left the room, pulling her phone out of her back pocket as she went.

Kim ran a hand through her short hair. Everything was moving so fast, and so slow. She was still trying to get her head around the pill bottles and Jared running away. How on earth was she screwing up so badly? A few minutes later, MaryAnn came back into the room.

"He can fit Jared in at three. He wants to talk to the two of you together, and Jared by himself."

Kim nodded, surprised. "Today? That's great." She glanced at the clock. It was nearly one o'clock. "Okay. You hungry, kiddo?"

"Yeah." Jared scooped Sadie into his arms and rubbed his face in her fur.

"I'll start grilled cheese, you can warm up some of that soup from last night." She wanted to bake something to relax, but there wasn't time. Grilled cheese would have to do.

Keith and MaryAnn stood.

Kim glanced over. "You staying for lunch?"

"No, we're going to head out. Let us know how your appointment goes, okay?" Keith leaned over and kissed her on the forehead.

"Sure, Daddy."

Her parents hugged Jared on their way out. Her dad spoke into Jared's ear, but she couldn't hear what he said.

Jared filled two bowls with soup, then microwaved them while Kim flipped the grilled cheese sandwiches.

"Aunt Kim?" He leaned against the sink, just a few feet away from her. His voice was barely louder than a whisper.

"Yeah?"

"I wouldn't have done it. I mean, I don't even know if that would have worked anyhow. I didn't want to do anything; I just didn't know *what* to do."

She set the spatula on the counter and put her hands on his cheeks. "You *talk* to *me*. That's what you do. No matter what. You stop worrying about whether you're causing problems, because you're not. You stop acting like you're a burden, because you're not. I love you. And if anything happened to you…" Her eyes filled with tears. "I can't lose you."

Jared's chin quivered. "I'm sorry."

Kim choked back her own tears. "I know. You don't need to be sorry. I just need you to understand that we're in this together. Taking care of you is my job. It's my privilege. Your job is being a kid and not trying to solve everything on your own."

A tear slipped down his cheek and Kim wiped it away.

"I know you had to be the grown-up for your parents, but you don't have to do that anymore. You don't have to try to protect me from anything. You don't have to worry about money or bills." Kim desperately hoped Jared heard what she was saying. Really *heard* her. He needed to know they were a team. No matter what. "You only have to worry about getting good grades and doing your chores. That's it."

Jared swallowed hard. "But—"

"Yes, I know I said grades. That doesn't mean I'm sending you back to that ridiculous shithole. We'll do some research and figure out how to homeschool or do cyberschool or something. Whatever." She grabbed his shoulders and shook him once. "The point is that we will figure it out together."

Chapter Fourteen

Pattie patted Nate's arm. "Come away from the window. You can't see anything anyway."

"I know. I just hope everything's okay." Nate could see so much of himself in Jared. He wanted to help the boy, but there was really nothing he could do. It was a helpless, crappy feeling.

"Sooooo, Kim seems nice."

"Mom. Really?" He finally turned away from the window and shook his head at his mother's not-so-subtle comment.

"What? I just said she seems nice. What's wrong with that?"

He sighed dramatically. "Nothing."

"Is she the one you had breakfast with?"

"Yes, Mother, Kim is the person I had breakfast with."

"She seems nice." Pattie smirked as she repeated herself, emphasizing each word.

"Yes, Mother, Kim is very nice."

"Very? I didn't say 'very.'" Her grin spread across her face like she'd just won something.

"You're exhausting, you know that?"

She laughed. "Think of it as payback for all those years of you incessantly asking 'Why? Why? Why? Why?'"

"Huh. I thought you were always big on encouraging kids to learn?"

"Smartass. Now are we going to get lunch or what?"

"Why? Why? Why? Why?" Nate dodged out of reach as his mother swatted at him. "I'll get my keys."

"You'd better be taking me someplace nice."

"Only the best for you."

"Yeah, yeah, I hear you."

"I'm serious. You can get anything you want off the McDonald's dollar menu. Anything at all."

"Ha, ha."

They went outside and Nate opened the car door for her. When he was on the main road, Pattie said, "You look a lot better than you did a few weeks ago."

"Okay… Where are you going with this?"

"It's just an observation. You ran right out of the house to go after Jared. You didn't even hesitate."

"I was going into the woods. Not a lot of paparazzi there."

"A month ago, you wouldn't have gone if it meant leaving the house. Is your anxiety better overall?"

"I'm not sure how to answer that. Either it's better, or I'm getting better at dealing with it. I'm not sure which."

"Did you find a new therapist?"

Nate slowed to a stop for a red light. "No. Not yet. I've been doing the exercises Dr. Ghirardelli gave me, and that's been helping."

"That's great."

He knew she was concerned, but holding back because she didn't like to nag. "I plan on finding someone local. I know I still have some issues to work through."

She patted his hand. "I should hope so. I didn't spend all

that time messing up your childhood for you to *not* talk about it in therapy."

He grinned. "Oh, I know. I won't let your efforts go to waste."

"Good. I've always said that if your kid can't bankroll a therapist for at least five years, you haven't done your job as a parent."

"Only five? Well, you've always been an overachiever." He smirked at her.

Pattie's mouth snapped shut and she glared at him. "Don't push it." She smacked his arm.

Nate grabbed his arm and yelled, "Ow!" He rubbed the spot and shook his head. He pretended to make a note on his hand. "One more thing for therapy."

"Brat."

The light turned green. He pulled into the parking lot and into a parking space. He turned off the ignition and hesitated. "Seriously, though, I don't know what I'd do without you. You're my rock."

"Aww, stop. You're going to make me wreck my mascara."

Nate took a breath. He wasn't sure if he should tell his mother a story that wasn't his. He figured the facts were public record, so he only gave her the barest minimum. "Jared's father murdered his mother, then killed himself. I can't even imagine how that would mess a kid up."

"Wow. Poor kid. It's a good thing he has his aunt. And his grandparents."

It was a good thing Nate had Pattie, too. "It wasn't easy when my father took off, but you held it together for both of us. I don't think I ever told you how much I appreciate that. I don't know how you managed to not badmouth him or tell me all the shitty things he'd done. You're the best mom ever, and I love you."

Pattie reached over and put her hand on his cheek. "Don't give me more credit than I deserve. I'm no saint."

He knew she didn't want to get all teary-eyed before they went into the restaurant, so he decided to lighten the mood. "Oh, believe me, I know that. You don't even qualify for sainthood after all those times you beat me with a wooden spoon."

"*Beat* you!" Her eyes widened.

He got out of the car and went around to open her door. "I'm glad you did. It gives me more to talk about in therapy."

She playfully glared at him. "You're rotten."

"Not my fault. It's genetic." He grinned and slung his arm over her shoulders as they walked into the diner.

Chapter Fifteen

Kim's leg jittered as she sat outside Sawyer Jensen's office. The door was closed, leaving her alone in the waiting room. Or lobby. Whatever it was. The office was inside a newer, rather industrial church building. The ceilings were high, and the walls were painted a warm, welcoming, soft brown. Religious decorations were grouped by someone who obviously had design experience. Kim looked around, recognizing some of the themes. Noah's ark, Daniel in the lion's den, and, of course, the birth and death of Jesus.

Kim couldn't keep herself distracted for long. She wondered what Jared was telling Sawyer, if anything. She hoped he was able to find some sort of rapport with the man. He seemed approachable and kind.

She checked her phone, scrolled through endless nonsense on social media, then checked the stats for her newest video. It was doing well, in spite of the fact that she'd done less promoting than she typically did. Relieved, she opened her email and sent herself some notes about her next video.

There was one window on the far side of the room. She stood and walked over to it, gazing out into the parking lot.

The weather had turned dreary and overcast, which only added to her down mood. The events of the day were catching up with her.

She slid her phone into her back pocket with a sigh. She wished she had something to occupy her hands, besides her phone. Maybe she should take up knitting. A black cat trotted across the parking lot and disappeared under a bush, capturing her attention for a minute or two.

Forty minutes later, a door clicked open behind her and she jumped, startled from her train of thought.

"Ms. Donahue? Come on in." Sawyer was youngish, probably not much over thirty. He was dressed like an older version of one of his teen clients. Faded jeans, Converse sneakers, gray t-shirt with a gray zipper hoodie hanging open. His hair was stylishly messy, and his smile was warm and genuine.

He stepped to the side of the door, giving her plenty of room to walk past him without feeling like they were too close. She appreciated that detail.

His office wasn't large, but it was comfortable. He had a desk off to the side, floor to ceiling bookcases covering one wall, and four comfortable chairs commanding the middle of the room, in a sort of circle. There were little tables between the chairs and boxes of tissues everywhere. Jared looked up from the chair he was in and smiled. Actually smiled. Nothing could have made her happier.

Kim gripped her purse and sat gingerly on the chair beside Jared.

Sawyer sat in the chair across from Jared. "I'm really glad you came in. Jared and I had a good talk. We talked through the events that occurred this morning, and the incidents that led us here, and it's my opinion that Jared isn't in any immediate danger."

"Thank you, Dr. Jensen."

His eyes widened a little and he held up a hand. "Sawyer, please. My dad is Dr. Jensen. He's a heart surgeon, so I feel like a bit of a fraud when someone calls *me* Dr. Jensen." He laughed easily.

"Sorry. Sawyer. I really appreciate you taking the time to see us today and talk to Jared. I..." She reached over and squeezed Jared's hand. "I didn't know what to do."

Jared's cheeks pinked. "I'm sorry, Aunt Kim," he mumbled.

"It's okay."

"I feel bad that I scared you."

"You don't have to worry about me."

Sawyer cleared his throat. "Ms. Donahue –"

"Kim, please."

"Kim. Jared's doing an excellent job of verbalizing his feelings right now. It would be helpful for both of you if you let him say what he needs to say, without trying to protect him from *your* feelings. He clearly understands the consequences of his actions, and how they affected you, this morning. It's good for him to get it out. You may certainly want to forgive him and let him know you're not angry, but it's not a bad thing to acknowledge your own feelings."

"Okay." She felt a little chastised, but it made sense. "So when I stop him and tell him everything's okay, I'm basically dismissing his feelings."

"Exactly."

"I'm sorry, Jared. I'll do better with that."

He nodded.

Sawyer looked up at the clock and tapped his palms on his knees. "Okay, folks, that was a great session. I do have a couple of openings if you'd like to come back. I'd recommend weekly visits for a couple of months, then bi-weekly, then monthly, then as needed. You don't have to decide now." He crossed the room and picked two thin books off a shelf. "I would like for you to take these and work through them together." He handed one to each of them. "It's set up with daily lessons, but realistically, a lesson every two or three days is more manageable for most families. It covers communication and feelings, how to listen effectively, those sorts of things."

Kim glanced at the workbook. "This is great. Thank you."

"Jared, I really enjoyed talking with you." He reached out to shake Jared's hand, then Kim's. He opened the door to the office and walked through the small waiting room Kim had been in and opened the next door that opened to the huge lobby. He spoke to a woman at a desk at the far side of the room, near the entrance. "Cindy? Give them a packet and if they'd like to schedule for next week, take care of that. Thank you."

Cindy nodded, her blonde curls bouncing. "Sure thing."

Sawyer clapped Jared's back, then went back to his office.

Cindy handed Kim a Ziploc bag with papers and brochures and a pen with the church's logo and website on it. "This is information about Sawyer and what to expect from this type of counseling, the services we offer, as well as information for other community services. All that good stuff."

"Okay, great." Kim fished her wallet out of her giant purse. "What's the charge for today?"

Cindy's smile was bright. "Oh, no charge. It's part of our ministry to provide mental health resources for members and their families. Of course we would love donations to the church. The amount would be at your own discretion. Would you like to schedule for next week?"

"Oh. Uh, we're not members."

Cindy's smile never faltered. "But MaryAnn and Keith are. Of course you're always welcome, too." She tapped the packet. "If it's something you'd like to consider, there's a brochure in here that gives an overview of our service times, youth activities, and outreach opportunities. More details are on our website."

Kim turned to Jared. He nodded and Kim pulled out her planner. "We'd like to schedule an appointment for next week."

"Wonderful." Cindy told her the available times, then put them on the calendar.

The phone rang, so Kim said, "Thanks so much."

Cindy nodded and gave a little wave as Kim and Jared walked away.

In the car, Kim said, "So? How was it?"

Jared buckled his seatbelt. "It was good. I want to go back."

"That's great. He seemed really nice." She pulled out of the parking lot. "No reciting a ton of Bible verses?"

"He did tell me one verse, but not in like a preachy way. That was pretty much it."

"Good. You had a good talk?"

He shifted in his seat. "I mean, he was asking me about hurting myself and all that stuff, so it wasn't a *good* talk. But he, like, *listened* to me."

"Good. Anything you want to share with me?"

"No," he mumbled. "I'm not going to… you know. I'm not. I wouldn't."

She reached over and squeezed his hand. "Okay. I want to stop at the store and get stuff to make cinnamon rolls."

"Awesome."

Kim drove to the store on autopilot. Thoughts swirled around in her mind. What if she hadn't come home? What if Nate hadn't seen Jared go into the woods and followed him? What if Jared had been more determined to hurt himself?

What if, what if, what if?

She was mentally exhausted but made sure it didn't show on her face. She agreed that she'd been wrong to shelter Jared from her feelings completely, but she certainly wasn't going to let him know exactly what was going on in her head. He was still just a kid and it was still her job to protect him as much as she could.

They walked through the store, picking up groceries without much conversation. It was an easy silence, though, not strained like it had been on the way to Sawyer's office.

Chapter Sixteen

Nate hugged his mom before she left. He was glad to see her, but he was also glad to see her go, so he could be alone. The day had been long and eventful, and he just wanted to crash on the couch and watch some mindless television.

He did exactly that. Until eight thirty, when a knock on the door made him bolt upright, his heart pounding. He squeezed the remote so hard the battery cover popped off and fell to the floor.

The knock came again. It didn't have the sinister edge he'd felt the first time when he'd been surprised. He grabbed the battery cover off the floor and set it on the coffee table with the remote, then walked to the door. Pulling back the curtain, he breathed a sigh of relief. He unlocked the door and smiled. "Hey."

Kim held up a plate. "Cinnamon rolls?"

"Come on in." He stepped back to let her inside. "Sorry the porch light wasn't on." He flipped the switch, illuminating the front porch and sidewalk. "I wasn't expecting visitors."

"Sorry to just come barging over. I would have called first but I don't have your number." She handed him the plate.

"What's the occasion?"

"I bake when I have a lot on my mind. And I wanted to thank you. For earlier. So I thought I'd share some cinnamon rolls. I hope you like them."

Nate grinned. Maybe having neighbors wasn't so bad after all. "Of course I do. What kind of weirdo doesn't like cinnamon rolls?" He'd been on a fairly strict diet during his time as Qaaxag, so he appreciated the treat.

"I'm sure there are a few."

"Did you have one?"

"No. I came over as soon as they were cool enough to ice. I didn't want to come over too late."

He jerked his head toward the kitchen. "Let me set these down. The plate's getting hot. Come on in."

"Sure." She stepped inside and closed the door. "I'm not interrupting anything, am I?"

"Nah, I was just staring at the TV." Nate walked into the kitchen and set the plate on the table. He pulled two small plates out of the cupboard and grabbed a stack of napkins. He got forks out of the drawer, then pushed it shut with his hip and gestured to the table. "Have a seat."

"Are you sure? I know it's getting kind of late."

He was glad she'd come over and was surprised to find how much he wanted her to stay for a while. "It's never too late for a cinnamon bun." He pulled the foil off and inhaled deeply. "They smell amazing."

"It's the cinnamon. It's from Saigon."

Nate raised an eyebrow. "Really?"

"Really. I get a lot of products to try out and review. One company sent me a bunch of gourmet spices and that was one of them. I used it once and swore I'd never go back to regular store-bought cinnamon. It totally turned me into a cinnamon snob."

He got his roll, then pushed the plate toward her. "Please."

She hesitated but did get herself a roll. "Thank you. I can bring you another one."

Nate laughed. "There are still four rolls the size of my head. No need to bring a replacement."

Staring at her roll, she said, "I really appreciate what you did this morning."

Uncomfortable, Nate shifted in his chair, poking at the cinnamon roll with his fork. "It's not a big deal."

"It is to me."

Nate felt a twinge in his chest. He didn't want any attention, especially for just doing the right thing. "Anybody would have done the same."

"I disagree. Not many people would have followed a teenage boy into the woods. But *you* did, and I appreciate it." She took a bite of her roll. "Mmm, they turned out really good."

Nate nodded. "Delicious. Thank you."

"You're welcome. Can I ask you a question? Jared said you were on TV? Some kind of alien show?"

He definitely didn't want to go there. "Yeah." He got up and got a bottle of water from the fridge. "Water?"

"Sure. Thanks."

He handed her a bottle and sat back down. He hadn't expected the conversation to head this direction. "I was an actor on this sci-fi show until I got injured." He patted his leg.

"Were you hurt on set?"

He took a long swallow of water. "No, it was, um, it didn't... wasn't during filming. It was, uh, a kind of car accident." He looked up. Her gaze was curious, but he didn't think she'd pry, so he could stop there. On the other hand, a simple google search would answer all her questions, with very little accuracy. "There was a... fan. I guess that's what you'd call her.

She was, um, unstable, and she fixated on my character and convinced herself that we were, um, *together*. She had sent a bunch of fan mail and weird stuff to the studio. Showed up in person a few times, but security always threw her out."

"Whoa." Her eyes widened.

"Yeah. Then one day I was walking down the sidewalk with one of the other cast members and this car comes barreling right at us. I barely had time to shove Katrina out of the way before the car hit me. This woman jumps out screaming that she's my wife and I'm cheating on her. Meanwhile, I've got broken ribs and a shattered leg. Paparazzi caught it all, of course."

"You're lucky you weren't killed." Kim's expression was horrified. Her fingertips touched the delicate necklace at her throat.

"I know. There was a cement bench that took some of the impact. If it hadn't been there…" he trailed off. "Anyway. With the injury and legal stuff, I couldn't go back to filming for a while. So they killed my character off and I moved here."

"Do you miss it?"

Funny, he'd never really considered whether he missed it or not. "The show? Yes and no. It was a lot of fun being a badass alien warlord. And the people I worked with were awesome. But being in the spotlight like that?" He shook his head. "I don't miss that at all. Every time I went outside there was someone shoving a camera in my face."

"I can't even imagine how much that had to suck."

"And every bit of my personal life was fodder for tabloids. Not that I had much of a personal life, but it got tiresome being accused of having affairs with every barista I ordered coffee from."

"Affairs? So you were in a relationship?"

Nate mentally kicked himself. He hadn't planned on

talking about *Daystar Rising,* and he definitely hadn't planned on talking about Miranda. "Yeah, with a costar. It wasn't serious, even though the tabloids had us getting married in secret ceremonies every other week." He took another long drink of water. "We kind of split after the *accident.*" He made air quotes around the word.

"That's a shame."

He shrugged. "Nah. It was about over anyway. Lots of reasons. That just helped it along." He didn't bother mentioning that while he was in the hospital, he found out Miranda was screwing people not-so-behind his back, including one of the show's producers… who happened to be working on producing another show that was destined to be a blockbuster. And had a role Miranda wanted. Whatever. It was in the past. Over and done with. Once he'd realized it hadn't been his heart that was hurt, only his pride, it was much easier to deal with.

Glancing up, he realized his mind had wandered and he'd been quiet too long.

Kim smiled. "Got stuck on Memory Lane?"

"Something like that." He drummed his fingers on the table. "Um, I kind of promised Jared I'd talk with him about the show. I should have cleared it with you first." At the time, it hadn't occurred to him that he was overstepping and possibly making a promise he couldn't keep.

She raised an eyebrow. "Yeah, you were in the woods with a troubled kid and didn't take the time to get my permission. Unacceptable." She shook her head. "It's fine, Nate. He really likes the show. What's it called?"

"*Daystar Rising.*" The words felt strange on his tongue. Like they referenced a different life.

"I watched a few minutes of it, but it's just not my thing. I'm more Hallmark movies and those old eighties rom-coms."

She sat back and winced. "Sorry. I'm not trying to be insulting. I'm sure it's a good show."

Despite the drama, it really *was* a great show, and he was proud to have been a part of it. "It wasn't insulting at all. Different strokes and all that." He finished his cinnamon roll and leaned toward her. "I'll let you in on a secret. I've never watched an entire season. And I stopped watching completely when I was written off the show."

She mirrored his position, putting her elbows on the table and leaning toward him. "That's quite a confession."

Suddenly it felt like they were too close, and the conversation was getting too deep. It wasn't, not really, but he was having a conversation with her he wouldn't have with anyone else, and it felt like too much. He changed the subject. "And that was quite a cinnamon roll. Not that you needed to do that, but I appreciate it." He sat back in his chair and stretched his leg out. "I'd like to make good on my promise to Jared, if it's okay with you."

She pushed her empty plate away and leaned back in her chair. "If you don't want to talk about the show, you don't have to."

"I get the feeling Jared's been let down a lot. I don't want to be one of those people."

Kim sat silent for a moment. When she spoke, her voice was quiet. "Thank you."

"Don't thank me for that." To his utter dismay, tears filled her eyes. "Kim?"

She blinked rapidly and swiped at her eyes. "Sorry. It's been a long day. I tend to get a bit emotional when I'm tired. And…"

He waited.

"You have no idea how right you are. He's been let down so many times. I mean, he's got me and my parents, but I've never felt like that was enough to balance out the damage his parents did." She wiped her face. "Sorry, I shouldn't be telling you this stuff."

He swallowed, hard. "It's fine, I've been told I'm a good listener." It felt like they'd crossed some sort of threshold. Leveled up. What it meant, he had no idea.

"You are. Not just for me, but obviously Jared thought so, too."

It was definitely getting too deep. Nate abruptly steered the conversation to what he hoped was a lighter topic. "Tell me more about your video series."

Chapter Seventeen

Kim let herself back into the house a little after eleven. She tiptoed upstairs and tapped on Jared's door. There was no answer, and for a second, her mind screamed that she shouldn't have left him alone. Her heart jumped into over-drive, pounding in her chest. She slowly turned the knob and pushed the door open a few inches. Jared was fast asleep, breathing deeply.

His covers were askew, his big, bare feet sticking out. Kim tiptoed over and fixed his covers, then leaned down and brushed his hair aside to plant a kiss on his forehead. He stirred slightly, then burrowed down into the covers.

Pulling his door closed behind her, Kim winced when the knob clicked into place. It sounded so loud in the quiet house. She froze and waited a beat, but there was no movement from inside his room.

Letting out a breath, she went back downstairs to the kitchen and started the dishwasher, then wiped down the counters while Sadie sat on the island and supervised. She readjusted the foil covering the cinnamon rolls, then took one last look around the room before turning off the light.

In her bedroom, she changed into yoga pants and a tank top and sat on the edge of the bed. She was too tired to sleep. Picking up a book, she moved to the chair beside the window and tucked her legs underneath her. The words on the page were meaningless, her mind unwilling to settle enough to read. She shoved the bookmark back into the same place and leaned her head back against the chair. Through a gap in the curtains, she could see the stars clearly, bright pinpoints of light dotting the black sky.

It was early morning before she crawled into bed and eventually drifted into a dreamless sleep.

The jangling of her phone woke her just before nine. The Caller ID showed the school's phone number. She sat upright and cleared her throat before answering.

"Yes?"

"Ms. Donahue?"

"Yes?"

"You're listed as Jared's contact person rather than his parents. Have you provided us with the proper forms that authorize you to receive sensitive information about him?"

Kim's jaw clenched. *We've had this conversation a dozen times, you hateful bitch.* "Why don't you check your files and let me know if you need any more pieces of paper." She hated this secretary with a burning, unholy passion. "What do you want?"

"We're calling to let you know Jared is absent today. His suspension ended yesterday, and he should be back in class today. This will be marked as an unexcused absence." The evil secretary's voice held a touch of glee.

"Why, exactly?"

There was a long pause. "Because he's not here."

Kim flung the covers back and stood, planting her fist on her hip. "What exactly qualifies you to classify this absence as unexcused?" She was tired and stressed. The perfect storm for not backing down to some jerk.

"Um…"

Kim was careful not to raise her voice. "No, not 'um,' I'm asking you a question. What criteria are you using?"

"Ms. Donahue, his suspension was over yesterday. When he didn't show up today, we assumed –"

"There's your problem, right there. He could be in the hospital, he could be sick, he could be doing any number of things that are, in fact, allowable absences. But by all means, please educate me as to why *my child* isn't in school today."

"Ms. Donahue, I don't know why he's not here. But it's very important that children maintain regular attendance. It's their best hope of academic success. It's also my understanding that he is not, in fact, *your* child."

Kim took a deep breath, swallowing back the "F" word that threatened to burst from her lips. Who did this woman think she was, lecturing her on the importance of attendance after issuing a bogus suspension? "Is there anything else?"

"No."

"Your own policy allows two days to provide an excuse. Which means this will not be marked unexcused until Tuesday at the earliest. I'll be checking EduSystem as soon as we hang up. If his absence has been prematurely marked as unexcused, I'll be forced to involve my attorney."

The secretary squawked. "Ms. Donahue-"

Kim hung up the phone and tossed it onto the bed. Her hand shook. "You've got to be freaking kidding me," she muttered to Sadie, who was stretched out across Kim's pillow. "I swear I'm going to end up smacking that woman."

Sadie blinked slowly and flicked her tail, in complete agreement.

Flinging open her closet door, Kim yanked hangers back

and forth. "Where is my red shirt? It's *red*. How hard should it be to find a red freaking shirt?" She blew out an angry breath and backed up to lean against the dresser. She took several deep breaths to calm herself. She'd overslept, she'd had an argument, she had work to catch up on, and the birds chirping outside were getting on her nerves. Even the bright sun streaming through the window was offensive. It did not bode well for a good day.

A sliver of red peeked out between two black sweaters. Kim pulled it out and held it up. Okay, at least she'd found her favorite red blouse. Maybe things would start looking up.

And she had lunch scheduled with her friend Tara. They hadn't talked in a couple of weeks, and she was in serious need of some girl time.

She lingered in the shower, letting the hot water pound against her aching shoulders. Shampooing her short hair only took a few seconds. She stepped out of the shower and wrapped herself in her favorite fluffy towel. She took her time applying makeup and fixing her hair. Finally, she dressed and took a look in her full-length mirror. Her shirt and a pair of red heels were bright pops of color against her black pants. She looked good and finally felt ready to face the day.

Jared was downstairs, a plate of cinnamon roll crumbs in front of him. He was looking at his phone, then glanced up and did a double-take. "Wow. You look like a lawyer or something."

Kim grinned and ruffled his hair. "I'll take that as a compliment." She popped a pod into the coffee machine and pushed the button to brew. "How many of those did you eat?"

Jared feigned innocence. "How many of what?"

Kim cocked her head and raised an eyebrow.

"I left you one."

"Jared! One? There were six rolls."

He blinked.

"I don't want to hear it tomorrow morning when you have nothing for breakfast." She tried to sound stern.

"We have popcorn."

"Popcorn? For breakfast?" She made a face.

"What's wrong with that?"

"Bleh. It's weird." She pulled her mug out of the coffeemaker and popped the pod out to throw into the trash.

"And it's Friday. Pizza night. So there will be leftover pizza for breakfast."

She blew on her coffee. "Pizza and popcorn?"

Jared smirked. "All the Ps. Breakfast of champions."

"You're goofy."

"Can I go to the library today?"

"Were you planning to be there long? I'm meeting Tara for lunch, so I could drop you off on the way and pick you up when we're done."

"Okay."

"We can hit McDonald's for you on the way home. What are you working on?"

"I have to finish that report for English Lit. We have to have three references from actual books, not online sources." He looked pained.

"Hey, back when dinosaurs roamed the earth, we didn't even *have* online sources."

"Then how did you google stuff?"

She laughed behind her coffee cup. "Google didn't exist."

"That had to suck."

She quirked an eyebrow at his language, then nodded. "It was a dark and difficult time. There was even a time you couldn't see who was calling when the phone started ringing. It was like Russian roulette. Was it a friend? A telemarketer? Who knew?"

He wiped a glob of icing off his plate and popped it in his mouth. "I was supposed to go back to school today."

She was surprised he'd brought it up. "I know. But it's Friday, so I figured another day plus the weekend would give us some time to look at our options."

His brow creased. "Options?"

"Yeah, I don't know. Transferring? Homeschooling? Sucking it up for the rest of the year? Changing classes? I don't know. That's why I'm meeting Tara. She'll have some good advice."

"Why?"

"She's a teacher. She quit teaching in public school to home-school her kids and now she teaches in a cyber school, so I'm sure she has some insight."

"Huh."

"Tell me about your report." She sipped her coffee while Jared launched into a surprisingly lengthy monologue about his report.

When he'd finished, she glanced at her watch. "Go get your stuff. Train leaves in fifteen."

He hopped off the barstool and headed upstairs.

Kim washed her mug out and turned it upside down on the mat beside the sink. Staring out across the yard, she watched a squirrel run into the woods and skitter up the side of a tree. She heard Jared moving around in the room above her head. Her heart squeezed in her chest. She'd never planned to have kids. Never wanted them. But she'd had Jared off and on over the years, and now that he was with her permanently, she couldn't imagine life without him.

A few minutes later, his heavy footsteps on the stairs pulled her from her thoughts.

"Ready?" He was at the doorway, his backpack slung over his shoulder.

"When we get home, that thing needs to go in the wash." She pinched a bit of fabric on his hoodie.

"Nah, it's got another week in it, at least." He lifted the sleeve to his nose and breathed deeply.

Kim scrunched up her face as she pulled the door shut behind them. "Absolutely not. Unless you want to sleep out here on the porch."

He shot her a rare devilish grin. "You think I won't?"

"I know you won't. Because you're doing laundry when we get home."

He tossed his backpack in the back seat of the car and got in the front. "Aye, aye, captain."

Kim tried to keep her emotions off her face. Guilt, mainly. Only three days of not being in that school and Jared was acting like a normal kid. It was a striking contrast to the sullen, withdrawn boy he'd been just a few days ago, quiet and unsmiling, hiding his face, trying to be invisible. How had she missed the signs that he was miserable? His bruises were fading, too.

"Aunt Kim?"

"Huh?" She startled from her thoughts.

"Road's closed. You have to go around the other way."

"Oh, shit. *Shoot*." On autopilot, she'd forgotten about the new route to the library. She pulled into a driveway and turned around. "I wasn't paying attention."

"Everything okay?"

She smiled over at him. "Yeah." She decided to heed the counselor's advice to be honest, and her own caveat to not be *too* honest. "Just thinking about all this school stuff, and a little frustrated because I'm so clueless about the options." She shot him a grin as she pulled up to the sidewalk in front of the library. "Lucky thing for you we have Google these days."

"I'd rather have a pet pterodactyl like you did."

She pretended to glare. "Pterodactyls won't research your reports for you."

"No, but they could eat anybody who had a problem with my paper."

Kim laughed. "I'll text you when I'm back."

"Lunch with Tara? The library closes at eight," he joked.

"Go. I'll be back around two."

Jared snorted. "No way you're back by two. Bet you a quarter." He pulled his backpack out of the backseat and trotted into the library, pausing at the door to wave.

Kim waved back and drove to Sonny's Diner. Inside, she scanned the tables until she found Tara in the far corner booth, talking on her cell phone. Kim approached and gave a little wave.

Tara grinned. "Gotta go. Kim's here. Love you." She ended the call and jumped up to give Kim a hug. "Do you know how long it's been since we've had lunch? Four months! That's entirely too long."

Kim hugged her back, tight. "Unacceptable."

They sat down. Tara said, "I just ordered us both water, I wasn't sure what you'd want."

"Water is perfect. Thank you."

Corinne, the waitress, stopped by, set their glasses on the table, and took their food orders.

"So? Tell me about the Jared situation."

Kim let out a deep breath. "I'll try to give you the short version."

Just as she finished her tale, Corinne appeared with their food and refilled their drinks.

Tara sat back. "Wow. That's a lot. I wish I could say I'm surprised at the suspension, but I'm not."

"Mrs. Edwards is the only one who's been in touch with

Jared to make sure he didn't fall behind. He's at the library right now working on a research paper for her."

"Good."

Kim poked at her salad. "I don't see how I can send him back there. If I let him go back and something happened... I'd never forgive myself."

"You've come to the right place." Tara fished around in her purse and pulled out a sheet of paper. "I actually emailed this to you before I left the house, so you don't have to try typing in all these links. Here's the cyber school we use. Since I'm on the faculty, I checked to see if I could pull a few strings. It's not the best time to switch, but this is a pretty critical situation. This is the crap cyber school was made for. Email her," she poked at the page, "and tell her I referred you. She'll answer all your questions and walk you through the process."

Kim blinked back unexpected tears. "Thank you."

"Obviously you have other options, but this is probably the simplest thing to get him through the end of this year. If it's not what you want, I can help you figure it out."

"You have no idea how amazing you are."

Tara snorted. "Oh, believe me, I know."

They laughed together and Kim felt the weight lifting from her shoulders.

"I feel so much better, just having this in my hand." She held up the paper. "I hate the feeling of floundering."

"It'll work out. Jared's a great kid, and you're a great parent."

"Guardian."

Tara shrugged. "Have you thought about adopting him? Making it official?"

Kim shook her head. Of course the thought had crossed her mind, but it had its downsides, too. "I don't want to affect his

Social Security survivor benefits. It's not a ton of money, but it'll mean a lot less in loans for college."

Tara took on a thoughtful expression. "Have you checked into that? Because I don't think adoption affects a child's benefits. Only a spouse if they remarry."

"Really?"

"I don't know for sure, but I seem to remember a similar situation back when I was teaching, where the kid's dad died, and when the mom remarried, her benefits stopped, but the kid's didn't."

"I'll definitely look into that. There have been lots of times this past year where it would have been easier to be his parent instead of his guardian. Thanks for the info."

"Hey, you don't keep me around just because I'm gorgeous."

They laughed and Kim pushed her empty plate away. "What's new with you? What are Kody and Kaylee up to these days? Has Mark's job gotten any better?"

Tara sighed and launched into her own tale.

It was nearly two thirty when they hugged in the parking lot. Kim squeezed her friend tight. "Thank you so much. I feel a lot better about the school situation now that I have some solid options."

"I'm glad I could help. I'll text you the dates for the kids' science fair if you really want to go."

"I do. It sounds fun. Tell Mark hello for me."

"I will. Say hello to the hot neighbor for me." Tara winked.

Kim felt her face turn red and she was having trouble not grinning. "I never said he was hot."

Tara laughed. "Didn't have to. It's all over your blushing face."

"Don't you have somewhere to be?" Kim shook her head. "I'll see you soon."

They blew air kisses on the way to their respective cars.

She drove to the library and as soon as she parked, she texted Jared. A few minutes later, he came out and got in the car, smirking and holding his hand out.

"What?"

"I knew you wouldn't be back by two."

"Blah blah blah." She handed him a quarter. "Don't spend it all in one place."

He snickered and slipped the coin into his backpack. "Can we stop at McDonald's?"

"Yep."

"Can I go over to Nate's when we get home?"

"Nope."

"Why not?"

"We don't know if he's home. We don't know if he's in the middle of something. You can't just drop over unannounced."

Jared curled his lip and raised an eyebrow. "You went over last evening. Unannounced."

"Yes, but I was taking him cinnamon rolls. I wasn't going to accost him with a million questions. And I was just going to drop off the rolls and come home, but he invited me in."

A wide grin split his face. "Did you kiss?"

Kim gasped, her mouth dropping open. "What? Where did you get *that*? No, we did not kiss. Or hug. Or anything else you may be conjuring up." Flustered, she abruptly changed the subject. "Did you get all three references you needed?"

"Of course. You left me there long enough to get three *thousand* references."

She pulled up to the drive-thru and ordered Jared's food. On the way home, he ate his fries. "These are actually fresh."

"That's a miracle."

With his cheeks stuffed full of fries, he asked, "Did your friend have ideas about school?"

Kim was surprised he'd brought it up. "Yes. She gave me contact information for a cyber school, and she said we should be able to get you enrolled even though it's so late in the year. Best case scenario is that all your credits transfer, and you don't have to repeat a bunch of work."

"So I don't have to go back?"

"I can't say that for sure. I have to call this lady, which I will do as soon as we get home. Even if it all goes smoothly, I'm sure we'll have to go in and clean out your locker and turn in your books. Stuff like that."

"Okay." His voice was suddenly small.

She hated that even the thought of school so altered his demeanor. She pulled into the garage and they walked into the house. Jared sat at the kitchen island with his food, dipping his burger into honey mustard sauce. Kim filled a glass of water at the fridge.

"Would it be okay if Isobel comes over sometime this weekend?"

Kim raised an eyebrow. "Isobel, huh?"

He rolled his eyes. "She's my *friend*. She does online school because her parents travel a lot. They just got back from two months in Costa Rica."

"That sounds exciting. What do they do?"

"Mercenaries or something."

Kim nearly spit out her mouthful of water. "Do you mean missionaries?"

"Oh. Yeah, that might be it. They help build orphanages and preach and stuff. Last year they were in Africa for like six months."

"How'd you meet her?"

"School. She didn't start homeschooling until like fifth grade."

"That's cool."

"So can she come over?"

"Sure. Tomorrow's good. Sunday afternoon, we're going to Grandma and Grandpa's for dinner though."

"Okay. I'll text her." He hopped off his stool and threw his trash away, all while texting one-handed. He stopped suddenly, his eyes widening. "I wonder if it would be okay to introduce her to Nate? Do you think he'd be okay with that?"

Kim shook her head. "He seems really private. I don't know if he'd appreciate being put on the spot like that."

"But…" The doorbell chimed, cutting off Jared's objection. He sighed, then went to answer the door.

A newly familiar voice drew her to the living room. Nate looked over Jared's head and held up a plate. "Returning this."

Jared was quiet, but Kim could see he was lightly bouncing on his heels, no doubt warring with himself about whether to ask Nate the questions he wanted to ask or be polite.

Nate looked back down at Jared. Smiling, he asked, "No unplanned hikes today, huh?"

Kim's breath hitched for a second, waiting to see how Jared reacted.

He simply shrugged both shoulders. "Nah, I won't be doing that again."

Kim crossed her arms. "Jared, you can let him inside."

Jared jumped, embarrassed. "Sorry. Yeah, come in."

Kim said, "Come on in the kitchen. I was just cleaning up."

Nate followed Jared into the room and held up the plate. "Where would you like this?"

Kim took it from him and put it in the dishwasher. "Thanks. I take it you enjoyed the rest of the cinnamon rolls."

Sadie jumped onto the island to investigate the new visitor.

Nate scratched Sadie's head, earning a purr. "I had one for breakfast and three for lunch."

Jared snorted. "Aren't you going to yell at him for eating so many at once?"

Nate raised an eyebrow. "How many did *you* eat?"

"Five."

"Five! Dang, you should enter an eating competition or something."

Kim said, "Don't give him any ideas."

"I said she should take it as a compliment," Jared grumbled.

Nate laughed. "I'm betting she didn't, though."

Kim sighed. "No, she did not."

After a moment, Nate said directly to Jared, "I didn't know if you guys were busy tomorrow, but if you're not, you could come over and I can show you some of the pictures and stuff I have from the show."

Jared's eyes were wide as saucers. "Yes! Um, well, crap." He glanced at Kim, then back at Nate. "My friend Isobel is coming over tomorrow and she loves the show, too, so I know she'd be super excited to know you were next door but I didn't say anything to her because Kim said you like your privacy and probably don't want people to know but I know Isobel wouldn't say anything and I didn't say anything, either, and I was going to ask if I could introduce you to her but Kim said I shouldn't be a pest and I'm not trying to be but you said about coming over and it would be so cool if I could come over and bring Isobel, but if not that's totally okay."

"Dude, oxygen," Nate said with a laugh. "Sure, you can bring your friend Isobel over, but only if it's okay with your aunt."

"It's fine with me, if you're sure you can handle it."

"Eh, it can't be any worse than the last con I was at. The fans wouldn't stop screaming long enough to ask any questions or hear the answers. It got so bad security ended up taking us off the stage early because the crowd was getting out of hand."

"That's stupid," Jared said.

"Most cons are great. The fans ask some really deep questions and it's usually a good time for everyone."

"If you liked doing that, how come you don't do them anymore? Or do they stop asking you after your character dies?"

Nate shook his head. "Depends. If the character was super popular, they'll keep inviting you to cons. I haven't gone because the last few haven't worked out with my schedule."

Kim held up a hand at Jared's expression. It looked like he was ready to start rattling off another list of questions. "You can bombard him with your questions tomorrow." She turned to Nate and shook her head. "I don't think you know what you're in for."

He grinned as he stood up from his stool. "It'll be great."

Jared was still over the moon. "What time can we come over?"

"How about noon? We can order pizza."

Jared's eyes widened. "Really?"

Kim put her hand on his shoulder. "We'll get some chips or something to go with it."

"Sounds great. I'll see you tomorrow, then."

Kim flicked her wrist and pointed. Jared got her meaning and jumped off his stool and walked Nate to the door. "Thanks so much. Isobel's going to be super excited."

"It'll be fun. I have some props I think you'll like."

"Cool." Jared's voice was full of star-struck wonder.

Kim hovered in the doorway of the kitchen, giving Nate a small wave and a shake of her head. She had a pretty good idea that Jared wouldn't be getting any sleep.

Nate smiled at her over Jared's head, and she was struck by

how different he was from a month ago. He even carried himself differently. Taller, more relaxed. Infinitely more attractive. She pushed *that* thought away.

Kim spent the evening editing a video to post automatically Monday morning, while Jared holed up in his room, undoubtedly writing a long list of questions for Nate.

In the morning, she woke up to the sound of Jared moving around. Squinting at the clock, she realized it was just after six. She flung her arm over her eyes and sighed before getting up.

Sadie stood up and stretched, then curled back up on Kim's pillow and went back to sleep.

Kim rubbed her face in Sadie's fur, envious of the option to go back to sleep. She got dressed and met Jared in the kitchen.

He rifled through the cabinets, impatient.

"Whatcha doing?"

"Trying to find something to take over for lunch. We don't have any chips."

"Let's run to the store. I'll get stuff to make cookies and we'll get some chips."

He was practically out the door before she had her shoes on. She had to chuckle at his enthusiasm.

They made a quick trip to the store, then she had Jared help her mix up the dough for peanut butter chocolate chip cookies.

"I hope Nate likes cookies," Jared said as he scooped dough onto the cookie sheet.

"If he doesn't like cookies, he's not someone we want to associate with."

A knock on the door cut off his horrified expression. "That's Isobel." He ran to the door and a second later, excited chatter filled the living room.

Kim smiled to herself as she put the tray of cookies in the

oven. It did her heart good to see Jared with a friend, excited about meeting Nate. She did feel a twinge of sympathy for Nate. This afternoon was going to be more than he'd bargained for.

Jared and Isobel poked into the kitchen.

"Hi." The pretty girl smiled at Kim.

"Hi, Isobel. It's nice to meet you."

"Something smells great."

"Thanks. Peanut butter cookies with chocolate chips."

Isobel nodded appreciatively. "Yum."

Jared interjected, "We're going to work on our list for Nate."

Isobel giggled and blushed.

Kim hid her laugh. Apparently, Isobel had a bit of a crush on Nate. Kim couldn't wait to see Isobel's reaction when she met him in person.

"Your mom's really cool." Isobel's voice carried down the hallway.

Kim froze.

Isobel gasped and kept talking. "Sorry, I meant your aunt."

Kim sidled closer to the stairs, her heart pounding.

Then Jared's voice, unbothered by the gaffe. "It's okay. I mean, she's pretty much my mom."

Putting a hand on the wall to steady herself, Kim wasn't sure what to do with the waves of emotion crashing over her. The timer dinged, and she pushed away from the wall and crossed the room on shaky legs. She was full of overwhelming love for the boy, while being crushed by the reality of the responsibility she'd taken on. There was so much more to this parenting thing than keeping a roof over his head and food in his belly. And right there, that offhanded comment she was never meant to hear, was all the confirmation she'd ever need that she'd made the right decision in taking Jared in and letting William go.

Chapter Eighteen

Nate spent the morning picking out boxes to set on the kitchen table for the kids to go through. There were bits of costume, props, and tons of photos. He hadn't gone through any of it and was surprised to find he was looking forward to it.

Talking with Jared had rekindled some of his enthusiasm for *Daystar Rising*, reminding him of the good times, especially when the show first started, and then when it became a megahit, practically overnight. Those days had been fun. Back before the fame had changed everything.

At eleven thirty, he ordered pizza for delivery. Four pizzas, to be exact, because he wasn't sure what everyone would want. He hung up and had to laugh at himself. He was nervous. It was ridiculous. They were his next-door neighbors. No big deal.

He was simply making good on his promise to Jared. Nothing more. It's not like he had anything to prove. No need to impress anyone.

Yeah, right.

At two minutes before twelve, he paced around the

kitchen, trying not to stare out the window, when he saw Kim step out onto the porch. A teenage girl, presumably Isobel, followed her, then Jared came out, carrying a box.

The pizza arrived at the same time. As Kim and the kids came onto the porch, Nate paid the driver and took the stack of pizzas. He held the door open with his back, letting his guests enter ahead of him.

"Kitchen's straight ahead." He glanced at Kim's backside, then mentally chastised himself. Nope, nope, nope, that wasn't a road he was going down. "What's in the box?"

Jared answered, "Chips, salad, and fresh-baked cookies."

"Cookies? Awesome."

Kim shot him a look over her shoulder. "I think you mean 'salad, awesome,' right?"

"Pssht, of course that's what I meant. What did I say?"

She laughed. It was a sound he wanted to hear more of. "No cookies until we've had lunch."

Nate slid the pizza boxes onto the table. "That's brutal. I can smell them. Are they fresh?"

"Took them out of the oven ten minutes ago." She nodded at the boxes he set on the table. "Wow, that's a lot of pizza."

"I didn't know what everyone would like. So there's a bit of everything." He turned and said, "You must be Isobel." He put his hand out to shake hers.

Isobel made a strangled noise, part laugh, part breathy sigh.

"I'm Nate Sanders. It's really nice to meet you."

She slowly reached out and shook his hand.

"Jared says you were just in Costa Rica. That must have been fun."

Isobel nodded. "Fun."

"What kind of pizza do you like?" Nate had the feeling she

probably would have eaten pizza topped with fried tarantulas and not notice. Or live tarantulas. The poor girl hadn't blinked since she got there.

"Yes."

Nate glanced over at Kim, who was biting her lips, trying not to laugh. "How about we sit down and eat, then you guys can start the interrogation."

Kim handed out the paper plates and napkins, while Nate opened the pizza boxes. "There's pepperoni, white broccoli pizza, a chicken bacon ranch pizza, and half mushroom, half plain cheese."

"No anchovy?" Kim asked.

"No. Sorry." It took a second before Nate grasped that she was joking. "Very funny. You're giving me a complex."

She laughed. "The chicken bacon ranch is my favorite."

"Mine's the broccoli."

Jared made a face. "Broccoli on pizza? What a waste." He shrugged. "Oh, well. Guess that means I get a whole pepperoni."

Nate looked at Isobel. "I guess you're stuck with the mushroom."

"Okay."

"I'm teasing. Have whatever you like."

"Okay." She took a slice of broccoli pizza.

From the corner of his eye, Nate could see Jared rolling his eyes and Kim smirking.

She turned away, though, and opened the bowl of salad. "Do you have some forks for the salad?"

"Sure." He set his slice of pizza down.

"Just tell me where."

"Top drawer, to the left of the dishwasher."

He rather liked the image of Kim making herself at home in

his kitchen, then almost groaned at the thought. His mother was going to have a field day with this.

Kim gave everyone forks and put a big spoon in the salad, then opened the bag of chips. After she filled her plate, she sat down across from Nate. They exchanged a smile.

"So," Jared began, "did you always want to be an actor?"

"Pretty much. I did some acting in high school and thought it would be an easy job."

Kim asked, "What's the hardest part?"

"Well, the constant blows to the ego are pretty hard."

"What do you mean?" Jared asked. "You have great reviews for Qaaxag."

"Sure, but over the years, I tried out for about three hundred other parts and got turned down and turned down and turned down. My first break was a cereal commercial."

"Toasted Fiber-Os," Isobel blurted out, then blushed beet red.

Nate grimaced. "Yeah. They're exactly as appetizing as they sound, too. Have you seen it?"

She nodded. "YouTube."

"Ah."

Kim raised an eyebrow. "Toasted Fiber-Os? I'm going to have to look that one up."

He felt his face heat. The thought of Kim looking him up unsettled him. Even though he might have recently found himself watching an episode of *Fifteen Minutes to Fabulous*. Or two episodes. Or ten. "The cereal sucks, but the acting was brilliant," Nate joked.

Jared said, "Then you got *Daystar Rising*, right?"

"Almost a decade later. I did a few more commercials and a really, really bad movie on SciFi."

"*Centipede Lava*." Isobel offered.

"What?" Kim said.

Nate sighed. "Giant prehistoric mutant centipedes are spit out during a volcano eruption in Hawaii."

"Wow. They were unharmed by lava."

"Right." He laughed. The movie had been awful and cheesy, but a lot of fun to make. It had developed its own small but devoted cult following, and for some reason, fans still clamored for a sequel.

"Because they were prehistoric."

Nate sighed heavily. "You're one of *those* people, huh? The ones who need their storylines to make sense?"

"Sorry."

Jared grinned. "It's online. Isobel and I watched it last night."

Kim shook her head. "Is that the god-awful noise I heard coming from your room at eleven o'clock?"

"Yeah."

Nate finished his slice of pizza and speared a forkful of salad. "I'm surprised you still wanted to come over after seeing that. It was bad."

"No, it was good," Isobel insisted.

Jared rolled his eyes again. "Oh, brother."

Isobel picked at her pizza. Nate guessed she didn't actually like broccoli.

They finished eating and Nate threw the paper plates in the trash while Kim put the forks in the sink. They crossed paths as he was heading back to the table and she was taking the rest of the salad to the fridge. Without thinking, he put his hand on her hip as he stopped and let her cross in front of him. She hesitated ever so slightly and glanced up at him. He couldn't read her expression to tell if he'd overstepped just a little, or a whole lot.

He busied himself lifting a box of memorabilia from the counter to the table and pulling items out. "I got to keep these weapons. And these scales are pieces from the suit of armor I wore in the war in season two."

"Whoa." Jared inspected the plastic pieces. "They look like real metal on tv."

"If they were real metal, I wouldn't be able to stand up," Nate joked. "I'm not exactly a bodybuilder."

Isobel said, "Did you work out a lot for the show? You were, I mean, um, Qaaxag, um, well, like, muscles and stuff."

Nate didn't have to look at Kim to know she was holding back a laugh. "Nope, it was all costume. I had a latex bodysuit they put me in. It was pretty cool. They made me lay in this gel stuff to make a mold, then they made the alien body so it would fit me perfectly."

"Oh."

He hid a laugh at her disappointment.

Jared was all ears. "That's so cool. How did they do the extra arms?"

"It was a combination of costume and green screen magic. Sometimes they had me stop and repeat an action with my arms in different positions so they could edit them together. It was always amazing to see how seamless it ended up being on the screen."

"Did you get to keep any of the swords?"

"Nope. They're too important to the storyline."

Nodding enthusiastically, Jared practically shouted, "That's what I said. I said the crystal alloy is going to be important in the final war and they're going to dismantle the ships and strand themselves on Earth in order to save it and fulfill the prophecy."

"Awesome theory."

"Do you know how it ends?"

"Nope. We got our scripts once a week and that's all the further ahead we were allowed to know. Pretty much only the writers knew what was coming."

"Do you know ahead of time if your character is going to die?"

"Nope. That's why everybody always flips to the end of the script first, to see if they're still alive at the end of the episode." Nate grinned. "Of course sometimes a character dies and then comes back in the army of the undead, so you never really *know* – know either way."

"Do you think they'll bring Qaaxag back?"

"I doubt it, but anything's possible, I suppose."

"How do they do the alien language? Like, did you have to learn the whole thing?"

Nate nodded. "Yeah. We actually worked with a linguist who came in and created the whole language so that we could actually say the words."

Kim raised an eyebrow. "So you're fluent in a language that doesn't really exist."

"Oh, it exists. People at the cons can carry on a whole conversation in Qaaxian."

"Goodness." She looked baffled by the concept.

"Hey, how many people have learned Klingon? Same sort of thing."

"Not that many," Kim said.

Nate and Jared exchanged a look, and Jared said, "Seriously, there are tons of people who speak Klingon. There's even a Klingon Language Institute where you can take classes to learn."

"You're kidding."

Nate held back a laugh at Kim's incredulous expression. "No joke."

"Wouldn't it make more sense to learn Spanish? Or French? Or Latin?"

Nate shrugged. "I guess that depends on what floats your boat. People really get into their fandoms."

"I suppose." She still looked skeptical.

Jared pulled an envelope of photos out of the box and looked at Kim. "We should go to a con. You'd have fun."

Isobel leaned closer to Jared so she could see the photos. Nate noticed the way Jared froze for a second, then held the stack of pictures so Isobel could see them better. He also noticed that Jared seemed far more interested in Isobel than the photos.

He looked over their heads at Kim and raised an eyebrow. She looked at them, then back at Nate, and mirrored his expression.

They spent most of the afternoon going through Nate's boxes of stuff from the set. It was almost six when Isobel's phone buzzed. She pulled it out. "It's my dad." She returned a text, then another, then looked up at Kim. "Can Jared come to dinner with us? My parents want to try the new Asian Fusion and said we can take him along. If it's okay."

Jared sat up straight, his eyes pleading.

Kim nodded. "Sure."

Isobel grinned and sent another text. "They'll pick us up in about ten minutes."

Kim said, "I guess we'd better head over before her parents get here."

Isobel fidgeted with her phone, her face turning red. "Um, would you, um, mind, um, I promise I won't like put it online or anything, but, um, maybe could I get a picture?"

Nate smiled. "Sure. Let's get one with you and Jared both, okay?"

She nodded furiously, still clutching her phone.

Kim reached over. "Here. I'll take the picture. Jared, do you want one?"

"Yeah!"

A minute later, Kim had snapped pictures on both phones and handed them back to the kids.

"Thanks so much, Mr. Sanders," Isobel said.

Nate chuckled. It was the first sentence she'd managed to speak without getting tongue-tied. "Please. Just call me Nate."

"Okay," she squeaked.

Jared pulled her toward the door. "Thanks, Nate. It was really cool seeing your *Daystar Rising* stuff."

"It was really cool showing it to you guys. Isobel, it was nice to meet you."

She giggled and followed Jared out the door.

Kim hung back while the kids headed across the lawn. "You handled that really well."

Nate chuckled. "Comes with the territory."

"Not bad for the ego, either, I'm guessing."

He shrugged. "At first, maybe, but after a while, you get it through your head they're interested in your character, not you. Then you figure out it's just part of the job. Kinda like people coming up to you when you're in a restaurant."

She nodded. "True. The kids had a good time."

"I'm glad. I did, too."

"Me, too."

Nate shoved his hands into his pockets. He was surprised at how much it meant to him that she'd had a good time today. "Hey, so, if Jared's not going to be home for dinner, do you want to grab something? All I've got is leftover pizza and something in the back of the fridge that was here when I moved in."

Kim looked up at him for a long moment, then nodded. "Sure. I'll grab my purse."

"I'll get my stuff put away and be over in like fifteen minutes?"

"Sounds good."

He stepped back into the house and watched her cross the lawn. Yeah, his mother was definitely going to have a field day with this.

Chapter Nineteen

"That was fun," Kim said.

Isobel nodded vigorously. "He's *soooooo* nice. And really friendly. And super cool."

Jared batted his eyelashes and clasped his hands to his cheek. In a high-pitched voice, he said, "And he's *soooooooooooo* handsome."

Kim laughed while Isobel glared at him, blushing furiously.

A car pulled in the driveway.

"Jared, take your key in case I'm not home when you get back. I'm going to grab dinner with Nate."

Isobel's eyes widened. "Are you *dating* him? Oh, wow, that's like super awesome."

"Not dating. Just dinner." She shooed the kids out the door, stopping Jared for a quick kiss on the cheek. "Have fun. And behave!"

He rolled his eyes but gave her a hug. "*You* behave." He made kissy noises.

She tilted her head and put her hands on her hips. "Watch it, mister."

Laughing, he followed Isobel to the car. Kim waved at her parents, then went back inside to freshen up.

In the bathroom, she swiped on some fresh mascara and lipstick, ran her fingers through her blonde pixie hair, and reapplied a spritz of hairspray. After a moment's thought, she changed into a deep burgundy silky blouse and picked a pair of heels that went with her dark jeans. Nate was tall, unlike most of the guys Kim had been out with. She usually wore flats so she didn't tower over anyone. Not that being 5'9" was a giant, but a lot of guys didn't want to look up at their date.

Back downstairs, Kim threw her phone and keys into her purse and fixed a stray piece of her bangs. She walked outside as Nate pulled along the front of the house. He got out of the car and walked around to open her door.

"Thanks." She got in and buckled her seatbelt while he got back in the driver's seat.

"You look really nice."

"Thank you." She noticed he had changed into a deep green shirt that matched his eyes. "So do you. I like that shirt."

"What, this old thing?" He grinned. "How about Italian? I wouldn't mind trying Asian Fusion, but I'm thinking Jared wouldn't be too happy to have us show up at the same place he's at."

"Italian sounds great. I bet Isobel wouldn't mind if we showed up, but yeah, Jared would be less than thrilled." Poor Jared. His crush on Isobel was so obvious. To everyone except Isobel.

Nate chuckled. "How about Carmine's? They have the best seafood ravioli in the world."

"That sounds incredible." Her stomach tensed in agreement.

Carmine's wasn't quite local, being a thirty-minute drive

away. Not too far… not too close. Kim's heart skipped a beat at the prospect of spending the drive with Nate.

"Carmine's it is, then."

Kim fidgeted with the strap of her purse and tried not to look at Nate's profile, which was rather handsome and distracting. Instead, she focused her attention on the radio. "I haven't been to Carmine's in ages. In fact, I think the last time I was there was when I was still in college."

"I took my mom there last month for her birthday."

"That's so sweet. Your mom seems really nice, by the way. I feel bad I didn't get much of a chance to talk to her the other day. But I really appreciate her coming over to let us know you'd gone looking for Jared. At least we knew pretty much where he was. Saved a lot of searching."

"I'm glad she was there, too. I didn't have your number, and I was afraid if I asked Jared for it, he'd bolt."

"I'm not sure what he would have done." Kim shuddered at the dark directions her mind wanted to turn.

"He seems to be doing okay today. Are things better?"

Kim looked over at him and her words caught, struck by his easy and unassuming good looks. His short blondish hair was just the right level of messy. She blinked, bringing herself back to the conversation. "Yes. I think so. We're working on getting him enrolled in a cyber school for the rest of this year. We'll worry about next year later."

"May I ask what happened? I know it's none of my business, so I won't be offended if you don't want to talk about it."

"No, it's fine. You know about Jared's parents. So do some of the kids, and quite frankly, middle school is brutal and some kids are just little jerks. He's been picked on and bullied all year, but he seemed to be handling it okay, and it got better for a while." She took a deep breath. "Then one of his friends decided they weren't friends anymore and wrote his number in the bathroom. He started getting these horrible text messages and all kinds of crap on social media. Messages telling him his parents died to get away from him, and that he should kill himself."

Nate puffed out a breath. "That's… wow."

"Yeah. I didn't know any of this until I got a call from the school the other day. They suspended Jared for getting in a fight. One of the kids who had been picking on him spit on him in the locker room, so Jared hit him."

"Hopefully the other kid's face looked as bad as Jared's."

She had to laugh a little. "That's exactly what I said. Not that I condone violence, but I'm a big fan of self-defense."

"Totally agree."

"The principal doesn't. Their zero-tolerance policy," Kim made air quotes around the words, "meant Jared got suspended. The other little brat got sent back to class."

"I wish I could say I'm surprised." His lips pressed together.

"Then you know what they did? He was suspended for two days. I kept him home yesterday, which would have been the third day, and they had the nerve to call to *notify* me he was absent. Then the old hag tried to lecture me on the educational importance of regular attendance."

"After they toss him for two days for defending himself."

"Exactly. And they weren't the least bit concerned about the messages he'd gotten. All of a sudden, their zero-tolerance turns into a cover-your-butt 'It didn't happen on school property' excuse." She realized she was practically yelling. Settling back in her seat, she said, "Sorry. The whole thing just pisses me off."

"As it should. The whole situation is ridiculous and unjust. No wonder the poor kid freaked out."

"My mom called the youth pastor at their church. He's a counselor, and he was able to squeeze Jared into his schedule. He didn't feel Jared was a real danger to himself, that he was overwhelmed and felt trapped. I think he's right. Once we started looking into alternate schooling, it's like Jared's a whole different kid."

"That's great."

"I'm so glad we have options these days. I can't imagine having to send him back there."

"Especially if the administration is that tone-deaf. Jared's lucky to have you in his corner."

"Thanks." His words warmed her. Kim couldn't think of anything else to say, so she didn't say anything as Nate pulled into a parking space, then went around the car to open her door.

On the narrow sidewalk, another couple was coming in the opposite direction. Nate stepped behind her and lightly put his hand on her side while the other couple passed. She couldn't ignore the tingle that ran up her spine from the contact, just like it had in his kitchen when he'd touched her.

Inside, they waited for a hostess to show them to a table in the busy restaurant. When they were seated, Kim tried to focus on the menu and not the phantom feeling where Nate's hand had rested.

A few minutes later, when they had both ordered the seafood ravioli and the waiter had delivered a basket of fresh bread and filled a glass of red wine for each of them, she finally allowed her gaze to meet his.

She said, "Good wine."

The corner of Nate's mouth lifted in a half-smile. "It's adequate. Something, full-bodied, blah blah, aromatic, something something."

Kim laughed. "Not an aficionado, I take it?"

"Nope, not even if I knew what that was."

She laughed again and spread butter on a slice of the warm bread.

"Tell me about you. What made you go into vlogging?"

"Originally, it seemed soooo easy. Make a video, post it, cash in the zillions of dollars in per click ad revenue. Turns out, it's actual work and you can't force something to go viral and become an overnight billionaire. Which kind of stinks, but the perks are pretty sweet. I'm my own boss, I get to be creative and do things that interest me, I make a living, and it's fun when someone comes up to me and tells me one of my videos helped them."

"Like the ladies at breakfast."

"Exactly. Of course every now and then you have to deal with a creep, but you know all about that."

He tipped his glass in her direction. "Boy, do I."

Kim wasn't sure if she was about to step onto a minefield, but she asked anyway. "Are you going to go back to acting?"

The waiter chose that moment to reappear, placing their plates of seafood ravioli in front of them. "Anything else right now?"

"No, thank you," they said in unison.

The waiter nodded and moved away to the next table.

Kim leaned toward her plate and inhaled deeply. "This smells incredible."

"I wouldn't steer you wrong." Nate speared a ravioli with his fork and lifted it. "That is really hot." He set the fork down on the edge of the bowl and took another slice of warm bread.

"I haven't baked bread in ages. Normally I stick to the sweet stuff, but I'm thinking I should make some bread."

Nate nodded. "If you happen to end up with an extra loaf or two, I can help you get rid of them."

"I'll keep that in mind." She cut into a ravioli and blew on it to help it cool.

Nate touched the stem of his empty wine glass. "To answer your question, I don't know. Sometimes I think it would be great to get back to acting, but I think I'd really like to get into directing. I was assistant director for two episodes of *Daystar Rising,* and that was awesome. It was right before everything went bad, so I'm sure I would have been able to direct more episodes as we went. But now I'll never know."

"Have you asked?"

His hand stopped midway to his mouth, as if he'd never considered it. "No."

"Why not? If it's something you want to do, it couldn't hurt to ask."

"They haven't called me, so they probably don't want bothered."

Kim lifted an eyebrow. "Or maybe they think *you* don't want to be bothered."

Nate stared down into his ravioli.

"I'm sorry. It's none of my business. I shouldn't have said that." Being bossy had its place in so many areas of her life, but sometimes it wasn't so great while having a conversation with another person. Which she usually realized *after* she'd put her foot in her mouth.

"No, you're probably right. It's been a tough year, and up to now, I haven't been able to reach out to anyone. For a lot of reasons."

"What are you afraid of?"

Nate looked up at her. "Getting run over again."

She held his gaze for a long moment. "Well. I have no response to that."

He finally grinned. "Yeah, I didn't think you would."

They finished their ravioli in silence occasionally punctuated with sounds of enjoyment. The waiter brought a dessert menu.

Kim leaned back in her seat. "I don't think I could eat another bite."

Nate shook his head. "Nope, me either. Besides, there's nothing they could have that would be as good as your cinnamon rolls."

"Aren't you sweet. I almost didn't think that was a hint."

He put a hand over his heart and looked shocked. "Kim. It hurts me that you would think such a thing."

Rolling her eyes, she couldn't ignore the swell of giddiness. She felt like a fifteen year old. Or fourteen. She was as bad as Isobel, blushing and falling all over herself. At least in her case, it wasn't a character that made her heart flip flop in her chest, it was the man. "Are you hinting for more cinnamon rolls, or would you like something else?"

For a brief moment, the expression on his face changed to something more serious and curious, and she realized her words could be taken as an invitation to more than baked goods.

She was glad for the dim lighting because her face was on fire. "Like… um… cake or something…"

The waiter brought the check. Nate grabbed it, handing the waiter his card before he could walk away.

"I'm not picky. Whatever you want to make, I'll be glad to make it disappear."

"Good. I have a few things I'd like to try that I haven't made before. You can be my guinea pig."

"Gladly." He signed the slip and put his card back in his wallet. "Ready?"

"Ready."

They were halfway home when Nate said, "Did you want to go straight home? It's early."

"Jared's probably home by now, I guess I shouldn't be out too long." The week's events were still too fresh for her to be comfortable with leaving Jared by himself for long. No matter how much longer she wanted to stay with Nate. She glanced over at his profile. "If you want to stop at the grocery store, we can get stuff to bake something. I mean, if you wanted to hang out at my place for a while." Once she'd said it, she felt silly. Until Nate's smile.

"That would be great."

"Really?"

He took his eyes off the road for a second and looked at her. "I can't think of a better way to spend the evening."

Kim couldn't keep from grinning. "Great. Now we just have to decide what we're making. Is there anything you don't like?"

"Bee stings, insomnia, rising gas prices, when you can feel a sneeze so your face is all messed up but then it goes away…"

She laughed, loud. "Okay, yes to all that. Are there any desserts or dessert ingredients you don't like?"

"I'm not a big fan of dark chocolate. Otherwise, I'm pretty open."

"Dark chocolate. Got it." She held up one finger to keep track of the things he didn't like. "What about coconut?"

"Love it."

"Pineapple?"

"Love it."

"White cake?"

"Love it."

He wasn't kidding when he said he'd eat just about anything, was he? "Good. I think I know what we're going to make." She'd seen a picture of a white layer cake recently that she thought she'd try out. It seemed like the perfect project for a kitchen date. Wait. Date?

"We?"

She forced her attention back on the conversation. "We. You don't think you're just going to sit there and watch me work, do you?"

"No, ma'am. I am an excellent stirrer, and I've won awards for measuring things. My skills are at your disposal."

"Awards for measuring?" She was pretty sure he was joking, but he looked serious.

"Yep. I'm the reigning Mr. United States Measuring Master."

"I want to see the certificate."

"Oooh, I'd love to show it to you, but it got destroyed in a tragic accident."

Definitely joking. She played along. "Really."

Nate nodded vigorously. "Yup. You see, the measuring competition was in the same building as a bodybuilding competition. Some poor lackey messed up and delivered the vat of body oil to our competition – which was dry goods only – and it spilled all over the stage and ruined the certificates."

"Tragic, indeed."

"So as much as I would love to offer you proof…" he lifted his shoulders in defeat. "I just can't."

Kim laughed. "Okay, Mix Master, are you planning to drive past the grocery store?"

"Oh, crap." Nate threw on his turn signal and checked his mirrors before barely making the entrance to the parking lot. "Glad you were paying attention."

"I understand. You were lost in your glorious visions of yesteryear."

"Exactly." He pulled into a parking space and hurried around the car to open her door. He grabbed a cart from the cart park next to the car. "What do we need?"

Kim tapped her phone. "I have most of the stuff at home,

but we need pineapple, whipping cream, and eggs. And cream cheese." She held out her phone so he could see the picture that went with the recipe she was looking at.

"That looks really fancy."

She shrugged. "It's not any more work than a regular cake."

"It is, though. See, for me, I'd walk over to that display buy a cake already made. Boom. Done. This is definitely more work."

"Okay, but my cake won't taste like processed crap."

"I kinda like processed crap."

Kim laughed. "I didn't mean to insult your palate."

"No, no, it's fine." He tried to look affronted. "We can't all be refined."

They steered into the baking aisle. Nate paused in front of the cake mixes. Kim looked back at him. "Um, no."

He raised an eyebrow and grinned. "You can make a cake without a mix? Are you some kind of sorcerer?"

"Yes. Now grab a bottle of eye of newt. It's to the left of the frog toes."

"I don't see any bat wings."

"That's okay, I have plenty at home." Kim set a bag of shredded coconut into the cart, absurdly happy that she and Nate could be in perfect sync with this weird conversation. It wasn't often she met a man who got her particular brand of humor and could roll with it so easily.

There were only a handful of other shoppers in the store, so they took their time gathering the rest of their ingredients and making their way to the checkout. One lone cashier looked bored out of her mind, so Kim skipped the self-checkout to give the girl something to do.

Nate piled the groceries on the conveyor belt and Kim handed the cashier her rewards card, then swiped her debit card to pay for the groceries as soon as she saw Nate reaching for his wallet.

He pushed his wallet back down into his pocket and loaded the bags into the cart. The cashier handed her the receipt. "Have a good evening."

"You, too," Kim told her.

Chapter Twenty

Nate opened Kim's door, then put the bags in the trunk. Being with her was fun. He was pretty sure this was the first time in his life he was really looking forward to baking a cake.

He pushed the cart into the corral and waited a second to make sure it wasn't going to roll back out before getting into the car.

Kim asked, "Does your mom do much baking?"

"Not really. She's an incredible cook, but she's more of a cake mix from the box kind of baker."

"That's how my mom is. She used to bake cupcakes whenever she was upset or overwhelmed. If we came home and Mom was baking, we knew to stay out of her way. She was an ER nurse, so she saw a lot of things no one should ever see."

"I can only imagine. And your dad was a cop, right?"

"Right. I think it helped them understand each other better because they both had these careers that were so intense but in very different ways. I always wanted to end up with a relationship like my parents, where they have such a deep respect for each other."

"What about your ex?" Nate remembered his name, but he

had no interest in using it. But he probably couldn't have been *all* bad if Kim had married him.

"It started out okay. No, that's not true. It started out great. He was attentive and interested in what I was doing. We enjoyed the same things. Everything was so easy, and we got married pretty quickly. That's when everything changed. All the things that were fine for a girlfriend were no longer okay for a wife. All my annoying habits," she made air quotes, "had to stop. I laughed too much, talked too much, ate too much, spent too much time with my family, the list goes on and on."

"Wow."

"Yeah. At first, I kind of bowed to the way he wanted things. After all, he was a lawyer. He was going to do great things, blah blah blah. He was the breadwinner, so I figured I should compromise on a lot of things. We went on for a while, and then the situation with my sister was the bomb that blew everything apart."

"How?" Nate imagined it was a hard situation, but couldn't connect the dots to how it could have made her marriage implode.

"That night, my sister and her husband were fighting. It got bad, so Jared ran to a neighbor's house. They called me to come get him and I called my parents to check on my sister while I got Jared out of there. William wasn't thrilled that I'd brought Jared home with me. Then my dad called and told me what happened. I had to sit Jared down and tell him his parents were dead. And my soulless husband wanted me to call CPS. He didn't even want Jared to spend the night." The anger and disgust in her voice still sounded raw, even after a year.

Nate slowed down to pull into her driveway. It was awful to know such horrible people existed in the world.

"He told me I had a choice. Either I called CPS and got rid

of Jared, or he was leaving and filing for divorce. I told him to go. I think it genuinely shocked him."

He turned the car off. "I'm sorry that happened to you."

Kim snorted. "It didn't happen *to* me. I was a willing participant, and if nothing else, I've learned a lot. Anyway. I didn't mean to talk your ear off."

"Hey, I asked."

"You did."

"Let's go bake a cake." Nate got out of the car, went around to open her door, then popped the trunk.

Kim was beside him, picking up some of the bags. He caught the scent of her perfume as he followed her into the house. It was light and floral.

They piled the bags on the kitchen island and Kim pulled a pink apron out of the pantry and slipped it over her head. She grabbed another one and handed it to Nate. "Wouldn't want to get flour all over yourself."

He tied the apron and laughed at the "kiss the cook" emblazoned across the chest. "Maybe you should wear this one."

"You'd rather wear the pink frills?"

He considered. "Nah, I guess not. Tell me what to do."

She grinned. "I like the sound of that."

"Now I'm scared."

Laughing, she gathered the rest of the ingredients from the cupboards, then pointed to a bright red mixer in the corner. "Pull that out a bit and plug it in."

"Nice."

"I couldn't live without my KitchenAid mixer. I use it all the time." She flipped a lever and pushed the head up, then twisted a silver bowl onto the mixer's base. "Alrighty, since you're the measuring champion, I'll tell you what to measure and you dump it in the bowl."

Nate flexed. "Measuring perfection, right here."

"Okay, Mister Perfect, let's start with the flour."

"Mister Perfect? I like that a lot. You can call me that from now on." He wiggled his eyebrows and grinned.

Kim gave him a side-eye. "I think I'll pass. What are you doing with the sugar?"

"Measuring it." He shook the measuring cup for emphasis.

"I didn't tell you how much."

Nate set the bag down. "Such a stickler for details."

Kim sighed heavily.

Nate tried not to smirk as she carefully watched him measure out the rest of the ingredients. "Okay, now how do you turn this contraption on?"

"Keep ahold of the head. It's heavy. Bring it forward into the bowl, then flip this lever to lock it in place."

"Okay." She wasn't kidding. The mixer head was much heavier than it looked.

She touched a lever on the side of the mixer. "Now this is your speed. Start on the slowest one and gradually work your way up to about four."

He moved the switch. "Holy crap this is loud."

She grinned up at him. "Now turn it back to zero, unlock the head and tilt it back."

He took the spatula she was holding out.

"Scrape the sides of the bowl, then mix some more." She turned to the island, where the round baking pans were.

"You're looking away? Are you sure you can trust me to do this?"

"I'm taking a chance," she deadpanned.

Nate scraped the bowl, replaced the head, and started mixing again. "It looks really good."

Kim leaned over, putting her hand on his back as she peeked around his side. "Smells good, too. This cake's going to be awesome."

Heat flooded from where her hand rested. He cleared his throat. "Of course. With my mixing skills and your expert supervision, it's inevitable." He grinned down at her and somehow managed not to lean over and kiss her. He reluctantly turned his attention back to the mixer. "I think we're good."

"I agree. Do you know how to unattach the bowl?"

"Pssssht. Of course." He tilted the head up and pulled on the bowl. "Nope, not even a clue."

Kim laughed. "Here." She used her hip to shove him aside and gave the bowl a quick twist, releasing it from the mixer.

"Impressive." Nate followed her to the island.

"How are your pouring skills?"

"Second to none."

"Try to split it as evenly as you can."

"You got it." Nate poured the batter into the pans, then held the bowl still while Kim scraped the remaining batter into the pan.

When the pans were in the oven and they'd mixed up the filling and set it in the fridge to chill, they sat at the island.

"Did you want something to drink?"

Nate hopped up. "I'll get it. Where are the glasses?"

Kim pointed to a cupboard and Nate pulled out two glasses. He filled them with ice and water.

The front door opened and closed, followed by footsteps toward the kitchen. "Nate! I didn't know you were here." Jared appeared in the doorway.

"Hey there. You want some water before I sit down?"

"Sure." Jared perched on one of the stools.

Nate filled another glass and sat down.

"I smelled something baking, so I thought I'd investigate."

Kim reached over and ruffled his hair. "You should have gotten home earlier. Nate was doing the baking."

Jared's eyes widened. "No way."

Nate pointed to his floured apron. "Way."

"You can help put it together if you want," Kim said.

"What's that mean?"

"It's a layer cake. So we have to cut the cake, put the filling in, then put the cake back together and then frost it."

Jared looked skeptical. "That sounds hard. I'll let the experts handle it."

Nate shook his head. "Uh-uh. You want to eat a piece of this cake, you have to work for it."

"Ugh, fine. When will it be done?"

Right on cue, the timer buzzed. Nate jumped up before Kim could, and squeezed his hands into her oven mitts to pull the cakes out of the oven. He slid the hot pans onto the wire racks Kim had set out.

"Now," Kim said to Jared, "we wait about ten minutes, then we can take the cakes out of the pans. After that, we have to let them cool completely."

"How long's that take?"

"Ideally, they should cool overnight."

Nate and Jared both exclaimed, "Overnight?"

Kim rolled her eyes. "I *said* ideally. We can put them in the fridge for about an hour and that should be good enough."

Nate bit down on his smile at her exasperation. "What shall we do until then?"

"We can play a game," she suggested.

Jared jumped up. "I'll go bring some games in."

Setting the oven mitts down, Nate reclaimed his seat and took a sip of water. He glanced at Kim and quietly said, "No Monopoly, right? Please?"

"You don't like Monopoly?"

"The last time I played Monopoly, I ended up with a broken

arm and my sister had a black eye. Monopoly tears families apart."

"I didn't know you had a sister."

Nate shook his head sadly. "I don't… anymore. Not since the Baltic Avenue incident."

Kim shoved his arm. "You had me going!"

He laughed, loud. "Sorry, I couldn't resist."

Jared came back and set a stack of board games on the table. "What do you want to play, Nate?"

Nate studied the boxes. "They all look pretty good. Which one do you recommend?" He was glad he asked when Jared's face lit up.

"5 Second Rule."

"Never heard of it. How do you play?"

Jared grabbed the box, opened it, and set a box of cards and a twirly tower thing in front of them. "You take a card, and then you have to name three things that fit the topic, but you only have five seconds to say them."

Kim chuckled. "It's harder than it sounds."

"Okay, you go first so I see how it works." Nate couldn't help but notice the excitement on Jared's face. A pang of sadness for the boy hit him. How many normal moments like this had he had with his parents? Nate guessed there weren't too many. Then again, maybe he was just being judgmental because he knew how their little family had ended.

Kim grabbed a card and a timer. "Name three superheroes." She flipped the timer. Tiny marbles made a zooming noise as they sped down the spiral tower.

Jared sputtered, "Uh, uh, Superman, Batman and, uh, Flash!"

"Oooh, you almost missed that one," Kim said.

Jared took a card and the timer and looked at Kim. "Three animals you would *not* want as a pet." He flipped the timer.

"Oh, crap. Bees, flies, and turtles."

Jared turned to Nate. "Your turn." He drew a card. "Name three mountains."

"What? Um, Everest, uh, Mount St. Helens, um…" This really *was* harder than it looked.

"Time's up!" Jared was gleeful.

"How come I got the hard question? I think that was rigged," Nate joked.

He reached for the timer and pulled a card for Jared. "Name three kinds of dogs."

"Pug, poodle, uh, um, uh, oh geez, Chihuahua."

"Sorry, dude, you missed the last one."

Jared groaned and drew a card for Kim. "Name three types of tree."

"Pine, Christmas, bonsai."

Nate and Jared looked at each other, shaking their heads. Jared said, "Sorry, nope. Christmas trees *are* pine trees."

"Phooey." She pulled a card for Nate. "Name three planets."

"Mars, Jupiter, and Pluto!" He smacked his palm on the island, startling the cat. He hadn't even noticed her getting up there. She gave him a filthy look and jumped down.

Kim and Jared exchanged a look. "Ooooh, sorry," she said. "Pluto is technically not a planet anymore."

"What? I refuse to accept that. It's an outrage, and a slap in the face to everyone on Pluto. I challenge." He couldn't keep a straight face.

Jared doubled over with laughter. "You can't challenge."

"Au contraire. I just did." He stifled his chuckling long enough to pull a card.

Before he knew it, an hour had passed. "Hey, the cake should be cool, right?"

Kim made a face. "I suppose if we had put it in the fridge, it would be."

"Oops. We never took it out of the pan, did we?"

"Nope."

Jared heaved a sigh. "Really?"

Nate tilted his head. "Hey, you're the one who distracted us."

Kim agreed. "Totally. It's all Jared's fault."

"Hey!"

They all laughed as Kim slid off the stool and took the cakes out of the pans. "I'll put them in the fridge now. Maybe a half-hour?"

Nate glanced at his watch. It was just before nine. "We could finish it up tomorrow afternoon. We don't want to rush perfection."

Kim smiled over at him. "They do look pretty perfect. I think tomorrow is a great idea."

Jared groaned, but Nate was pleased. An afternoon like this evening was definitely something to look forward to.

"Can I help you clean up?" he asked.

"Of course." Kim opened the dishwasher. "I'll rinse, you load."

Nate stood beside her, loading dishes, feeling rather at home in her kitchen.

"Does that mean you're leaving now?" Jared sounded disappointed.

"Not right this minute, but probably soon."

Kim walked past Jared and ruffled his hair again. She did that a lot, but the boy didn't seem to mind. "You're going to see him again in like eighteen hours. I think you'll survive."

Nate put detergent in the dishwasher's cup, then said, "Anything else to go in here before I start it?"

"Nope. Go ahead, thanks."

He closed the door and pushed the buttons to start the

machine, then pulled his apron off. "What should I do with this?"

"I'll just hang it up. We'll need them again tomorrow."

"You don't trust me with the filling?"

"Nope." She took his apron and hung it with hers on the back of the pantry door.

Jared reluctantly slid off his stool. "I'm going upstairs. If you're leaving."

Nate nodded. "I am. Good night, I'll see you tomorrow."

"Night!" Jared grinned and went upstairs with the stack of board games.

Nate leaned against the counter. It felt like the most natural thing in the world to reach out for Kim and pull her to him. She didn't hesitate, wrapping her arms around his waist.

"This was fun," she said, looking up at him.

Nate nodded and leaned down. His heart pounded as his lips touched hers. For a second, he wondered if he'd made a huge mistake, if she wasn't interested in going there, and another second later, she returned his kiss, and he had no more doubt.

Her fingers spread over his back while his one arm circled her waist and the other traveled north to rest on the back of her neck. Encouraged by her response, Nate deepened the kiss and tightened his hold on her.

"Oh, geez, really?" Jared's voice from the doorway propelled Kim backward.

Her face blushed bright red as she wiped her lips. "Uh…"

Jared rolled his eyes. "That's so gross," he said, but he didn't seem to be bothered by the situation.

Nate shrugged, sort of concerned and sort of amused at Kim's reaction. He hoped she wasn't truly bothered by Jared coming in. It's not like they were doing anything wrong.

Picking up his glass and walking to the fridge, Jared said,

"I'm just getting water. Believe me, I'm not coming back down-stairs for *anything*. Not even if you pay me."

Kim shook her head, her face still red.

Nate reached out and she let him pull her next to him. He took it as a good sign.

"Good night!" Jared called loudly as he left the room.

Kim covered her face with her hands and leaned into Nate's chest. "I'm mortified."

Nate chuckled. "He seemed to take it pretty well."

She laughed, too, the sound muffled through her hands. She finally looked up at him, the faintest pink still staining her cheeks. "He didn't seem surprised, did he?"

"Not even a little bit."

Her face turned serious. "You don't think he was upset, do you? I mean, I didn't think so, but if I need to have a talk with him…"

"I think he's fine." He put his forehead against hers. "Think he's staying upstairs?"

"Yup." She rose up on her tiptoes and kissed him.

Following her lead this time, he rested his hands on her hips while her arms wound around his neck and her hands tangled in his hair.

It pleased him greatly to see she was a little breathless when she pulled back.

"I guess I should go," he said reluctantly.

Kim nodded, her eyes still closed. His shirt was fisted in her hands. She slowly let go and smoothed his shirt.

Pressing a quick kiss to her lips, he loosened his hold on her, and she stepped back slightly and finally looked up at him. "Wow," she breathed.

He let out a breathy laugh-sigh and nodded. "Yeah, wow," he whispered back.

They stood for a few more minutes, enjoying the moment,

until they heard Jared's chair scrape across the floor over their heads.

"I'll see you tomorrow."

Kim nodded and walked him to the front door.

He kissed her again, then left. The dew soaked his shoes as he crossed the yard to his porch. He couldn't wipe the grin off his face.

Chapter Twenty-One

As soon as the door shut, Kim pressed her fingers to her lips and giggled. Holy crap, was he a good kisser. She wrapped her arms around herself and sighed, feeling like a teenager again. Glancing out the window, she watched Nate's silhouette open his door and go inside. Holy crap, that man was fine. She laughed at herself again. She was worse than a teenager.

She locked the doors and turned off the lights before heading upstairs. Tapping on Jared's door, she waited until he told her to come in, then opened the door.

He sat at his desk, but his laptop was closed. Sadie stretched and yawned from her spot on Jared's pillow, then jumped down and left the room.

"I'm going to bed."

"Okay. I'm going to finish this." He held up a book. "It's really good."

"*Flowers for Algernon*. It's a great book, but kind of deep for bedtime, isn't it?"

Jared shrugged.

"Don't stay up too late." She crossed the room and swiped his hair away from his forehead so she could plant a kiss there.

When she straightened, Jared made a face and rubbed at the spot. "Eeewww, you were just sucking face with those lips. Now it's like Nate kissed my head and that's so weird." He snorted and laughed.

"Very funny." She planted her hands on her hips and waited until he looked away, then she grabbed his face and planted kisses on his cheeks and forehead while he squealed and hollered and laughed.

He pretended to gag.

"Good night, goofball."

"Good night." He turned his attention back to his book.

Kim pulled his door shut behind her and once again it hit her in the middle of the chest like a ton of bricks how much she loved this kid.

Later, climbing into bed, she was overwhelmed by gratitude for the absolute perfection of the day they'd just had. The rude little voice inside her head tried chattering about how it wouldn't last – couldn't last – and it was only a matter of time before something horrible happened to put her back in her place. She shoved the voice aside. No, she wouldn't always be so blissfully happy, but that wasn't going to lessen her joy.

Stretching in the morning, her cheeks ached from all the smiling. In her dreams, she'd relived the kiss a hundred times, and now she couldn't wait to get the day started so afternoon would hurry up and get here.

The morning passed in a flurry of vacuuming and dusting and catching up on laundry, including Jared's nasty hoodie.

"Jared, take that basket upstairs, please."

"Yup, I'll take it up after I eat." He set the basket at the foot of the stairs and poured a heaping bowl of cereal. Around a mouthful, he said, "The vacuum won't pick anything up in my room."

Kim raised an eyebrow. "Like what? You have to actually bend over and pick up wrappers and stuff."

"Yeah, I know. I mean like normal stuff." He shrugged.

"I'll take a look at it. Finish your cereal."

When he had slurped the last of the milk out of the bowl and put it in the sink, they went upstairs.

"Here's your problem." Kim tapped the clear plastic canister.

"What?"

"It's full. You have to empty it."

"Oh."

She swished her hands. "Get your trash can."

Apparently enlightened, Jared got his trash can and emptied the vacuum tank into it. "I didn't know that would make it stop sucking stuff up."

"Now you know."

"I'm guessing I have to run it again."

"Yes, Sherlock, you have to run it again. Get the hallway, too."

With a tortured sigh, Jared plugged it back in and turned it on.

Kim was glad the solution had been that simple. She'd spent way too much money for that vacuum, and it hadn't lived up to the hype.

After the house was cleaned, the couch cushions were fluffed, the laundry was put away, and the dishes from lunch were in the dishwasher waiting for a full load, Kim finally sat down and leafed through a magazine she'd had for two weeks. Flipping absently through the pages, she kept an eye on the clock and her phone. It was almost twelve thirty.

The knock on the front door sent a thrill through her. She stood, waited a beat, smoothed down her shirt, then walked to the front door. One more deep breath, not wanting to seem too eager, and she pulled it open.

"Hey." Nate was a vision in his jeans and t-shirt that clung to him.

Keep your eyeballs in your head, Kim told herself as she stepped aside to let him in.

"Hey, yourself," she answered.

"I only had a sandwich so I'd have plenty of room for cake." Nate rubbed his belly.

Kim's eyes followed his movement. She wouldn't have minded – *stop it! Look up. Up. Step away from the abs.*

"Great. Filling. We need to do the filling."

He looked at her curiously. "I thought we made the filling already?"

She pointed at him. "Yes. You are correct." Feeling like an idiot, she abruptly turned and walked into the kitchen. "We need to slice the cakes." She pulled both cakes out of the refrigerator and set them on the island, then turned back and got the bowl of filling out.

"Aprons?"

"Behind that door." She pointed.

Nate brushed against her as he passed to get the aprons, his hand trailing across her back. A few seconds later, he gave her the pink apron and slipped his over his head and tied it.

Kim tied her apron and hoped her hands weren't trembling as she selected a serrated knife. "Okay. First I'm going to level the cake by taking off this top part that's domed." She carefully cut the cake. "And now I'll go through the middle so we can make our layers." She sliced the cake and ended up with two perfectly even layers. "You can do the other one."

"This could be dangerous," Nate said. "How do you know what's level? Just eyeball it?"

"Yup."

He bent over and studied the cake at eye-level for a minute. "What if I mess it up?"

"Don't."

His eyes went to hers. "Geez, now I'm really nervous."

She laughed. "C'mon, you're stalling."

He mimicked her earlier motions and sliced the top off the cake, then bent down to examine his work. "I don't think that was quite even."

"It's pretty good, though. I'm impressed."

"Really?"

"Yup. Now go right through the middle."

Nate worked the knife through the center of the cake. When he'd come through the other side, he made a face. "That's definitely not as good as yours."

"Psssht, of course not." She inspected his layers. "It's not quite even, but it's not too bad."

"It's off by a mile."

"It's off by about a half-inch. It'll be fine."

Nate rubbed his hands together. "Okay, what's next?"

"Now we put the bottom layer on the cake plate."

She pointed and Nate did.

"We're going to try to put a third of the filling at each level."

"Should we separate it?"

"What's the matter, Master Measurer? You can't eyeball thirds?"

He grinned. "Nope, but I could measure it out."

Kim grabbed three bowls out of the cupboard. "There you go."

"Perfect." He separated the filling into three parts. "I'm a little particular about such things."

"I see."

He turned the cake plate around and back. "Should it go all the way to the edges, or more in the middle…?"

"Almost to the edge, but not quite. Just leave about that much." She held her thumb and index finger about a half-inch apart.

"Aye, aye, captain." Nate used the spoon she handed him to glop the filling onto the cake and smooth it around. "Are you trusting me to put the next layer in place?"

"Of course." Kim sat on a stool and sipped at a glass of water. "You're doing great."

"Will I get brownie points if I say it's because I had a great teacher?"

"Yep."

"Then it's because I had a great teacher."

They laughed together as he put the next layer together.

"Now gently – and I do mean *gently* – press down on your cake to make sure it's not going to slide around." She watched him do exactly as she'd said. "Nice."

"Great teacher."

She laughed again. "You're dangerously close to sucking up."

"Ah. Too far. Got it."

Jared shouted from the hallway, "You aren't making out, are you?"

Rolling her eyes, Kim said, "No, it's safe."

"Oh, cool, the cake's almost done." He sat on one of the stools.

"How come I'm doing all the work?" Nate jokingly grumped.

"What are you talking about? I'm supervising."

Jared said, "It looks really good."

"Thank you. I've been slaving away on it all afternoon."

Kim chuckled. "Little dramatic, don't you think?"

Nate pointed to himself. "Actor, remember?"

When the cake was assembled, Kim got the bowl of frosting. "I can do the frosting since I didn't help with the filling."

"I'll supervise." Nate grinned and took Kim's stool.

Kim frosted the cake and turned it around, making sure she'd covered the sides evenly. "Jared, you can do the coconut."

"Cool." He hopped off his stool and stood beside her.

"Wash your hands first."

He did as she said, then she handed him the bag of shredded coconut.

"Just put some in your hand and press it into the frosting. Like this." She took a small handful and demonstrated.

"Okay."

Jared's first handful was thick. Kim stifled a laugh when he looked up, wrinkling his nose at the mess. "Can I take some of it off?"

"Nope, it'd just pull the frosting off. It's fine. Keep going."

He overcompensated on his next handful, only sticking a few sparse shards of coconut to the cake. He grunted, then tried again.

"Perfect." Kim nodded. He did a great job on the rest of the cake. "We'll just eat that section first."

Nate lifted his hand. "I love coconut. I'll eat that piece."

"Not quite yet. Jared, sprinkle a little bit over the top, then we're done."

Finally finished, the cake looked delicious. Kim got a knife from the butcher block. "Nate, will you grab plates out of that cupboard? Jared, please get the forks."

After a brief flurry of activity, they crowded around while Kim cut the first slice and lifted it to a plate.

"How perfect is that?" she said. The four layers separated by white frosting looked like they belonged on the pages of a food magazine.

She plated two more slices and they sat down. "Okay, guys. Moment of truth."

They all dug their forks into their cake and ate the first bite in silence.

Jared broke it with an enthusiastic, "This is freaking delicious!"

Kim agreed. Nate nodded as he took another huge bite.

She watched Jared and Nate lapse into another conversation about *Daystar Rising* and the makeup for Nate's costume. The words blurred and faded to background noise as she just enjoyed the moment. It was so comfortable, having Nate in her kitchen, making silly jokes and baking a cake. And making out against the counter was pretty great, too.

She felt her face grow warm as she thought about the kiss. Kiss*es*.

Pulling her attention back to the conversation, she tilted her head. "Wait. Did you say you had hair extensions?"

"Yup. I had dreadlocks, and when we first tried just a wig, it kept coming off. So they decided to give me extensions."

"Wow."

"It worked much better, and I eventually got used to wearing them when we weren't shooting."

"You had to keep them in?"

"Yup. I had dreads. This long." He motioned to a spot at the middle of his back.

"Here, look." Jared held his phone out for her to see a photo he'd pulled up.

"Wow. That's… wow."

Nate laughed. "Gee, thanks."

"No, no, it's not bad, it's just so completely different."

Jared swiped and tapped at his phone and held it out again. "Here's Qaaxag in full costume."

Her eyebrows jumped halfway up her forehead. "Wow."

He looked muscular and buff and just pretty fine in his shirt-less photo. The fact that he was bright blue with blue and silver dreads did nothing to diminish the sexiness of the photo.

Nate snorted. "That was a totally different 'wow' than the other ones."

Jared rolled his eyes. "Close your mouth, Aunt Kim, you're going to drool on the cake."

She laughed. "Stop."

"Spoiler alert. I don't actually have six arms. And my abs don't really look like that."

Kim pretended to pet the photo. "I bet if I squint real hard they'd be close."

They both laughed hard, while Jared made gagging noises and poked his finger toward his throat. "Eww, are you guys going to make out again?"

Nate wiggled his eyebrows. "I sure hope so."

Kim blushed again and cleared her throat. "Are we done with the cake? It needs to go in the fridge."

Wrapping his arm around her waist, Nate pulled her against his side. "It was delicious. Great team effort." He lifted his hand to Jared for a high five.

Jared returned the high five, then got the plastic wrap out of the pantry and pulled off a sheet to cover the cake.

When it was covered, Kim picked up the plate and Nate opened the fridge for her to place it inside. He shut the fridge and gave her a high five. "Teamwork."

When she high fived him, he grabbed her hand and laced his fingers with hers, and planted a quick kiss on her lips.

"Um, hello? Impressionable child present," Jared said.

Kim pretended to glare and joked, "Impressionable child is going to end up getting himself grounded."

Jared laughed. "Oh, I forgot. Isobel asked if she left the

dragon scale you gave her on the table. She couldn't find it and we didn't see it in her parents' car."

Nate shrugged. "Maybe. We can go over and check the box."

They all put their shoes on and walked over to Nate's house. Kim's heart skipped a beat when he grabbed her hand and held it as they walked. She was definitely infatuated, and her romantic heart saw a great deal of potential.

Chapter Twenty-Two

Nate let go of Kim's hand to open the door, catching a hint of her flowery perfume as she walked past him. "The big box is still on the kitchen table. You can check it first."

"Okay." Jared took the lid off and rummaged through the contents. "I don't see it."

"Is it the one I autographed for her?"

"Yeah."

Nate put his hands on his hips and tapped his fingers. "You know what? I think it's over on the counter behind the other box." He pointed.

Jared went across the kitchen and shifted the box. "There it is! She'll be so happy." He pulled his phone out and started texting.

"I didn't want to pack it away, but since the box was in front of it, I totally forgot about it."

"Crisis averted. I can't believe she left it behind," Kim said.

Jared glanced up from his phone and said, "Eh, she was more focused on the selfies."

Nate drummed his fingers on the table. He didn't want

them to leave. "I don't have any games, but if you guys aren't busy maybe we could watch a movie or something."

Jared looked at Kim. "Can we?"

"Sure."

It didn't look like she was in any hurry to go, either, which pleased him a great deal. He said, "If it gets too late, we can even order pizza."

"Trying to sweeten the deal?"

He gave her another quick kiss. "I think it's already a pretty sweet deal."

She laughed. It was definitely one of his favorite sounds. "What are we watching?"

Nate turned the television on and connected to his movie account, then handed the remote to Jared. "You can pick, but your aunt has veto power."

Jared settled into the oversized recliner and began scrolling through the options.

Nate's breath caught in his throat. He couldn't remember when he'd ever been so… content. It meant the world to him that Jared was comfortable and that Kim was close. He could get used to this. He cleared his throat. "Drinks?"

"I'll help you." Kim followed him back into the kitchen.

When they turned the corner of the doorway, out of Jared's sight, Nate grabbed Kim's face and kissed her. Her arms went around his waist, her fingers digging into his back, pulling him against her. He loved the taste of her mouth, the faint flavor of the cake only making it better.

He pulled back a little, and they smiled against each other's mouths. "It'd be too easy to get carried away."

She shook her head and whispered, "Not with a chaperone two feet away."

Taking a deep breath, he nodded. "Drinks."

"Make mine a double," she joked.

Reluctantly, Nate let go of her and poured three huge glasses of tea. He gave her another quick kiss before carrying his and Jared's glasses to the living room.

"How about this one?" He'd selected an action hero movie.

Kim said, "Ick. Haven't you already seen it a thousand times?"

"Maybe a hundred."

"Fine."

"Nate?" Jared asked.

"Fine by me." Truth be told, he couldn't care less what movie they watched.

Nate put his arm on the back of the couch and Kim immediately settled in the crook of his arm, tucking her legs under herself and leaning her head back against his shoulder. He could get used to this.

The movie started. Nate had seen it a few times himself, so he didn't bother trying to pay attention when a much more interesting option was curled up against him.

In spite of the frequent shouting and gunfire, Kim dozed off and snuggled even tighter against him, her forehead on his neck, her arm flung across his waist. His fingers stroked her arm, toying with the hem of her sleeve.

Trying not to disturb her, Nate shifted to prop his feet on the coffee table. He glanced over at Jared, who was glued to the screen. Finally, the hero prevailed, and the credits began rolling up the screen.

"I love that movie." Jared looked over.

At his voice, Kim stirred and sat up.

"Welcome back."

She gave a little laugh. "Sorry. I guess I was just too comfortable."

"You won't hear any complaints from me."

"Until your arm falls asleep."

"Can I use your bathroom?" Jared asked.

"Of course. Through the kitchen, to the left." Nate waited until Jared was out of earshot, then said, "Do you guys want to go out and get pizza?"

Kim looked up at him, the surprise evident. "Out? You're really getting the hang of this."

"I'm trying. But I haven't been out in public today." He'd told her about his goal to go out somewhere public every day.

"Sure, if you want. Pizza's a great motivator." She sat back against the couch and took his hand. "Is it getting easier?"

He loved that she took him seriously without coddling him. Her style, her personality, was exactly what Jared needed in a parent, and exactly what he needed in a… friend? "Yes. I still get a little jittery, but it's nothing like it used to be."

"That's good."

"Jared can pick the place."

"Thank you for being so good to him."

A knock on the front door immediately set him on edge. Nate frowned. "I'm not expecting anyone."

He mentally counted to five as he walked across the room. Stalkers didn't knock. They just ran you over on the sidewalk. Pulling the door open, Nate was nearly knocked over by the petite brunette that barreled into his arms.

"Natey! I've missed you *so* much!" Miranda fisted a hand in his hair and trapped his lips against hers.

Nate pushed at her waist and turned his head, trying to free himself. "What are you doing here?"

She finally let go and pouted her lips. "I missed you, baby."

Nate's mouth flopped, but he couldn't form words. He wasn't the least bit happy to see Miranda, but she didn't seem to notice. He repeated, "What are you doing here?"

Miranda put her hand on his chest and practically purred, "Didn't you miss me? I got your messages."

"I didn't send any messages." He stepped back, away from her touch.

Miranda's attention was diverted when Jared came back into the living room. Kim stood, and wouldn't meet his eyes. He followed her gaze to the suitcase he hadn't noticed Miranda bring in.

Jared frowned, looking back and forth from Nate to Kim.

After a long and awkward moment, Miranda stepped toward Kim and demanded, "Who are you?"

Before Nate could intervene, Kim put her hand on Jared's shoulder and nudged him toward the door. "We should go."

Miranda stepped into Kim's path. "I'm Miranda. Nate's girlfriend."

"No, no, not my girlfriend. Ex-girlfriend. Kim…" Nate put his hand on her arm.

Kim didn't pull away, but she didn't exactly encourage his touch. He hated to think what she must be thinking about the situation. She gave Miranda a slight nod of her head but said nothing. Her expression was unreadable.

"Dennis wrote you back into the next season. It'll be nice to have you come home." Miranda kicked off her high heels and settled onto the couch, tucking her legs under her, right where Kim had been sitting.

It annoyed Nate to see her there, like she was violating Kim's territory. Her words finally filtered through his annoyance. "What did you say?"

She giggled, but it wasn't a joyful sound. It was downright predatory. "Dennis is bringing you back to California where you belong. I asked him to let me give you the news. I have the letter here." She fished an envelope out of her purse and held it out.

Kim gently pulled out of his grasp. "I'll talk to you later."

She nudged Jared, who went out the door and straight over to their house without saying goodbye.

Nate followed her onto the porch and pulled the door shut behind them. He took her hand. "Kim. I had no idea she was coming."

Nodding, she said, "I know. But she's here now and it sounds like you have things to talk about."

Nate leaned in for a kiss, but Kim turned her head and slid her hand from his grasp. "I have to go."

He watched her walk across the yard to where Jared waited on her porch. He gave Jared a wave. The boy halfheartedly returned it, but Kim didn't turn around. The door closed behind her and Nate took a deep breath, dreading going back inside to face Miranda.

He went inside and sat on the chair Jared had occupied.

"Who was that?" Miranda's eyes narrowed.

"Kim."

"And what is she?"

His teeth clenched. "She's none of your business. What's in the envelope?"

Miranda flicked her wrist, pulling the envelope back against her chest. "Come and get it."

"No."

She pouted. "Oh, come on, Natey. You're no fun."

"I'm not playing games."

She heaved a sigh, then said, "It's exactly what I said. Dennis wants them to write you back into next season."

"Qaaxag's dead." He'd always known a return was a possibility, but he wasn't sure it was something he wanted.

"That's the beauty of dying off-screen. They figured out a way to bring you back. This is from Dennis." She shook the envelope back and forth. "It has all the details. But we can talk about that later. I want to talk about us." Her voice dropped, husky.

"There is no us."

"There used to be an us, and it was amazing."

"Until you found someone else to be amazing with."

"Don't be like that, Natey. You said you forgave me." She trailed the corner of the envelope down her cleavage.

Nate squeezed the bridge of his nose. "Give me a break, Miranda. We're over. We're not getting back together. Ever. So can we just skip the nonsense?"

The seductive sex kitten was gone. Angry, she spat, "Fine." She flicked the envelope at him. It landed on the floor. "It's all in there. Dennis wants you back in a week. Two, tops. Filming starts in three weeks."

"That's not going to work."

A half-horrified, half-disgusted expression settled on her pretty face. "Don't be ridiculous."

"Look. You don't understand what I went through."

She rolled her eyes. "I was there by your side through it all. I know it was tough, but it comes with the territory. You don't think I've had creepy people come up to me? I've been afraid plenty of times, but you don't see me running off to some shitty Podunk town and hiding."

He couldn't believe how he'd ever gotten involved with her. How had he overlooked her shallow, selfish disregard for everyone around her? He picked the envelope off the floor and held it in his hands. The weight suggested it held several sheets of paper. He wanted to tear into it, but not with her here.

Nate scowled at the shoes and purse dropped haphazardly on his floor. "Where are you staying?"

"You're kidding me, right?"

"No."

Her tone was venom. "Don't be stupid. I'm staying here with you."

"No, you're not."

"What do you expect me to do, Nate? Sleep under a bridge?"

His head pounded. The thought of her sleeping under a bridge didn't bother him at all. "Get a hotel room. Sleep in your rental car."

"I took an Uber."

"What the heck, Miranda?" He got to his feet and yanked his phone out of his back pocket. There were only two hotels in town. He tried both of them, but they were both fully booked for a business convention. There was no possible way this was going to end well for him. The knot in his chest tightened, constricting his breath.

Pacing around the kitchen, he angrily tapped at his phone, trying unsuccessfully to find a hotel room anywhere in a fifty mile radius. There were no vacancies. And no flights out until morning. He cursed. His home was supposed to be his sanctuary. Right now, it was anything but.

"Relax." From behind him, Miranda slipped her arms around his waist.

He jerked away from her. "Don't."

"Why not?" She pressed herself into him. "Everyone will think it anyway."

Stepping back, he rammed his hip painfully on the corner of the island counter. "Ouch. Dammit, stop."

"Why are you so angry?"

He raised his voice. "Because I don't want you here."

Instead of being deterred, his words only seemed to be a challenge. "Once you calm down, you'll be glad I'm here."

He stared at the phone in his hand, tempted to call his mother and ask her how to get out of this. Inspired, he tapped out a text, asking his mother if Miranda could stay with them. A few minutes later, the flicker of hope was squashed with the news that she was out of town.

Out of options, Nate resigned himself to the fact that Miranda would be spending the night.

Chapter Twenty-Three

Kim knew she wasn't fooling Jared by pretending everything was fine, but she did it anyway. "How about we get some pizza?"

"Sure."

"You can pick where. I'm going to the bathroom, then we can go." She knew her fake cheery voice was shrill and unconvincing. But she couldn't let herself admit that she was upset. Jared had shown her pictures of Miranda, and it was bad enough knowing she was Nate's ex. But when she showed up in person, in all her perfect movie star glory, it was a bit much to stomach.

Taking her time in the bathroom, she wet a washcloth and patted her face, being careful not to disturb her makeup. When she thought she could put on a half-genuine smile and face Jared, she dried her hands and turned off the light.

In the car, she could feel Jared staring at her. "What did you decide?"

"Little Caesars. If that's okay."

"Perfect." Their pizza was edible, and they were always fast. Get in, get out. That's exactly what she wanted to do.

"Are you okay?"

She rolled to a stop at a red light and glanced over at him. "I'm fine. We don't even know the situation."

"He wasn't happy to see her. I could tell."

Kim watched the light turn green, then pressed the accelerator. "It's not my business."

She could see Jared's scowl from the corner of her eye, but he didn't say anything else. They ordered their pizza and ten minutes later, they were back on the road. As she pulled into the driveway, she looked over and saw Nate and Miranda walk across the porch and get into his car. She couldn't help but notice they hadn't taken Miranda's suitcase with them.

"Aunt Kim?"

Jared's voice yanked her back to herself. "What." She turned the key off and tried to pull it out of the ignition, but it wouldn't budge. "What is your problem?!" she yelled at the key.

"You didn't put it in park."

"What?"

"The car. You didn't put the car in park." He tapped the gear shift.

"Oh, geez." Kim put the car in park and shook her head. "Sorry." In the rearview mirror, she watched Nate's car pass behind hers. "Grab the pizza, please." She shoved her door open and fumbled with the house key.

She opened the door and held it for Jared. "I'll get the plates and napkins if you want to start a movie or something."

Jared took the pizza into the living room and turned on Spongebob.

Kim handed him a paper plate and napkin, then took a slice of pizza, but had no desire to eat it. Sadie jumped up onto the couch beside her and curled up.

"He really likes you."

She took a tiny bite. "It's not a big deal. They dated for a long time and we just met. So… it's fine."

Jared was already finished with his first slice. "Just don't dump him until you know what's up."

"Dump him? We're not even dating."

Even with his cheeks plumped with a massive bite of pizza, Jared managed to look skeptical. He rolled his eyes. "You have to talk to him."

"Don't talk with your mouth full."

Kim stared at the inanity on the screen, her mind going back and forth, back and forth. No, he definitely hadn't been expecting Miranda, and he didn't look particularly happy to see her. That could have been because he wasn't happy to see her, or because he wasn't happy that she and Jared were there when she showed up. A million scenarios played out in her mind, none of them particularly comforting.

One episode blended into another, and Kim still didn't have a solid handle on how she felt. All she knew was that the situation sucked, and it didn't feel good.

Jared let out a massive yawn, and she glanced at her watch. "It's ten thirty. Time for bed."

He flipped off the television and picked up his plate.

"I'll get the trash."

"Thanks." He stopped while she pressed a kiss to his forehead.

"Good night. Love you."

"Love you, too." He headed for the stairs and stopped. "It can't be as bad as it looks."

Kim managed a smile. "Maybe not."

His footsteps tromped up the staircase and his door clicked shut. Kim picked up the paper plates and napkins and piled them on top of the pizza box. In the kitchen, she put the leftover pizza in the fridge and threw the trash away. She wiped down the counters, checked the lock on the back door, and turned off the light.

Double-checking the lock on the front door, she turned off the lights and paused. A pair of headlights passed the house and pulled into Nate's driveway. She knew she should just walk upstairs, but she stayed glued to the window.

Nate got out of the car and walked around to the passenger side and opened Miranda's door. She flung her arms around his neck and he picked her up, carrying her like a groom carting his bride over the threshold. He closed the car door with his foot.

Kim was glad she couldn't see his face in the darkness. He carefully made his way up the front porch, set Miranda on her feet, but she clung to him. The door opened and they disappeared inside.

Squeezing her eyes shut, Kim turned away from the window, angry at herself for standing there watching. She liked him. They'd kissed. Big deal. There was no commitment, no understanding, no *mis*understanding except in her own head. No reason to feel like he'd somehow betrayed her. He hadn't.

It sucked.

But that was that, and she wasn't going to waste any more time wallowing. She texted Tara, and a few minutes later got a reply.

> he's a dirtbag and doesn't deserve you
> anyway

The message that boosted her spirits enough that she went to bed. With Sadie curled around her head, purring, she actually fell asleep in good time.

Chapter Twenty-Four

"C'mon, baby, stay with me," she slurred.

Nate dropped Miranda onto the bed and yanked her arms from around his neck. "Let go."

She was like a drunken octopus. He'd no sooner remove one tentacle than another was groping him somewhere else. "Natey, I've missed you so bad."

"Get some sleep." He turned to leave the room.

"Baby? I'm gonna—"

Before he could grab the trash can, Miranda vomited, the putrid stench of recycled alcohol filling the room. She puked all over herself and his comforter, thankfully missing the pillows and carpet.

Angry as he was, Nate helped her to the bathroom.

"I'm sorry, baby. Help me get this off." She plucked at the fabric of her dress.

Clenching his teeth, Nate unzipped the back of the dress. "That's it. You're on your own." He left her leaning against the counter, fumbling with her clothes. Hopefully she didn't fall and crack her head open on the tub or toilet.

Nate pulled the comforter off the bed, trying not to barf. He was glad he'd listened to his mother and gotten the heavy-duty washer and dryer. He grabbed another blanket and slung it over the bed, then threw his pillows in the closet. The last thing he wanted was for his pillows to end up smelling like Miranda.

And now, thanks to her, they'd probably never end up smelling like Kim. Darkly, he tossed another old blanket onto the bed to protect the sheets and heard the water running in the sink.

"You okay?"

"Yeah," came her weak reply. Good. He hoped she felt as miserable as he did. Or, preferably, worse.

He was just straightening the fresh comforter when Miranda stepped out of the bathroom wearing only tiny panties that left nothing to the imagination.

"For crying out loud!" He reached into the closet and ripped a t-shirt off its hanger and threw it at her. "Cover yourself."

Her eyes brimmed with tears. "Don't you want me?" A lone tear escaped, trailing down her face.

Nate had never been one to hurt someone's feelings. Still, he honestly answered, "No."

The vulnerable sadness vanished, replaced with a hard, almost sinister expression. She tossed the shirt he'd given her onto the bed. "You might as well have sex with me, Nate. She's going to think you did anyway."

Without answering, Nate scooped up the puked-on comforter, stepped into the hallway, and slammed the door shut. He stormed into the laundry room, shoved the comforter into the washing machine, filled the detergent cups, and started the wash cycle.

It was almost midnight. Nate was tired and angry. He grabbed the afghan off the couch and went out to his car. He wanted to be as far away from Miranda as possible. Reclining the passenger seat all the way back, Nate managed a few uncomfortable hours of fitful sleep.

The sky was lightening when he pried his crusty eyes open. The pounding in his head made it feel like he'd been drinking himself, but all he'd had was water. He stretched and glared at his watch. Almost six, and he was no less angry – or tired – than he had been when he'd come outside.

He shoved at the pillow behind his head and picked up his phone. He thought about texting Kim. But to say what? *Hi, just FYI I slept in my car last night.* Yeah. Like she'd buy that.

The front door opened and Miranda walked out, holding a cup of coffee, wearing nothing but his shirt. His jaw clenched. She had an entire suitcase full of clothes, but she walks outside like this. What was she trying to punish him for? Turning her down? Granted, it wasn't something she was accustomed to, but this was overkill. Even for her.

He kept his head down and pretended to be asleep.

Chapter Twenty-Five

Kim made a disgusted snort. She made the mistake of looking out *that* window on her way to the kitchen. There stood Miranda, on the front porch with a cup of coffee, disgustingly beautiful with her tousled hair and bare legs, wearing what was obviously one of Nate's t-shirts.

"Whatever," she grumbled.

In the kitchen, she slammed the cupboard door after choosing an "extra caffeine energy boost" coffee pod. She shoved it into the machine and slapped the button to begin brewing.

"Shit!" she yelled as the coffee began dripping into the empty space where a mug should be. Fumbling in the cupboard, she shoved a mug into place to catch the rest of the coffee. It took seven paper towels to mop up the coffee that had flooded onto the counter and dripped down the cabinet to the floor.

"What's going on?" Jared's sleepy voice was coming down the stairs.

"Sorry, I didn't mean to wake-"

"Kim! Kim! Come look!"

She made a noise. "I've already seen it."

"What the heck is he doing?"

He? Kim hustled to the window in time to watch Nate disappear into his house. "Where was he?"

"In his car."

"Why was he in his car?"

Jared shrugged. "I think he was sleeping in there. He had a blanket."

Kim tried to ignore the little burst of hopefulness that flared in her belly. "That doesn't make sense." She let go of the blinds and they snapped back into place. "Okay, let's stop being creepy. Why are you up?"

Jared raised an eyebrow. "Because it sounded like a herd of elephants came through the kitchen."

"Oh. Yeah. Sorry. Crap." She remembered the coffee mess. "How about pancakes?"

"We're out of syrup."

"How is that possible? I just bought syrup."

"Like a *week* ago."

Kim sighed and looked through the cupboards. Normally she enjoyed stress-baking, but she wasn't even in the mood for that. "How about Dunkin Donuts?"

His eyes widened. "Really? Yes!" He ran for the stairs before she could change her mind.

She finished cleaning up the coffee mess and dumped out the half a cup that made it into the mug. "Well, that's a waste," she muttered as the dark liquid circled the drain.

Jared was back downstairs and ready to go. Kim tilted her head and pointed to her robe. "It'll be a minute."

"Fine." He slumped onto the couch.

She went upstairs and got ready in record time. She needed coffee.

They made a quick run through the drive-thru and went

back home. Kim tried not to look across the yard, but couldn't resist. Not that it mattered. There was nothing new to see.

After eight, a loud vehicle drove past the house. Kim abandoned the video she was preparing to upload and went to the window. Miranda stood on Nate's porch, fully dressed and gesturing wildly. He leaned against the railing with his hands in his pockets, just watching her rant.

It pleased Kim greatly to see that Miranda looked unhappy.

Chapter Twenty-Six

"You're such a fool. I can't believe how stupid you are!" Miranda screamed at him.

His head thumped, he was tired, and he wasn't interested in listening to her crap. "You have a safe trip."

"You're making a huge mistake."

He pulled her suitcase onto the porch and handed it to the Uber driver. Her mouth was still going, but he couldn't care less what was coming out. He just wanted her gone. Gone, gone, gone.

Miranda changed tactics. She burst into tears. "You know it's only because I still love you. Natey, please."

He hated that nickname with the burning passion of a thousand burning Qaax suns.

"Baby, please. I miss you so much. Please come home." She grabbed for his hands, and he stuffed them deep into his pockets.

"I *am* home." He sighed. "Was that everything?"

She sniffled.

Rolling his eyes, he told the Uber driver to wait. He had a sneaking suspicion she'd left something behind just to have an excuse to come back. He was correct. Her purse sat on the far kitchen counter, hidden by the refrigerator.

He carried it out and, ignoring her pouting, handed it to her and opened the car door. "Bye." He shut the door and walked around to the driver's side. Handing the driver some cash, he said, "Here's a little extra to make sure she gets to the airport on time. I don't care what she says, do not bring her back here."

The driver counted the money and shoved it in his pocket. "You got it."

Nate felt bad for what this driver was about to endure and handed him another twenty. "I mean it. Lose this address."

"You're such an asshole!" Miranda screeched from the passenger seat as the driver winced.

Nate turned and walked toward the house, not taking a decent breath until the car was out of sight. Good riddance.

A long, hot shower and a fresh shave later, Nate went over in his mind a hundred times what he was going to say to Kim. And a hundred times, it sounded like crap. He had no idea what he was going to say that could possibly convince her he hadn't slept with Miranda. Especially since bringing it up at all seemed to sound an awful lot like guilt talking.

He put on his shoes and decided it was time to man up, walk across the yard, and knock on her door. Instead, he vacuumed the living room, put the comforter in the dryer, started a load of laundry, and checked his email.

It was nearly eleven when he decided that a food offering was in order. He left the house, but instead of going next door, he got in the car and drove to a sub shop. Standing in line, he stared at the menu. This was a stupid idea. He didn't know what Kim would want, let alone Jared.

"Can I help you?" A teenage boy pulled on a pair of plastic gloves.

"I don't think anybody can," he muttered.

"Excuse me?"

He looked up and forced a smile. "Sorry. Yeah. Three turkey subs, please. No. Wait. Two turkey subs and one ham sub."

The kid behind the counter hesitated before writing anything down. "Two turkey, one ham. You sure?"

"Yes." Crap. That meant if they both wanted ham, one of them would be stuck with turkey. "No. Make that two ham, two turkey." He'd rather have turkey, but at this point, he'd eat a sub made of dung beetles if it meant she'd sit down with him.

"Four subs."

"Yes." He could have the extra sub for lunch another day. If there was an extra. Maybe there would be three extras. Or maybe all four of them would end up smashed in his face.

"Sir?"

"Sorry, what?"

"Do you want everything on them?"

"Yes, please, but could I get the oil on the side?"

"Sure." The kid waited again. "Two ham, two turkey. Everything on them, oil on the side for all four."

"Yes."

"Is that everything?"

"Yes." He glanced around. "No. Wait. Chips." He grabbed a bag of plain chips, then a bag of BBQ. "Okay. This is it."

"You sure?"

"Yes."

He hesitated again. "Sure?"

"I'm sure. Four subs and chips. That's it."

The kid rang the order into the cash register. Nate handed him the money.

"It'll be about ten minutes."

"Great. Thanks." He took the chips outside and put them in the car, then went back in to wait for the subs.

Driving back home, he imagined any number of scenarios. None of them ended well.

"Okay," he said to the empty car, "so I can explain about yesterday. No, that's stupid. Hey, Kim. I know it looks bad that my ex-girlfriend showed up and threw herself at me, then spent the night at my house, but gee, you just can't believe your own eyes, right?" He stopped at a stop sign and smacked his palm against the steering wheel. This was going to suck.

Assuming she'd talk to him at all.

He pulled into his driveway and glanced in the rearview mirror. "Good luck, buddy. You're gonna need it."

Subs and chips in hand, Nate crossed the yard. He hesitated on the porch, but sucked it up and knocked. He heard Jared inside, yelling, "I'll get it."

A second later, the door opened.

"Nate!" Jared grinned. "Aunt Kim, it's for you," he yelled. "Come on in. Ooh, did you bring lunch?"

"Yeah."

He stepped inside.

"Who is-" Kim appeared in the doorway to her office and jerked to a stop. "Oh."

"Hi."

"Hi."

Nate held up the bag. "I brought lunch."

"Oh."

"Subs," he said stupidly, as if the 200-point font, bright red word "SUBS" emblazoned on the bag hadn't given it away. "And chips. I wasn't sure what you'd want."

"Okay." She was still in the doorway.

"Can I come in?" He was already inside, but just barely. He hadn't wanted to barge in if she didn't want him there.

"Sure," Jared said, looking back and forth between the two adults.

Nate waited for a response from Kim.

She gave her head a shake. "Sure. Yeah. Come in."

He didn't budge until she walked toward the kitchen, then he followed her and set the bags on the island.

"I got ham and turkey subs. You guys can have whichever you want."

Jared grabbed a turkey sub and the bag of BBQ chips. "Thanks, Nate," he said before disappearing into the living room.

Kim reached for a sub, then yanked her hand back like they were poisoned.

"What?"

"Which one will your... never mind. I'm not very hungry."

Confused, Nate stared at the remaining subs, trying to understand. Realization dawned. Four subs. The three of them, plus Miranda. Great. He hadn't seen that coming.

"No! No, no, no. No." Nate took a step toward her and stopped. He didn't want to crowd into her space, but he didn't want her to take off, either. "No. It... I got two ham and two turkey so if you both wanted one or the other... I didn't disappoint either one of you."

Her brow creased and her gaze went back to the subs.

"I figured I'd have the extra for lunch tomorrow. Or dinner tonight. Whatever. But no, it's not... Kim, I wouldn't..." He had no idea what to say.

"Oh."

"I like both. It doesn't matter what I end up with." He wanted to reach out to touch her but figured it wouldn't go well.

"So where-" she cut herself off.

"Gone. She's flying back to California. Nothing happened. I swear."

Kim let out a humorless part-laugh, part-sigh. "It's none of my business. You don't have to tell me anything."

Part of him wanted to just grovel and beg her to understand. Another part of him decided a different tactic was in order. If he acted guilty, she'd probably assume he was. He felt bad about the situation – about the inevitable misunderstanding – but he had done nothing wrong. "No, I don't. But I know how it looks, and I know how I'd probably feel if the situation was reversed. I like where we are, and I don't want this situation to mess it up. So I'm telling you. Nothing happened."

Kim seemed to relax a little bit, although she was still staring at the sub.

He lowered his voice. "I didn't *want* anything to happen."

"So I shouldn't believe what I saw."

"There was nothing to see."

"I couldn't help but seeing it. I was going up to bed when you guys got home and… I couldn't help myself. She was all over you. I watched until you got in the house and it sure didn't look like you didn't want anything to happen." She held up a hand. "I know. It's my own fault for gawking out the window. But it makes it hard to think it was all innocent."

"Am I just wasting my breath if I tell you what was going on?" Irritation gnawed at him. At Miranda, at himself, even at Kim for jumping to conclusions, no matter how reasonable.

"Maybe." She was back on the defensive, crossing her arms and avoiding eye contact. She moved to the side of the island and leaned against it, putting it between them.

"She hadn't eaten all day, which I didn't know. So we went to the Clubhouse to get food. She had a few drinks and they hit her a lot harder than I expected. I had to carry her out to the car, and she wasn't any better by the time we got home. I put her in bed and she puked all over the place. After she got cleaned up and passed out, I went out and slept in my car."

"Why? Why wouldn't you sleep on the couch?" She sounded skeptical.

Nate ran his hand down his face. He could feel the heat spreading across his cheeks. The mere thought embarrassed him, let alone saying it out loud, but it was the pure, unvarnished truth, and Kim deserved nothing less. "Because she kept coming on to me, and I didn't want to wake up to her doing something I didn't want done."

That finally brought Kim's eyes to his. "Oh."

Chapter Twenty-Seven

She believed him.

Maybe she was being naïve or stupid or just full of wishful thinking, but she did. Her mind argued with itself. On the one hand, he owed her nothing, so he had no reason to lie. On the other hand, maybe he thought his chances of getting into her bed were better if he made her believe he hadn't slept with Miranda. That didn't seem right, but on the other hand…

"I need more hands," Kim muttered.

"What?"

"Nothing." If they did end up in an actual relationship and he went back to California to act or direct, what then? She'd have to trust him.

"Will you talk to me?"

Kim heard the hurt in his voice. She was taking too long talking to herself, and he was probably thinking the worst. "Sorry. The voices in my head are having a conference."

"What are they talking about?"

"Most of them are arguing about whether or not we should trust you. There's one, though, that's getting really loud and obnoxious."

"About whether to trust me?"

She shook her head. "No. About why there's no roast beef sub."

Nate blinked and raised an eyebrow. "I was afraid that was going to be a problem."

"I mean, if you're going to suck up with food… good effort, but…" She gave an exaggerated shrug.

The tension left his posture and he relaxed, leaning on the island. "How do I come back from this faux pas?"

"Since it would be silly to send you back out for a different sub when these are perfectly okay, how about you buy me dinner?" She came around the corner of the island to stand next to him.

He rubbed his chin and looked to the ceiling. "Geez, I don't know."

"Sorry, that's the deal. Take it or leave it." The lighthearted mood felt right.

"Nope."

Before Kim could respond, Nate's hands were in her hair and his mouth pressed against hers. She melted against him, her hands going around his back and grabbing fistfuls of his shirt.

When he pulled back, she grinned up at him. "Okay. You win."

He chuckled. "I'll still buy you dinner."

"Good." She reached over and grabbed a sub. "I'm starving."

"Me, too. I didn't have breakfast."

"I had a handful of M&Ms."

"Breakfast of champions," Nate joked as he picked up a sub and settled onto one of the stools.

"Drink?" Kim went behind him to the fridge to fill her glass.

"Sure. Whatever you've got."

"Tea it is."

She filled both glasses and set them on the counter and wrapped her arms around him from behind. "I'm glad you came over."

"Me, too." He leaned back and looked over his shoulder, touching his forehead to hers. "I'm sorry the whole mess happened at all, but I'm glad it's resolved."

She squeezed him in a tight hug, then picked up her glass and sat down to eat.

A few minutes later, Jared poked his head around the corner. "Is it safe to come in?"

Kim's mouth was full, but she nodded.

"Good. I didn't want to walk in if you guys were making out. Or fighting."

"Nope, just eating lunch," Nate said.

Kim pointed to the chip bag. "Did you eat all the chips?"

"There's some left." Jared shook the bag and what sounded like three crumbs bounced around inside.

"That's not 'some.' That's none."

Jared peered into the bag. "Okay, it's almost none."

"Did you finish that essay?"

A few of Jared's teachers were willing to work with him on keeping up with his assignments.

"It's almost done. I just have to format the references."

Kim raised an eyebrow.

"Fine, I'll go do it now." He ran upstairs.

Nate cleared his throat. His face was serious. "So. The unexpected visit. What she said was true. They're thinking about writing my character back into the show."

"I thought he died."

"Since it was all off-screen, they can spin it into a plot twist and bring him back."

"The decision is up to you?"

"Yes and no. They could leave him dead. Or find another actor for the role."

"That's a big deal. What are you thinking?"

Nate crumpled his sub wrapper into a ball. "I'm not sure what to think."

"Have you called the writer or producer or whoever?"

"Not yet."

Kim didn't want to sound condescending by asking him why he hadn't called yet, so she stayed silent and waited for him to continue.

"I'm going to call this afternoon. I'm not sure what to say. I guess just find out what he has in mind and go from there."

"That sounds like a plan." She reached over and rested her hand on his forearm.

"I really wasn't expecting this. I figured once I was gone, I was gone for good."

"Hopefully when you talk to him, he'll have some solid answers for you. He'll have specifics, right?"

"Yeah."

Kim picked the wrappers off the island and put them in the trash can, then put the extra sub in the fridge. "What's your ideal situation?"

"I really don't know. It could be a good thing to go back, or it could be a huge mistake."

"What if... No, you got a letter. Never mind." She felt bad about almost voicing her skepticism.

Nate snorted. "What if she made it up? Believe me, that thought crossed my mind. More than once. But I'm sure it's legit."

"Will the offer still stand once Miranda gets back to California and talks to them?" The woman oozed vindictiveness.

He shrugged. "I'm not worried about that. Miranda is drama, and everybody knows it. She's cried wolf too many times for anybody to take her seriously without solid evidence."

Kim felt an unwelcome pang of sympathy for Miranda. "That would suck, not having anyone believe you when you say something."

Nate answered, "It sucks more when someone makes up lies about you."

The pang vanished. "True."

He stood. "We're okay, right?"

Kim stepped easily into his arms. "We're good." She meant it. She trusted him, and would continue to do so until she had a reason not to.

"I'm going to go call Dennis. Pick you up at six?"

"Perfect."

"You decide where we're going. Jared can come, too, that's up to you."

Kim lifted up onto her tiptoes and kissed him. "Good luck. I hope they tell you what you want to hear."

"Me, too. I just wish I knew what that was."

She knew the feeling.

Chapter Twenty-Eight

"Nate! Good to hear from you. How've you been?" Dennis's enthusiasm blasted through the phone.

"Good, good. You?"

"Good."

Nate wondered if he should start a drinking game for every time they use the word "good" in this conversation.

"I guess you heard from Miranda, huh?"

"Yeah, she just kind of showed up on my doorstep yesterday and tried to wreak havoc."

Dennis chuckled. "That's our girl. You two patch things up?"

Nate bristled. "She didn't exactly leave on good terms this morning."

"Ooh hoo, this morning? Long night? I'm sure you guys will work out whatever issues came up... or didn't come up..." The *wink-wink, nudge-nudge* was practically audible.

"I really just wanted to talk about your thoughts on *Daystar Rising* and see what you had in mind for Qaaxag."

"No small talk, eh?"

"Not about Miranda. That ship has sailed and sunk." As

much as he liked and respected Dennis, he was drawing his line in the sand.

"Too bad. You guys were a publicity dream. Ah, well." The sound of rustling papers came across the line. "I had some ideas about Qaaxag." His voice shifted to all business. "We could easily bring him back and use some of the clips from the starship explosion to make it look like the whole thing wasn't destroyed. Qaaxag and a couple of the other officers managed to take one of the escape pods and land on the surface of Andalaria. Captured by natives, nursed back to health, blah blah blah, they steal a supply ship and head back to Earth just in time for the war. From there, we can have him save the day, or end up being killed on screen, maybe betrayed by a trusted friend. Could go any number of directions. Or we could leave him dead. Or…"

Nate finished for him. "Or recast."

"That's a possibility. Bringing him back is great for the storyline."

Nate understood what Dennis was hinting at. "Leaving him dead isn't really an option."

"Probably not. But we do have some contract issues with recasting."

Nate let his head roll back and stared at the ceiling. "Now it's making more sense."

"Hey, contract or not, you're my first choice. It'd be near impossible to write decent dialogue with a different actor."

"Have you talked to Jerry?"

"Nope, figured I'd wait and see what you wanted to do."

"Okay." Jerry had been Nate's agent for years.

"You want me to talk to him?"

Nate closed his eyes. "Yeah. Go ahead." He knew the words were as good as a contract for Dennis.

"Great!" Dennis's voice boomed through the phone. "Glad to have you back on board."

"Thanks." He forced more enthusiasm into his voice than he was feeling. He hung up and called Jerry to give him a heads up, but ended up leaving a voicemail. He was glad a decision had been made, but he had no idea if it was the right one. Right for the show? Sure. Right for his bank account? Definitely. Right for him? Undecided.

He picked up his phone and made one more call.

"Hey, you."

"Mom, I need some advice." Maybe he should have called her first.

Nate told her the whole tale.

After a lengthy silence, she said, "Hmmm. What's the problem, then?"

"Am I doing the right thing?"

"Why do you want to go back to the show?" Leave it to Pattie to answer a question with a question.

"It's a better way of ending Qaaxag's story. It's better for the fans. It's a shitload of money per episode."

"How many episodes?"

"I don't know. A whole season is twelve."

"Why *don't* you want to go back to the show? Something to do with a next-door neighbor?"

He thought about it. "Sort of, but not really. I'm not making any major decisions based on someone I've only known a month. Mostly I don't want anything to do with Miranda, and it feels like a package deal."

"But in reality, it doesn't have to be."

"No."

"What's your plan afterward? To stay in California?"

That was one question Nate knew the answer to. "No."

"Because of Kim?"

"No. Home is here."

"How long would you be gone?"

"If I'm in the whole season? Up to six months."

"That's a long time, but it's not forever."

"Thanks, sensei."

Pattie laughed. "You're welcome, grasshopper. How are things with Kim?"

He gave her the entire story. "Last night sucked, but we had a long talk, and I'm pretty sure she believes me that nothing happened. I'm taking her out to dinner tonight."

"Good. I like her."

"I can hear the 'Don't screw this up, Nate' in your voice."

She chuckled. "When have I ever gotten involved in your love life?"

"Technically, never. You're great about not giving me advice until I ask for it, but you can't disguise your opinions. Your poker face is terrible."

"Can't argue with that. At least you never have to guess what I'm thinking."

"Not at all." He walked out to the back porch. "I like her, too."

"I know."

"You don't have to sound so smug."

She laughed again. "Everything will work out the way it's supposed to."

After they ended the call, Nate pondered his mother's words. There wasn't much he could do, at least until he heard from Jerry. In the meantime, his backyard was in desperate need of cutting. He popped on his headset and spent the next two hours mowing the grass and contemplating the return of Qaaxag.

Chapter Twenty-Nine

Kim uploaded her newest video segment and finished adding photos to her monthly newsletter, then scheduled it for distribution. Pleased with the day's work, especially since she'd really only worked half a day, she shut down the computer and went to check Jared's progress on his report.

His bedroom door was ajar. "Jared?" She pushed it open. He wasn't there, and his bathroom door was open.

A spike of panicked déjà vu sliced through her, but she forced herself to breathe and stay calm. He could have gone anywhere. She went back downstairs. "Jared?"

Nothing.

When she'd checked every room in the house, her determination to stay calm was swallowed by the overwhelming fear that he'd run away again. She ran out the front door and scanned the road, then dashed around the far side of the house. Turning around the back, she was halfway across the back porch when she heard laughter.

Jared stood beside Nate on his mower. They were looking at something on Jared's phone.

Nate looked up and saw her, raising his hand in greeting.

Much to her horror, Kim burst into tears.

Nate tapped Jared's arm, and they both hurried over to her.

Jared was the first to speak. "What's wrong? What happened?"

Kim wiped furiously at her face and shook her head. "Nothing, it's fine. I'm just overreacting."

"About what?"

A fresh stream of tears blurred her vision. "No, I'm being ridiculous." She took a shuddering breath and Nate put his hand on her back.

"What happened?"

"I just… I went upstairs and Jared's room was empty and I didn't know he'd gone out, and I –"

"Are you freaking kidding me?" Jared shouted. "What, now I have to ask permission to go into the yard?"

Shocked, Kim gawked at him. "Of course not."

"I screw up once, and you're never going to let me forget it, are you? Maybe you should get me microchipped so you can track me on your phone!" Jared stomped into the house, slamming the door behind him.

Kim's mouth hung open. She snapped it shut and looked up at Nate. "What just happened?"

From overhead, a window opened and Jared yelled, "F-Y-I, I'm going to the bathroom to take a crap!" The window slammed shut.

Kim wiped her face and glanced up at Nate again. "Guess we need to have another talk." She took a step, but he caught her upper arm. "What?"

"It's none of my business."

Her hackles raised. "But you're about to butt in anyway." She yanked her arm from his grasp.

Nate's voice was quiet. "Maybe you should give him some space."

"No. He doesn't get to talk to me like that and slam stuff around." She turned toward the door.

"Overreacting and ridiculous. I'm pretty sure that's what you said?"

She whipped back around. "It's a lot easier to parent when you don't have any kids."

"Which is why it's easier for me to be a little more objective. He wasn't doing anything wrong."

"Well, thank you *so* much for your input." Her voice dripped sarcasm.

"Kim."

She planted her fists on her hips. "Yes, please, do go on."

"Hey, I'm on your side."

"Really? It sure doesn't feel like it."

He put his hands on her shoulders. "Kim. Look at me."

She glared up at him.

"You can't freak out every time Jared leaves your sight."

"Every time? Really? I was fine when he was with Isobel's family."

"You knew exactly where he was."

"Do you have a point?"

His hands dropped. "Nope, guess not. You go do your thing. Good luck with that."

Kim felt tears stinging the backs of her eyes again. "I'm glad you're on my side. I'd hate to see how mean you'd be if you weren't." She spun on her heel and went into the house, slamming the door behind her. She heard Nate's heavy sigh, then his footsteps as he walked off the porch.

A minute later, his mower started back up.

Hesitating at the bottom of the stairs, Kim let out a breath and went to the kitchen instead. It probably wouldn't do any good to confront Jared while he was still angry. Or while she was still upset. Especially since she wasn't so much upset with

Jared as she was with Nate. Who did he think he was, telling her how to feel?

Sadie trotted down the stairs and meowed, undoubtedly voicing her judgment about Kim's overreaction just like Nate did.

A little voice in her head suggested maybe they were right. She told the voice to shut up.

Chapter Thirty

Nate finished mowing and hosed the loose grass off the tractor before pulling it into the garage. He was going back and forth between being irritated and feeling like maybe he'd over-stepped. Kim was wrong – if she kept freaking out, she'd push Jared away and cause more problems. And she was right – he didn't know what it was like to be a parent.

He really didn't know what it was like to become a parent overnight like she had.

In the shower, he decided he'd apologize. Regardless of whether he was right or wrong, handling Jared was one hundred percent her call. They weren't even in a relationship. So what the heck was he thinking?

While he dressed, he wondered if they were still having dinner. How was *that* going to work? Should he just go over at six, like nothing happened, or text her and ask? No, he decided, that would give her the opportunity to cancel. If she didn't text him first, he wasn't going to initiate a new conversa-tion. He would just show up on time and see if she'd let him take her to dinner.

At five before six, he second-guessed himself for the

millionth time, but walked out and crossed the lawn and knocked on her front door.

She opened the door, surprised to see him. "Nate. I didn't think..."

"Gotta eat, right?" He leaned against the door jamb. "We still on?"

"Yeah, come in. Let me get my shoes and see if Jared's going."

Nate took that as a good sign, that maybe she and Jared weren't still mad at each other. Kim put her shoes on and went upstairs. A few minutes later, she came back down and smiled. "He's getting his shoes on."

"Good. Where are we going?"

"Jared's vote is for pizza, no surprise. I could eat pasta. If we go to Archie's, we're both covered."

"Perfect. I have to ask though, can this count as a two-apology dinner?"

"Two?"

Nate reached out and put his hands on her hips. "I overstepped this afternoon. By a lot. I'm sorry. It's not my place to tell you how to do anything. Especially when it comes to parenting."

She leaned into him and put her chin on his chest. "You weren't wrong, though."

"I was wrong to open my mouth. It wasn't my place."

"No. It wasn't. But I do appreciate your willingness to be honest with me."

"You do?"

She poked him in the side. "Looking back, I can appreciate it. In the moment, not so much."

"Since you've conceded, that means this dinner *does* count for both apologies."

"Fine. But I'm getting dessert."

"I would expect nothing less." Nate kissed her, glad to have the unpleasantness of the afternoon behind them.

Jared came down the stairs and groaned. "This again? Can't you guys have some kind of warning?"

Kim pulled back from Nate and shook her head. "Nope. At this point, you should just assume that's what's going on and announce your presence accordingly."

Jared rolled his eyes but he was smiling. "I'll just get a collar with a bell."

Nate's phone vibrated in his pocket. He glanced at the screen. "I have to take this." Stepping out onto the porch, he swiped to accept the call.

"Jerry, hey."

"Good to hear from you, Nate. It's been too long."

"I know."

Never one for small talk, Jerry said, "Got a call from Dennis. He wanted four episodes, same compensation as before. I pointed out the show's increased popularity and he was too quick to agree to another twenty-five percent, so I played hardball and got you forty."

The air whooshed from his lungs. Forty percent per episode? That was a fortune. Then he registered the bit about the contract only lasting four episodes. "So they're going to kill me off."

"Probably. Might as well enjoy it while it lasts, right?"

"Right. Four episodes?"

"Yeah. Did you want to negotiate that?"

"No. Four's good."

"You'll have to be in LA by the tenth. Most of the filming will be in Jordan and Puerto Rico."

"Okay." That meant a minimum of eight weeks, most of it out of the country.

"I'll email the details over. Sign them and get them back."

"I will. Thanks, Jerry."

"You got it."

Nate disconnected the call and ran his hand down over his face. He hated the nagging thought his mind had latched onto. If Kim had become important to him in such a short amount of time, how quickly would he move on and forget all about her?

Chapter Thirty-One

"Everything okay?" Kim stepped onto the porch, Jared close behind her.

"Yeah." He shoved his phone back into his pocket. "Sorry. That was my agent, so I had to take it."

"Of course. Bad news?" Kim put her hand on his arm. He looked nervous. Or apprehensive.

"No, not at all."

"Good news then?"

"I think so."

She got the impression he didn't want to talk about it right that moment, so instead of pressing the issue, she jiggled her keys. "Alright, let's go."

In the backseat, Jared said, "Hey, guess what?"

"What?"

He held up his phone. "I just got a welcome email from the cyber school."

Kim reached her hand back over her shoulder and Jared high-fived her. "Awesome."

"I guess I finished that essay for nothing," he grumbled.

Nate said, "That was fast."

"We put in for an expedited admission. Thankfully Tara helped with the process."

"Great."

"It helped a lot, since they were pretty hesitant in the first place, with it being so close to the end of the school year. I don't know what we would have done otherwise. Apparently the threat of physical harm isn't a good enough reason to miss school, and getting a restraining order against another class-mate is almost impossible. Especially when the school won't cooperate."

Nate shook his head. "I don't understand how they can say they have a zero-tolerance policy, then only selectively enforce it."

She'd pondered that inconsistency a million times. "It's all a bunch of feel-good crap they spew but it doesn't do anything except make the administrators feel like they're heroes."

Jared snickered in the back seat. "Calm down, Aunt Kim. You're going to end up with high blood pressure or something."

She huffed out a breath. "Yeah, I'm good. The whole thing just pisses me off."

"You don't say."

Kim shot him a look, then put on her turn signal. "Fine. I'm done. It's handled. We'll get you withdrawn from there tomorrow and hopefully your supplies will come in the next day or two."

"The tracking says it should be delivered tomorrow."

"Good."

Nate said, "What supplies do they send you?"

Jared jumped in. "I get a laptop and printer and all the books and workbooks, we only need regular stuff like paper and ink and pens and things like that."

"How do they do classes?"

"There's chatrooms so all the students can post and there are video lessons, and all kinds of stuff. And you can email the teachers any time. It's pretty cool."

"Sounds great."

"I just hope my credits I already have transfer so I don't have to repeat a lot of work. That would suck."

Kim grimaced. "Language."

"Suck isn't bad."

"It's not bad, but it's impolite."

"Fine. That would *stink*."

Kim saw Nate trying to hide a smirk. "Not helping."

He held up his hands in surrender. "Sorry."

She found a parking space at the far side of the lot.

Nate shrugged. "I didn't expect it to be this packed on a Monday night."

Inside, the restaurant didn't seem that full. The hostess led them past a room where raucous laughter spilled through the doorway.

"I guess that explains that."

Nate slid into the booth across from Jared and patted the seat next to him. Kim slid in beside him and picked up her menu. "What are you getting?"

Jared poked at his phone. "Pizza."

She studied the pasta selections. "How about you?"

Nate's hand rested on her knee, sending a tingle up her spine. "I think I'll get a stromboli. You?"

"Linguini alfredo with chicken and bacon. It looks fantastic."

They ordered their food. Kim reached under the table and put her hand over Nate's. Jared was engrossed in his phone. "So that call with your agent was about going back to the show?"

"It was. I talked to Dennis earlier, and we talked about

different directions the character could go. His ideal solution was for me to come back and resolve the storyline."

"Fans not happy with the off-screen death?"

"No. But beyond that, it will tie up a lot of other loose ends if he comes back."

"Cool." She was familiar enough with the business to know that giving customers a satisfying ending was the most important thing, whether it was seeing the results of a home makeover or watching the hero save the heroine and live happily ever after.

"I gave Dennis the ok to talk to my agent, and that's who called this evening."

"And?"

"They want me for four episodes, so I'm guessing they're going to kill me off in a blaze of glory."

Jared piped up. "I thought you couldn't know if you were going to be killed off until you got the script?"

"Normally, yes. And I don't know if they're going to kill me off for sure. It's an oddly specific number of episodes, though, since the regular season is twelve." Nate leaned in. "And I'm sure I don't have to tell you this, but this is all confidential. Tell no one. Not even Isobel."

"Can I tell her you're going back on the show?"

"Yeah, you can tell her that."

"Good, because I kind of already did."

"Jared!" Kim scolded.

Nate squeezed her knee. "If it was a big secret, I would have said so."

She picked at the homemade bread the waitress had left when she brought their drinks, trying to phrase the question so it didn't sound nosy. Or needy. "How long will you be away?"

"About eight weeks. Most of the filming will be in Jordan and Puerto Rico."

Scrunching up her nose, she asked, "Why Puerto Rico and not Florida? I'd think the scenery would be similar."

"Lower production costs."

"And Jordan, I assume for the desert?"

"That, and Petra. Its archaeological treasures rival Cairo."

"You've been there before?"

"We filmed there in Season Two and did some sightseeing. It's incredible."

"I'm jealous." She smiled as she said the words. It was true – she would love to travel to the Middle East, and it would be an amazing trip to take with him.

"Don't be. I'll be covered in rubber and dreadlocks and leather, sweating to death in heat over a hundred degrees."

"That part doesn't sound fun." She couldn't imagine shooting her own show in conditions like that.

"It won't be. I'll spend four or five hours in makeup for an hour or two of shooting, then another couple of hours getting it all off."

"Do you know when you're going?" She almost held her breath, waiting for his answer.

"I have to be in LA by the tenth."

"Oh." She took a long sip of her water. The tenth was less than a week away.

"I know. It's sooner than I expected. But that means I'll be back sooner, right?" His smile seemed forced.

If he was trying to be cheerful, the least she could do was reciprocate. "Right." She sat back as the waiter dropped off their food. "Do you film continuously, or will there be breaks?"

"There are some breaks, but they're usually only a couple of days. Maybe when we're filming in Puerto Rico we could meet in Florida? You and Jared could do Disney or something."

Jared made a face. "That's for little kids." His eyes widened. "Oh! Except for Harry Potter World. That looks amazing."

Nate put his fork down and reached under the table to squeeze her leg again. "I'll let you know the minute I have the schedule and we can figure something out."

Kim didn't want to start thinking about making plans and then having them never end up happening. Especially when Jared was involved. "We can talk about it later."

He rubbed her knee and nodded, seeming to understand. "Okay."

Jared pointed at his glass and cast a spell, then laughed. "It didn't work."

"They probably have spell blockers so people don't conjure up their own food." Kim deadpanned.

"Good point."

They ate their food in relative silence.

"That was delicious." Kim pulled her napkin off her lap and leaned back in the booth.

The waiter appeared with a folder. "Dessert menu?"

Kim held up a hand. "Not for me, thanks."

Nate shook his head, while Jared looked back and forth between them. Nate said, "Go ahead."

Jared grinned and reached for the dessert menu. "Can I please get the chocolate lava cake?"

The waiter nodded and left the table.

"You guys are going to be so jealous when you see the cake."

"I'm too stuffed to be jealous," Kim said.

Nate leaned back and put his arm around her. "I'll probably be jealous. I'll just look pathetic and make you feel sorry for me until you give me a bite."

"You can have a bite," Jared said earnestly.

Kim jumped to her feet. "Restroom." She hurried away

from the table to the restroom and locked herself in a stall. She leaned against the wall and took a deep breath, trying to fend off the tears that threatened to flow. For his entire life, Jared's only positive male role model had been her father. Now he was getting as attached to Nate as she was. And he was leaving. How had she let this happen?

She pulled herself together and went back to the table.

"Everything okay?"

She gave him a bright smile. "Of course." Jared's lava cake had arrived. "That looks delicious."

"Do you want a bite?"

"Sure." She reached over with her fork and took a small piece. The warm gooey cake melted in her mouth. "That's so good, but it's rich. I think one bite is plenty."

Jared shook his head. "No way one bite is enough." He shoveled another forkful in his mouth. "Did you want a bite?" he asked Nate.

Nate held up a hand. "No thanks. I'm too stuffed to even try one bite."

Kim muttered, "Oh, sure, showing off your self-control."

"You have a little something here." He wiped a tiny crumb from the corner of her mouth.

"Thanks." She wiped her mouth with her napkin.

The waiter brought the bill and handed it to Nate.

"I'll leave the tip," Kim said.

"Nope, this is my sucking up dinner, it won't count if I let you contribute."

"But then you'll still owe me a dinner, so that would be a win-win for me."

"Not for me."

Kim laughed. "And that's my problem how?"

"I guess it's not." He handed the black folder to the waiter as he walked by. "No change, thanks." Nate turned to her and grinned. "But I just took care of it, so the point is moot."

"Ooh, bonus points for correct usage of 'moot.'"

"I learned it from Rick Springfield."

"Getting the girls with proper grammar since the early eighties."

"Hey, some of us can't rely on good looks and charm, so we use what we can."

She nudged him with her elbow. "Oh, please. You've got plenty of good looks. Charm is debatable."

"Well, I won't be sad. One out of two ain't bad."

Kim laughed again. "That's not quite how it goes."

"Close enough."

She nodded in agreement. "Close enough. Shall we go?"

Chapter Thirty-Two

Nate put his hand on Kim's back as they walked out of the restaurant. She hadn't seemed like herself since he told her how long he was going to be gone. And she'd shut him down when he suggested meeting in Florida.

He ran his hand up until it rested on the back of her neck. "Hey."

"Hey." She looked up at him and waited until he opened her driver's door.

Jared had already jumped into the backseat.

He searched her face, but her expression gave nothing away.

Before she got in the car, she rose up on her tiptoes and gave him a quick kiss.

Walking around the front of the car, he decided to take that as a good sign. Maybe. Or maybe it was a kiss goodbye. Oh, crap.

He tripped on the pavement and grabbed the hood of the car to right himself.

"You okay?" Kim asked as he got in the passenger seat.

"Yeah, I'm good." He fastened his seatbelt, then turned

toward her. "What are you thinking?"

She raised an eyebrow and subtly inclined her head toward Jared. "I'm thinking it's a good thing I didn't order a whole dessert for myself."

He stayed quiet while she backed out of the parking space. "I agree. Even one bite and I'm pretty sure I would have exploded. Or you would have had to roll me out to the car."

Jared piped up. "You guys are wusses. I had my whole dinner *and* a whole dessert and I'm fine."

Nate chuckled. "False. You had dessert minus one bite."

"Ooooh, he's got you there," Kim joked.

The lighthearted surface banter continued all the way back to the house. Kim pulled into her driveway and turned the car off. Jared jumped out, shouting his thanks as he dashed up the sidewalk.

Before Kim could reach for the door handle, Nate touched her arm. "Hang on."

She took a deep breath and settled back in her seat, fiddling with the strap on her purse. "Yes?"

"Tell me what's up."

"What am I supposed to say, Nate? It sucks that we're just getting to know each other and you're going to be leaving. I really like you, but I'm not sure how that's going to play out when you're away. Jared really likes you and it sucks that you won't be around. That's all. And I don't want to fill his head with false promises that sound great but never pan out."

"They're not false promises." Nate didn't like what he was hearing. Why didn't she believe him?

"Maybe not now. But it's easy to say we'll plan a trip and then there could end up being a production delay or we just get busy and it doesn't work out the way we'd like it to."

"What are you saying?" He didn't like this at all.

"I'm saying we'll just stay where we are until you leave,

and then we'll play it by ear. No plans, no promises. Then it goes the way it's going to go and we don't end up with hard feelings if it doesn't meet our expectations."

Nate propped his elbow on the door and ran his hand over his face, then rested his chin on his fist. "Don't you think that's kind of pessimistic?"

"I think it's kind of realistic."

"You don't think at this point we should have some expectations about the future and making some decisions to make an effort?"

She finally turned to face him. "This isn't just about me. Or us. Everything I do, every decision I make, every person I get close to – it all affects Jared, and he's my priority. I have to do what's best for him."

"Come on, Kim, do you think I'd do anything that would hurt him?"

"Not intentionally, no."

That stung. Hard. "Then what? You think I will anyway? You think I'm that much of a jerk."

She turned and stared at her purse, then started picking at the stitching with her fingernail. "That's not fair and you know it," she said quietly.

Silence stretched out for long minutes, filling the car like a physical presence.

When he couldn't stand it anymore, Nate said, "I'm sorry you feel that way."

Kim rolled her eyes and grabbed the door handle. "Thanks for dinner." She got out of the car and walked fast, not looking back when she went inside and closed the door.

Nate shook his head and walked to his own house. Inside, he grabbed his phone and called his mother, filling her in on the entire evening.

Her annoyance came across the line loud and clear in the

long pause. "*I'm sorry you feel that way.* Really, Nate? That's what you said?"

"What's wrong with that?"

Another annoyed pause.

"Now you're mad at me, too?" What had he done to turn the entire universe against him?

"It's dismissive and obnoxious and passive-aggressive. It means you're right and she's wrong and you can't grasp how she could be stupid enough to feel the way she does."

"What? That's not what I said at all."

"It is, actually."

"No, it's not." His voice rose.

Pattie's volume matched his. "Don't you raise your voice at me. I'm not the one being a jerk."

"Thanks for all your support," he snapped.

"You need to think about it from her perspective. She's absolutely right. She can't prioritize some guy she's known for a month over her *child*."

"Why does everyone think I'm going to hurt Jared? Where is that coming from?" He was definitely yelling.

"Go think about it. We'll talk tomorrow when you're less shouty. It's getting on my nerves. Love you." The phone went dead.

Nate glared at it. "Are you freaking kidding me?"

Chapter Thirty-Three

"Wow." Tara was outraged as only a best friend can be. "*I'm sorry you feel that way*," she mocked.

"I know, right? Like I'm supposed to get all excited and start making plans to take Jared to Disney and then what?" In her bedroom, Kim curled up in her comfortable reading chair and hugged a decorative pillow to her chest.

Tara sighed. "Okay. I mean, his comment was stupid and ridiculous, but I'm sure he meant well."

Kim groaned. "Whose side are you on?"

"Hear me out. If he wasn't interested, this would be the perfect exit. He could totally ghost you and have a thousand legit reasons. No cell service overseas. Long days of filming. His dreads got caught in a wind turbine. Whatever. But he's trying to think of ways to keep this thing going."

"Yeah, for now." She did *not* need Tara going to bat for Nate. Right now, she just wanted to vent and be mad.

"What are you worried about? If he likes you, and you like him, this could work."

"Or it could not."

"You're not usually such a pessimist."

"Realist." Kim picked at the fringe on the pillow. "He's going to be with Miranda 24/7."

"So she's a tramp. Nate's a good guy. He can handle her."

Kim snorted.

"Give him some credit. He could have slept with her and completely justified it, but he didn't."

"I know."

Tara's long sigh came over the line. "I wish I had some sage advice. It sucks. All you can do is decide if he's worth the risk."

"If it was just me, it wouldn't even be a question."

"You sure about that?"

"Fine. I'd still have questions. But I'd be more likely to take the leap."

"So leap. Let things with Nate keep growing. That doesn't mean you have to throw all caution to the wind or make Disney plans with Jared. Just take it day by day."

"Easier said than done."

"It always is."

After they disconnected, Kim stared at her phone. She opened the window to text Nate, then closed it. Then opened it again and texted,

You still up?

A minute passed, then her phone chimed with his return message.

At fire pit. Come outside?

Okay. Give me 5.

She went to the bathroom, then checked on Jared. His room was silent, so she tiptoed down the stairs and slipped her shoes on, then grabbed the afghan from the back of the couch and quietly went out the back door and across the dewy back yard.

The glow from the small fire illuminated Nate. He sat on a bench with his feet propped up on the stone wall of the pit. He looked up as she approached, a hesitant smile on his face.

"Hey."

Kim sat beside him on the bench. "Hey."

"I—" they both said at the same time.

Nate continued. "Please. Let me. I'm sorry about earlier. I was being a jerk."

"I'm sorry, too. I wasn't giving you much credit."

"I wasn't being very respectful of your point of view with Jared. I hope you know I'd never want to hurt him in any way, and I didn't want to think my leaving potentially could."

She wanted to make him understand where she was coming from. It wasn't about whether or not he wanted to hurt Jared, because of course he didn't *want* to. "I know you wouldn't want to, but I have to be careful, regardless of the best of intentions."

"I get that and I shouldn't have been dismissive earlier."

Kim raised an eyebrow. "I appreciate the rapid shift in perspective."

He grimaced. "You can thank my mom."

Laughing, Kim said, "Why?"

"She may or may not have said I was acting like an idiot. She also may or may not have told me to adjust my attitude and then hung up on me."

"Your mother hung up on you? Ouch, that's brutal."

"Yeah. She can be ruthless."

Kim spread the afghan over her lap. Nate put his arm on the back of the bench. When she leaned back into him, he put his arm around her shoulders and pulled her close.

"I don't want to fight with you."

Kim snuggled into him and shifted the afghan to cover both of them and rested her arm across his waist. "I don't want to fight with you, either."

"Good." He pressed a kiss to her forehead.

The fire crackled and sent up a shower of sparks as a log shifted.

"What do we do?"

Nate's fingertips ran across her shoulders. "That's your call, Kim. We can keep going like we are and then pick it back up when I get home, or we can put a label on it now."

Kim sat back and looked up at him. "What kind of label?"

Even the glow of the fire couldn't disguise his blush. "I don't know. I guess that depends on your intentions." He grinned down at her. "Are they honorable? I have my virtue to consider."

She covered her mouth with her hand and laughed. "Are you afraid I just want you to be my mistress?"

"Will you ever make an honest man of me?"

"We'll see."

"Ouch." He tapped his chest. "You wounded me right here."

"Be reasonable. I have the offer from the duke to consider."

Nate sighed. "He does have better lands than I. How many sheep did he pledge for your hand?"

"Nine. And fourteen ducks."

"Aw, man. How can I compete with that?" He pretended to consider. "I can go as high as six sheep, but I could also throw in three goats and some chickens."

"No ducks?"

"No."

She giggled. "How disappointing. I do like ducks."

Nate lowered his voice and looked around like he was making sure no one was watching them. "You do know that the duke's ducks were gotten through unscrupulous means, don't you?"

"Gasp." Kim put her fingertips to her throat. "How dare you disparage the duke's ducks."

"My disgust is for the dastardly duke, definitely not the duke's delightful ducks, my dear."

The sound of their laughter filled the darkness.

Wiping her eyes, Kim managed, "Dreadful," which sent them both back into gales of laughter.

When the last of the giggles were finally under control, Kim snuggled back into Nate and watched the dancing flames. Dampness drew close around them, chilling the air.

"Are you excited about reprising your role?"

Nate nodded. "I kind of am. It'll be better for the fans, that's for sure."

"You don't think there'll be any backlash, like people mad and feeling like they were tricked by his first death?"

"Nah. Since it was off-screen, the writers just had to make sure the characters would believe he was dead. Others weren't convinced without his body, so they'll probably play it up from that perspective."

Kim tried to focus on the positives of the situation. "I bet it'll be nice to see your old friends, too."

"Yeah. It's hard to keep in touch when you leave the show. Just like leaving any job with coworkers you like."

"What concerns you?"

Nate drew in a long breath and let it out slowly. "Besides us? I'm not looking forward to being back in the spotlight and potentially attracting another stalker." He shifted in the seat. "I can't explain it. She had a freaking *shrine* in her living room. One picture from when she'd met me in person at a con blown up in about ten different sizes. Pictures of me from magazines, from the internet. Stacks of them. She had framed one of those generic 'Thanks for writing' letters we send out when fans write in. Then there were the diaries. She wrote letters to herself from me..." He shuddered. "I only saw the police pictures and it was bad enough. I'm sure it would have been a lot worse to actually see it in person."

Kim snuggled closer. "I'm so sorry you went through that."

"I'm a little worried I'll be jumping at every little thing and I won't be able to concentrate and do my job."

"I bet once you're there and working, it'll be fine. Don't let the anticipation get to you."

"I'm trying not to." He squeezed her shoulder. "And what concerns you?"

"Miranda," she answered without hesitation. "I know I'm not supposed to say that. And it's not that I don't trust you. She bothers me, I don't trust her, and I know it's my own issue to deal with, but there you have it."

Nate didn't argue. Instead, he validated her concerns. "I don't trust her either. And I don't want to be with her. Kim, even if I had never met you, I wouldn't have slept with her when she showed up at my house. I don't know if it makes you feel better or worse, but you have nothing to do with why I'm not interested in her."

"I think it helps."

"Good."

They lapsed into silence, both of them gazing into the fire. It did make her feel better that she wasn't the only reason he wasn't interested in Miranda anymore. Then he'd have more than one reason to turn her down when she inevitably came on to him again. She tried to ignore the sharp pang of jealousy. She couldn't control what Miranda did. She couldn't control what Nate did. Nate couldn't control what Miranda did. They could only control their reactions.

Kim decided that her reaction was going to be to trust him until she had a good reason not to.

She felt his arm tighten around her shoulder and his lips pressed against the top of her head. "I'm glad we're not fighting anymore."

"Me, too." She turned her face up and kissed him.

Chapter Thirty-Four

After Kim went home, Nate made sure the last of the fire was out before going inside. It was after midnight, but he picked up his phone and texted his mother anyway.

You were right. Don't get cocky.

He knew it would make her smile when she saw it in the morning.

Climbing into bed, Nate was content. He was still anxious about returning to the show, but making things right with Kim, and talking about what they both wanted, went a long way toward his peace of mind.

The next day passed in a flurry of phone calls and emailed contracts and confirming travel plans. By late afternoon, the details swam together in his head. Everything was coming in on California time, stretching into the evening, when his phone started blowing up with text messages from his old – now current – castmates. It was nice, but a little overwhelming.

He replied to nearly everyone with the same copied and pasted message, assuming no one would compare notes.

The phone dinged again, and he was tempted to turn it off and deal with it later. This time, though, the message was more than welcome.

Fresh from the oven!

Followed by a photo of a pan of cinnamon rolls.

Those four words took the edge off his anxiety and helped remind him to keep his focus on what was important. As large as it loomed in his life, *Daystar Rising* was temporary. It had an easily defined beginning and end. The relationships he'd formed were just as temporary. He'd discovered that when he'd been injured, then left the show and his contact with everyone fizzled out. It wasn't good or bad, it just was.

He ignored a new stream of text messages and put his shoes on. Shoving his phone into his pocket, he grabbed the doorknob, then stopped, pulled his phone out and set it on the table. There would be nothing coming in that couldn't wait a few hours.

It was still light outside, but the sun was sinking into the horizon when he trekked across the lawn and knocked on Kim's door.

Jared opened the door with a sour look on his face.

"What's up?"

"She won't let me have a cinnamon bun."

"That's brutal."

Jared left the door hanging open and walked back to the kitchen. Nate closed the door and followed him. His heart melted when Kim turned and smiled up at him, then turned her face up for a quick kiss. He obliged, then inhaled deeply. "Smells incredible. Why are you torturing the boy?"

She rolled her eyes. "I'd hardly consider it torture. I told him he had to wait until I got them iced."

"I don't know. That's pretty rough."

Jared crossed his arms. "I even offered to put the icing on."

"Before I took them out of the oven."

Chuckling, Nate said, "Are they cool enough now?"

Kim touched the tops of the rolls. "Barely."

Jared jumped off his stool and grabbed a knife and the bowl of icing. "Close enough."

"Hang on. We have to put them on the plate first." Kim flipped the rolls out of the baking pan and arranged them on a platter.

"Now?" Jared asked hopefully.

"Don't get carried away. And wash your hands first."

"Fine." Jared washed his hands, then got busy icing the rolls.

"How was your day?" Kim asked.

"Good. Lots of phone calls and emails and texts. Your cinnamon rolls came at the perfect time because I was ready to smash my phone with a hammer. How was yours?"

She wrapped her arms around his middle. "Great. I recorded four videos and got two of them edited. Which is why we're having cinnamon rolls at nine o'clock instead of a decent supper."

"Seems nutritious enough to me."

"Me, too," Jared said. He finished icing the rolls and set the platter on the island.

Kim said, "We should get some plates."

Nate and Jared exchanged a look, then looked at Kim. "Why?"

She rolled her eyes. "Fine. No plates."

They each took a cinnamon roll and dove in.

"These are fantastic," Nate said around a mouthful.

Jared mocked Kim's voice. "Don't talk with your mouth full."

Nate couldn't help but laugh at Kim's expression. "Sorry."

"Mm hmmm." She leaned forward and tapped her finger on Jared's forehead. "Well, if either of you want to keep getting cinnamon rolls, you might want to rethink your strategy."

"Sorry," Jared said, but the corners of his mouth were twitching.

"I can tell," Kim said drily.

Nate finished his roll and licked the icing off his fingers. "These are fantastic."

"You already said that."

"They're so good I had to say it twice." He reached over and wiped a spot of icing from the corner of her mouth.

"I was saving that."

"Sorry."

She stuck her tongue out at him. "Next time, you make the rolls."

"Okay, but they'll be from a tube."

"That's fine."

Jared said, "I'll help. Those big ones aren't too bad. And the icing that comes with them is good."

Nate watched Kim narrow her eyes in a mock glare. "Really? Then why'd I waste my time on these?"

"Because you're awesome."

"Nice save," Nate said.

Jared hopped off his stool and got the plastic wrap from the pantry. "I'll cover these."

Nate pulled the platter toward him. "What, it's a one-roll limit tonight?"

"It's always a one-roll limit for me," Jared grumbled.

"Oh, yeah," Kim said. "Except last week when you ate nine of them before I got up."

He shrugged. "When opportunity knocks…"

Nate laughed and pulled Kim to his side. "He sounds like you."

"I'm not nearly that sarcastic."

He raised an eyebrow.

"Okay, maybe I am."

"Maybe?"

Jared went upstairs.

Nate waited until he heard the bedroom door close, then turned to Kim. "Want to sit on the porch?"

"Absolutely. Let me grab a glass of water. You?"

"Sure."

Nate took one of the glasses and followed Kim out to the porch swing. They settled in beside each other, his long legs propelling the swing while Kim tucked her legs underneath her.

Chapter Thirty-Five

Kim took a long sip of her water. "I've been thinking about something that my friend Tara said, and it kind of stuck and I keep thinking about it."

"She's the one who helped get Jared into the cyber school?"

"Yes. She asked if I had ever considered adopting Jared."

The porch swing creaked as it moved back and forth. "Had you? Before that, I mean?"

Kim swirled her glass, sending the ice cubes clinking into each other. "It feels horrible to say that I hadn't really thought about it. I mean, of course it crossed my mind, but he's my *sister*'s kid. I'm his aunt. I'm his legal guardian. It didn't seem like an issue and I think I didn't think about it because I'm not trying to replace his mom."

"Why did she bring it up?"

"I was telling her about the comments the school made –"

Nate interrupted. "What comments?"

"The evil psycho secretary kept making comments about whether I had the proper forms on file to discuss Jared with them, since I'm not his parent." She rolled her eyes, the mere thought of the bully secretary making her angry all over again.

"But she has to know the situation. The school's not *that* big."

"Oh, she knows. She's just an evil, horrible, hateful person."

"Wow."

"That's what made Tara bring it up. I already have permanent guardianship, but she wondered if Jared really feels like it's a permanent situation. I know there are times he kind of walks on eggshells, like if he doesn't toe the line, I'll send him away. I hate that he could ever think that, but I get where it comes from in his mind. Maybe it would help him really know that I'm not going anywhere."

"But?"

"I'm worried about how he'd interpret it. What if he sees it as an attempt to replace his mother? Or worse. What if he's ok with it and then feels guilty, like *he's* betraying his mother by seeing me as a mother figure?" It was the first time she'd given voice to all the thoughts in her head. Why did everything have to be so complicated?

"That's tough. I wouldn't have thought of that, but I can see where it's possible. Is he going to be seeing the counselor again? Maybe you could see if you can schedule an appointment to have this conversation with him present?"

"That's a great idea."

"No matter what, he's going to have a lot to process and work through. So figure out what the best thing is for the both of you, and stick to it."

Kim let the creaking swing soothe her for a minute. "It's hard to make huge decisions like this without knowing the long-term consequences."

"A crystal ball would make life a lot easier, wouldn't it?"

"Yes. My horoscope was no help. Today's was something like, 'Keep your eyes open and new opportunities will present themselves.' Very helpful and so specific."

"Did it at least give you your lucky numbers so you can play the lottery?"

"Nope."

"Maybe those come in fortune cookies." He shook his head. "How do they get away with calling those things cookies?"

Kim laughed. "Right? They're tasteless and have that weird texture that's crunchy, but not exactly in a good way."

"Definitely not cookie material."

"Not at all. Probably not food material at all."

Nate looked thoughtful. "Maybe they'll be useful for postapocalyptic sustenance."

"I can see it now. A whole group of survivors eating fortune cookies and getting bits of wisdom like, 'You may feel like an outcast, but soon you'll be in charge.'"

"Way to raise suspicion. 'Nice fortune, Carl, how about you take the first watch tonight?'"

Kim shifted and leaned into his arm. Bursts of yellow light blinked over the grass as fireflies searched for mates.

"I remember chasing lightning bugs and putting them in a jar when we were kids."

"We did that, too."

Nate nudged her with his shoulder. "Got a jar?"

Grinning, she got up. "I'll be right back." She went inside and grabbed a glass jar from the pantry, then came back out. "You can't catch lightning bugs unless you're in your bare feet."

Nate kicked his shoes off and stuffed his socks into them. "I don't remember the grass being this cold and wet when I was a kid."

Kim cupped her hand and scooped a bug out of the air, then tapped her hand against the jar until he fell inside. "I'm sure it was, we just didn't care."

"That's true about a lot of things. It'd be nice to be so carefree again."

"Maybe." Kim shrugged and put another bug in the jar.

"Hang on, I got one." Nate stood beside her and put his bug in the jar.

Kim felt the heat radiating from him and all she wanted to do was drop the jar on the ground and kiss him.

His voice brought her back to herself.

"I think he's trying to escape."

Kim tilted the jar and thwarted the bug's exit. "Did you know fireflies are actually beetles?"

"Huh. I did not know that. I thought beetles had hard shells."

"You're thinking of tacos."

They both laughed. The lightning bugs took advantage of the distraction and escaped.

Nate pointed to the jar. "They all got away. And now I'm hungry for tacos. And my feet are wet and cold."

"Anything else you want to whine about? This was your idea, you know."

"I didn't think it through."

Kim reached out and caught another lightning bug and tapped it into the jar. "Let's see how long it takes to get ten, then we can quit."

"Don't let them escape this time."

"You wanna hold the jar?"

Nate laughed and ran off to catch bugs.

Kim took off after him and they laughed as they tried to catch more uncooperative lightning bugs and put them in the jar, while trying to keep the bugs already in there from escaping.

"How many is that?"

Kim held the jar upside down and counted. "7... 8... 9. We need one more. Ah, crap! No, come back! Okay, we need two more. Hurry, I think they figured out how to get out the bottom."

Nate ran over and put a bug in the jar. "One more."

Kim put her finger in the way of an escaping bug. "Hurry."

"Got one!" Nate tapped the tenth bug into the jar and quickly counted. "Ten!"

They high-fived and sat back on the porch swing. They sat down and watched the glowing bugs climb up the side of the jar, and one by one launch themselves back into the night.

"That was fun," Nate said.

Kim chuckled and leaned against his shoulder. "It was. But you were right. My feet are freezing."

"Wait, what was that first part again?"

"Don't get cocky." She let him pull her closer and the sudden unwelcome image of William's face popped into her head. Never in a million years would he have taken his shoes off and run around the backyard catching lightning bugs. It was so nice to spend time with a man who was secure enough to be silly.

A man who didn't see Jared as baggage to be tolerated.

The nagging voice of doubt reared its ugly head and reminded her that this was too good to be true. And when something seems too good to be true? It usually is.

Chapter Thirty-Six

Nate stared at the empty glass jar, his mind drifting, wondering why he was leaving a woman who was willing to run barefoot through the wet grass and catch fireflies, even if it was temporary. He didn't need the money. He didn't need the inevitable drama.

So why? The answer came, sounding like a sage old karate sensei. *To prove you aren't running scared anymore.* So who am I trying to prove it to? He asked the imaginary wise man. *To yourself. To prove you're not unworthy of her.* Ha, he snarked back to the voice, I'm not worthy of her. I don't think anyone is.

The wise man made a noncommittal grunt and said no more.

Nate wasn't sure if that was a good sign or a bad one. Probably neither, since he was arguing with himself. Which probably wasn't the best sign, either.

"Where'd you go?"

Nate startled. "Oh, sorry. My mind was wandering."

"Unsupervised?" She teased.

"It's a good thing you said something, otherwise I might have ended up in Milwaukee."

"You'll have to tie a rope around it so it can't wander too far."

He chuckled. "I'll have to try that next time. Tether it to my spleen or something."

"What does a spleen do, anyway?"

"I have no idea."

"Do you have your phone?"

"No, I was tired of the constant stream of calls so I left it at home. Why?"

"I figured we could look it up."

Nate was confused. "Look what up?"

"The spleen. To see what it does."

"It's probably something really boring. I mean, with a name like 'spleen' how exciting could it be?"

"It could be intentionally misleading. Like the whole Iceland/Greenland thing."

He considered her theory. "You're saying the spleen is actually fascinating."

"It could be. We don't know."

"All right, what does the spleen do?"

"Maybe it's the source of human magic."

"Then why aren't all humans magical?"

Kim sighed. "Genetics, obviously. It's like eyes. Everybody has them, but only certain people have green ones."

"A green spleen would be magical?"

"I think a green spleen would be diseased, but I'm just guessing."

Nate nodded. "I think you're right. Green organs generally aren't healthy. Unless you're Vulcan. That's what Mr. Spock is."

Kim rolled her eyes. "I know what a Vulcan is. Geez. Were his organs green? Or was it just his blood?"

"Hmm. Well, in humans, blood is red and organs are kinda red. So I'd say yes, Vulcan organs are green."

She laughed. "I love how you speak with authority on Vulcan anatomy."

"We all have our areas of expertise."

"Does Qaaxag have red blood?"

"Nope. It's blue."

"Ah. So blue organs."

"Presumably." Nate pulled her closer.

"Wouldn't that suggest oxygen depravation?"

"No more than green suggests disease and rot in a Vulcan."

"Oooh, clever comeback."

He grinned. "I thought so."

"How do you know his blood's blue?"

"Battle scenes. And I think it was blue in the original book series. Our makeup team is brilliant. By the time they were done, I was convinced I was actually bleeding." The more he talked about it, the more he looked forward to playing Qaaxag again.

"That sounds so fun. Essentially playing dress up as an adult. Where else can you do that?"

"ComiCon."

"Oooh, or the Renaissance Faire."

Nate raised an eyebrow.

"What? I could totally pull off a tavern wench costume."

He couldn't keep his eyes from glancing downward. He cleared his throat and forced his gaze away.

Kim laughed. "Or not."

"No, you could totally do that." He felt his face heating. "I think they're two different kinds of crowds."

"I've never been to either one."

"I've only been to cons."

"I think the Ren Faire is in the fall, isn't it? Maybe we should go. I bet Jared would have a blast. We can walk around eating turkey legs."

Nate laughed. "That does sound kind of awesome." His mind zipped back to the idea of Kim in a tavern wench costume. He had a feeling that particular mental image wasn't going away any time soon.

"I'll check the dates, but I'm pretty sure it runs for a good while in the fall."

"That sounds right." He relished the feeling of her snuggled into his shoulder.

"It's getting chilly."

"I know."

Kim said, "Maybe running through the wet grass barefoot wasn't the best idea."

He shook his head. "Nope. It was a great idea."

"It was."

"We'll have to work on your jar skills, though. Way too many escapees."

She lightly smacked his chest. "I didn't see you catching lightning bugs *and* wrestling with the jar, mister armchair quarterback."

"Psssht, I could have."

"Then you're in charge of the jar next time. And I'll be watching your every move."

"It'll be flawless. Just like *all* my moves." He faked a yawn and stretched the arm that was behind her. "Smooth as silk."

She laughed loud. "I thought you didn't want me to worry while you're away. It's like Casanova himself just took over your entire being."

"Uncanny, isn't it?"

"I'm swooning."

It was Nate's turn to laugh. "Don't worry, I won't be using my overwhelming charisma on anyone while I'm away."

"Well, *that's* a relief," she deadpanned. "What mortal woman could possibly resist?"

"I'm going to assume you're hiding behind biting sarcasm because you don't want to be consumed by the fiery jealousy you must be feeling."

Kim tilted her head to look up at him and blinked slowly. "Yes. Yes, that's it, exactly. You've discovered my innermost secret."

He sighed. "It's a gift and a curse, to know women so well."

She laughed again, leaning into his chest to muffle the guffaws.

"You mock me."

"You've given me no choice."

He laughed with her until his stomach hurt.

She finally wheezed the last laugh and wiped her eyes. "Oh, gosh, that was hilarious."

"Hey, now."

"Sorry." Another laugh escaped.

"Yeah, you sound real sorry."

She wrapped her arms around his middle and squeezed tight.

He rested his face against the top of her head and breathed in her shampoo. "There'll be a whole world full of disappointed women, cuz all this awesomeness –" he patted his chest, "is coming back home to you."

She shifted and looked up at him. This time, there was no teasing in her smile. "I know."

Nate's heart jumped. There was a lot of commitment in that simple phrase. A lot of trust.

The fame, the big fat paychecks, the open doors… none of them were worth as much as that.

Chapter Thirty-Seven

Kim felt the mood shift. In an instant, the teasing playfulness that had defined the evening was gone, replaced with a seriousness that felt like a Big Talk was coming. She studied Nate's face. He was doing the same, tracing every detail of her face with his gaze.

He put his fingertips under her chin and leaned down to kiss her. It was one of those perfect, magical kisses that stole her breath and made the whole rest of the world fade away to nothingness. It stopped time.

When their mouths parted, she had to catch her breath. Her fingers clutched his shirt, but she didn't let go because they were trembling. Her eyelids were heavy as she lifted them to look up at Nate.

He rested his forehead against hers and said, "It's temporary, right?" The fire crackled in agreement.

She uncurled her fingers from his shirt and wrapped her arms around his neck. "Absolutely. People make relationships work all the time with much bigger obstacles than this."

"True."

"And it's not like we won't talk. We'll be texting and video chatting and talking and emailing the whole time." Maybe it wouldn't be so bad. They were still getting to know each other, so it could actually be really good for them to be limited to phone calls.

Nate nodded. "Yeah, the only time I can't be in touch is when we're shooting. In the grand scheme of things, that's a small part of the time I'll be gone."

"Exactly. Even with the time difference in Jordan, it'll be fine. And Puerto Rico's in the same time zone, so that'll be easier yet. This won't be bad at all."

He let out a long breath. "So you're feeling okay about it?"

"I am. I told you before, the only thing under my skin a little bit is Miranda, but I know that's totally my own issue. I trust you."

"Good."

They sat without talking for a long while, listening to the creak of the porch swing and the crickets chirping. The sky had faded from deep blue to black, with stars dotting the darkness.

"It's getting late," Nate said.

"Yeah, but I hate to move."

"Me, too. But I kind of have to pee."

Kim laughed. "So do I."

"That settles it then, huh?"

"I guess so."

Reluctantly, Kim pulled herself away from Nate's side. After a quick kiss goodnight, he jogged across the grass and she went inside. Checking the locks, she turned off the downstairs lights and went upstairs.

Jared's room was silent. She tiptoed in, kissed his forehead, straightened his covers, and backed quietly to the doorway. She paused, watching him sleep for a minute. There was nothing she wouldn't do for this boy, and she couldn't possibly love him any more fiercely than if he'd come from her own body.

Sadie wound around her feet, purring loudly. Kim pulled the door shut and reached down to scoop the cat up. Sadie pushed her nose into Kim's armpit and kneaded her arm.

"Ow, take it easy." Kim closed her bedroom door and set Sadie on the bed. She immediately curled up on Kim's pillow, flicking her tail around to cover her face.

"You know you're going to have to move, right?" Even if Sadie could understand the words, Kim knew it wouldn't matter. The cat wasn't moving until she felt like it.

She mindlessly performed her bathroom routine, then slipped between the covers and lay her head down on the five-inch sliver of pillow Sadie had left for her.

The rhythmic purring lulled her to sleep.

In the morning, her head was still on the edge of the pillow, but Sadie had moved to the foot of the bed and stretched out to her full length.

Kim's first thought was of Nate's kiss last night. Her second was that they only had five days until he left for LA. She sighed and flung the covers back, glad she'd created several videos ahead so she could spend as much time as possible with Nate.

As if she'd summoned him, her cell phone dinged with an incoming text message.

Good morning, beautiful.

She held the screen out to the cat. "Aww, you see this? How sweet is he?"

Sadie rolled to her other side, clearly unimpressed.

"You're just jealous." Kim rubbed the cat's side and was rewarded with a purr.

Good morning yourself

A few seconds later, he called.

"I'm heading up to my mom's neck of the woods to meet her for lunch. Do you want to go along?"

She was conscious of the fact she hadn't yet brushed her teeth. "You want me to go along to lunch with your mom?" She wasn't sure what to think of that.

"Yeah. Then I thought we could check out a brewery that's up that way."

"A brewery?"

"They do tours."

"Oh." She looked down at her pajamas. "When were you thinking of leaving?"

"Around ten thirty?"

"Okay. Wait." How would Jared be able to go to a brewery?

"Brewery tour is for all ages."

"You read my mind." She was struck by how thoughtful it was that he'd checked on the age limits before even asking her.

"I checked the website to make sure. And wear sneakers."

"Why?" That seemed like an odd rule.

"Safety issue. Feet have to be completely covered."

"Okay."

"I have about a thousand messages to return, so I'll pick you up at ten thirty, okay?"

"See you then."

Kim hung up and rushed to the bathroom to brush her teeth. Having a conversation before brushing her teeth grossed her out, even one on the phone.

If she was to wear sneakers, she assumed jeans would be an appropriate choice. She pulled on her favorite pair and picked a plain shirt that she dressed up with a multi-strand long necklace.

After she put on her makeup and styled her short hair, she went to wake Jared.

He was already sitting up at his desk, working on some sort of document.

"Whatcha doing?"

"Book report."

"When's it due?"

He clicked his mouse and a calendar appeared. "Next week."

"Nate wants to take us to lunch with his mom and then to tour a brewery."

He scrunched up his face. "Do I have to wait in the car or something?"

"Nope, the tour is open to all ages. We have to wear sneakers, though, so no sandals."

"Why?" His expression was the same as hers had been a few moments ago.

"Safety issue."

He shrugged and turned back to click the calendar away. "When are we leaving?"

"Not until ten thirty, so you have plenty of time."

Sadie jumped up on Jared's desk and flicked her paw, knocking a pen to the ground. She looked pleased.

Jared picked it up and set it in front of the cat, who knocked it down again. He laughed and picked it back up. "Don't you dare knock it down again," he said sternly as he put the pen in front of her a third time. Sadie flung it to the floor and he laughed.

Kim watched this for a few minutes, then went to her office to do some work before it was time to leave.

Chapter Thirty-Eight

Nate finished returning calls and replying to emails and texts. He'd signed the contracts his agent had forwarded and scanned them and sent them back. Welcome back messages were the bulk of the texts, so he could deal with those later.

When he looked up, it was almost time to leave. He closed the laptop and grabbed his keys, then took a last look in the hallway mirror and ran a hand through his hair to make sure it was just so.

He pulled into Kim's driveway. She and Jared came out the door before he had a chance to go knock, so he went around and opened Kim's door while Jared jumped in the back.

While he was pulling away from the sidewalk, Jared said, "Are you sure I'm allowed to go into a brewery?"

"I'm sure."

"Why am I allowed in a brewery but not a bar? Aren't they afraid kids will try to drink the beer in a brewery?"

"Nope. I did the tour a lot of years ago, and it's not like there's a beer fountain you can drink out of."

"Oh." Jared sounded disappointed.

"They talk a lot about what happened to the company during Prohibition, so if you like history, that'll be interesting."

"How did they keep being a company if beer was illegal?"

Nate glanced into the rearview mirror and grinned. "I guess you'll find out."

Jared's eyes widened. "Were they bootleggers?"

"I don't remember the whole story, so you'll have to wait and see."

"Huh. And I thought this was going to be boring."

"Jared!" Kim scolded.

Nate laughed. "I hope it's not."

"Is your mom going on the tour?" Kim asked.

"No, we're just meeting her for lunch. I wasn't sure when I'd be able to get up here before I left, so I figured we'd just make a day of it."

"She's not upset that we're coming, is she? I mean, she probably wanted to spend some time with *you* before you leave, not all of us."

"She's excited you and Jared are coming." In fact, she was probably more excited to see them than she was to see him.

"You're not just saying that, are you?"

"Nope. I think she wants to interrogate you. See whether or not to give you her stamp of approval."

"So I shouldn't be surprised if she puts a bag over my head and drags me into a dark room."

Nate blew out a *pffft* and said, "She won't do the dragging herself. Bad knee."

"Ah. Henchmen."

"Exactly."

"I hope they don't mess up my hair."

"Nah, I think they're pretty good about stuff like that."

Jared said, "You guys are weird."

Nate reached over and squeezed Kim's hand. He knew

Jared wouldn't admit it in a hundred years, but he loved this kind of interaction. And so did he. Normal, everyday, nothing special, just riding in the car, talking and laughing. He hadn't even left for California yet, but he already couldn't wait to get back home.

The forty-five minute trip passed quickly. He pulled into the parking lot and waved to a red SUV. "There she is."

"Here we go."

He could tell Kim was nervous by the way she touched her hair. "It's just lunch. It's not like you're asking for my hand in marriage." He paused, then added, "You aren't, are you?"

That made her laugh. "Not today. I still haven't decided what to do about the duke."

He pressed a kiss to the back of her hand. "Shall we?"

"We shall."

Jared jumped out of the car and went to the sidewalk by the time they had gotten their doors open. Nate pushed the button on his keychain to lock the car and reached for Kim's hand. His mother waited up ahead.

From behind them, he heard a loud motor approaching too fast. He turned and the edges of his vision went fuzzy and dark. A Cadillac sped toward them. The same green Cadillac that had run him down.

There was too much blood in his head. It pounded against his eardrums. The sun glinted off the car's grill, blinding and menacing.

A strangled noise caught in his throat.

The sickening squeal of twisting metal.

Shattering glass.

The pain of landing on concrete.

Screaming.

Blackness.

Silence.

But only for a moment.

Slowly, far away sounds filtered back into his awareness, getting louder as they came closer.

"Nate! Nate!"

It sounded like Kim. But it couldn't be. In his mind's eye, she was trapped under the car. She needed him.

He struggled to come back to himself. Had they both been hit?

Where was Jared?

Jared! He thought he said it out loud but he couldn't be sure.

"Nate?"

It was Jared's voice. He sounded scared.

Nate couldn't force his eyes to open. Was he dead? Were they all dead? Would Jared sound scared if they were dead?

A sliver of blinding light sliced through his eyelids as he pried them open.

"Nate?" This frightened voice sounded like his mother.

His eyes finally cooperated and slid open. He gasped in a breath and reached up to shield his eyes. It was so bright. Oh, no. Bright white light. They were dead, weren't they?

A face came into view, blocking out some of the brightness. Kim, her face etched with worry.

Another face on the other side of him. His mother, her expression matching Kim's.

"Nate?"

"Is he okay?" Jared's voice from somewhere above. Behind? Beside? Nothing was oriented properly.

He blinked a few times and the sky with puffy white clouds came into focus.

"What happened?" His voice was clear.

"I'm not sure. You turned around and then you yelled and passed out."

Nate struggled to sit up. "Did she hit us?"

"Who?" Kim's hands were on his shoulder.

"Should I call an ambulance?" A strange man's voice asked.

Pattie answered. "No, I think he's okay. Thank you."

The fog slowly cleared from his mind. He struggled to his feet and looked around. Parked beside his car was the shiny chrome grill he'd seen careening toward them. The car was green, but it was a classic Chevy Chevelle. Probably a '69. Definitely not a Cadillac.

There had been no accident.

Relief was short-lived. In that instant, he had been completely and utterly useless. What good was a man who froze and passed out and couldn't do anything to protect the people he loved?

"What happened?" his mother asked.

Nate shook his head, his gaze still on the car. The chrome mocked him. "I thought… never mind. I don't know."

Kim slipped her hand into his, but he pulled away. Undeterred, she reached again and refused to let go. "It's okay."

He tore his focus from the car to her. "It's not okay, Kim." He yanked his hand away from hers, a little more forcefully than he should have. "It's never going to be okay."

Chapter Thirty-Nine

Kim watched him walk away, stalking across the parking lot, away from the restaurant. She turned to Pattie and raised her hands in silent question.

Jared stepped closer to Kim. "What's wrong?" His voice was a whisper.

"I'm not sure."

Pattie put her hand on Jared's shoulder and gave him a smile. "Why don't you and I go in and get a table?"

Kim nodded. "Good idea."

Nate leaned on a stone wall at the far side of the parking lot, his back to them.

Jared hesitated, but followed Pattie into the restaurant. Kim looked both ways, then crossed the parking lot and came up behind Nate and put her hand on his back. His back moved with a big sigh.

"Sorry."

"Nate, you have nothing to apologize for."

"Don't I?" he snapped, then dropped his head. His fingers gripped the edge of the wall, his knuckles white. "Sorry," he mumbled again.

"Look at me."

He didn't move.

Kim wished she could see inside his head, to know what he was thinking so she'd know how to make him feel better. "Nate. Talk to me. Please."

"I thought that car was going to hit us. And what did I do? I passed out. What good is that?"

Kim knew pointing out that it didn't happen that way wouldn't make him feel any better. "I don't agree with your conclusion, but I don't think you're going to listen to reason right now. Let's go inside and have a nice lunch, okay?"

He pushed back from the wall and faced her. "Why would you even want to spend any more time with me?"

She wrapped her arms around him, tight, and kissed his cheek. "Because you're my ride home."

It earned her a surprised smile that quickly vanished, but it was real.

"Your mom and Jared went in to get a table."

With a heavy sigh, he let her lead him toward the restaurant.

She was glad he didn't pull his hand from hers this time. Lacing her fingers with his, she walked beside him without saying a word.

In spite of her earlier reservations, she was glad of two things – first, that Nate hadn't been alone when he panicked, and second, that his mom was here. Pattie was funny and warm and kind. They were a good team, keeping the conversation light, trying to draw Nate in, but neither of them pushing him.

Pattie spent a lot of time talking to Jared about school and didn't bat an eyelash about the switch to online learning. They'd gotten some less than supportive comments about it, mostly from people who didn't use the internet on any sort of regular basis themselves.

After lunch, Kim and Jared hung back while Pattie and Nate said goodbye. Then Pattie hugged Jared, then Kim, and whispered in her ear, "You're good for him."

Kim hugged her back, the lump in her throat making it impossible to answer. She swallowed it down, then managed, "Thanks."

Nate's mother's approval meant a lot. Even more than she'd expected it to.

They all waved goodbye, and Kim grabbed Nate's hand. He didn't pull away, but he didn't return her squeeze.

He also didn't meet her eyes as he fumbled with the keys to unlock the car. He did open her door for her, but he did so without a word. She climbed in and he shut the door.

Jared was already buckled in the back. "Is Nate going to be okay?"

"He's going to be fine," she answered automatically.

"Is there anything we can do?"

She'd been wondering the same thing. "Just be normal, I guess. Not make a big deal out of it."

"Wh-" he cut himself off as Nate got in the car and instead of whatever he was starting to say, said, "I was looking at the brewery tour on my phone. It's built into caves in the side of the mountain and it stays forty-seven degrees all year round."

"That's really... *cool*," Kim said.

Jared groaned. "You didn't."

"I did."

Nate hadn't backed out of the parking space.

"Everything okay?"

He nodded. "Yeah, I mean, if you guys would rather head home..."

"I'd really like to do the tour. If you want to go home, we'll go home, but I don't think that's the best idea. Do you?"

He finally met her gaze. "Probably not. But maybe…"

"What?"

He sighed heavily. "Maybe you should drive."

"Sure." Kim unclicked her seatbelt. She was concerned that he didn't feel up to driving, but she still thought the best course of action was to keep everything light.

They switched seats and Kim grinned at him. "Sorry, but I've got to adjust this seat. I've never had to adjust it this way – I'm always the tall one."

He laughed a little. "There's a button on the side of the seat."

She adjusted the seat and mirrors. "Okay, where to?"

"It's already in the GPS. You'll turn right out of the parking lot."

The GPS estimated a thirty-minute drive. The longer they were in the car, the calmer and more talkative Nate became.

They came into a small town and Nate pointed. "The brewery is up here, but we'll have to go past and park down there."

Kim followed his finger and saw the sign for parking. "Got it." She turned into the parking facility and found a space.

The brewery was a few blocks uphill. Kim groaned. "Couldn't they have the parking lot a little closer? Ugh."

Nate finally gave a genuine smile. "At least it'll be downhill on the way out."

"That is literally the *only* upside."

"Come on, it's not that bad," Jared called from his spot already up the hill.

"Talk to me in twenty years," Nate answered.

He laughed and ran ahead to the doors of the brewery.

Kim reached over and took Nate's hand. He squeezed it but

kept his gaze on the sidewalk. "Thanks."

She tilted her head. "For?"

He shrugged. "Just for being... I guess for not being weird about..." He waved his hand to encompass the day.

"Nate, it's okay."

He looked like he was going to argue.

"It's okay," she repeated, squeezing his hand for emphasis.

Holding the door open for her, he kissed her cheek as she walked past him and said again, "Thanks."

They found Jared waiting impatiently beside the check-in counter. Nate paid for their tours and they put their wristbands on and waited for the tour guide.

A small crowd gathered, about a dozen people. Precisely on time, a middle-aged woman in a brewery shirt introduced herself as the tour guide. She led them down a flight of stairs, chatting the whole way, pointing out significant photos that hung on the walls, giving them a brief history of the brewery's founding family.

She herded them into a damp stone-walled room full of barrels and kegs, gave another part of her speech, then led them into a cavern cut into the rock.

"We're actually inside the mountain at this point," she told them, patting the damp stone wall for emphasis.

Her speech was peppered with a huge amount of history, but her enthusiasm made it all very interesting. Kim glanced over at Jared, who listened with rapt attention, especially when she started talking about Prohibition and how the company was ordered to suddenly stop producing alcohol, but they needed to still stay in business.

Kim nudged Nate and cocked her head in Jared's direction. "I think this counts as an educational field trip."

He grinned back at her. "I had no idea he'd be this interested."

Chapter Forty

Nate was happy to see Jared enjoying the tour. Just being with Kim and Jared helped his mood immeasurably. Especially when Kim shivered in the cool, damp caves and wrapped her arm around his waist.

He put his arm around her shoulders and hugged her close to his side.

"What about you," he asked when the tour guide paused in her speech. "Are you having a good time?"

"Oh, this is great. I wouldn't mind another ten or fifteen degrees, but I'm not complaining."

The tour moved above-ground, into the factory part of the brewery, where they saw how the beer was bottled and packaged. Jared was enthralled with the bottles being flipped upside down and pushed along a long chrome track until the spot where they were flipped back up, filled, then capped. He'd taken dozens of pictures throughout the tour.

The tour ended in the tasting room, where Jared got to sample a birch beer and a root beer, while he and Kim sampled actual beer.

"This one's not bad," Kim said, holding her little plastic cup out.

"I don't think you'll like this one. It's bitter."

They swapped cups. Nate finished Kim's sample, while she took a dainty sip of his and made a face. "You're right. That's awful."

"One more?"

"Sure."

They got back in line and made their selections from the ten available beers. He said something and made Kim laugh so loud heads turned in their direction.

"Are you guys allowed to drive now?" Jared side-eyed them.

Kim laughed. "Yes. I'm a lightweight and even I can handle two dixie cups of beer."

Nate nodded. "It would take a bunch of these to be impaired."

Jared looked skeptical. "The root beer is really good."

"Oh, good. We can still have a couple of samples, I think I'll try that. What about the birch beer?"

"It's weird."

"Have you ever had it before?" Nate asked.

"I don't think so." He made a face. "And I probably won't ever have it again."

Kim went over to the counter to get another sample, leaving Nate and Jared on a bench near the windows.

"Are you okay? Aunt Kim told me not to say anything, but... are you?"

Nate's heart squeezed. The last thing he wanted was to make Jared uncomfortable. He glanced around, but nobody was close enough to hear him. "I have panic attacks, ever since the accident."

"Why do you call it an accident? She ran over you on

purpose." There was no malice or judgment, simply matter-of-factness in his voice.

Nate considered his question. "I think it's easier to call it an accident because I get less questions that way. At least, from people who don't already know the story."

"I guess that makes sense."

"Anyway. Sometimes something will just trigger an attack out of nowhere, and there's not much I can do about it."

"Are you going to break up with Aunt Kim because of it?"

Nate sat up straight. "What? Why… What made you say that?"

Jared ignored the question. "She doesn't like you less because you passed out."

"No, but-"

"Would you break up with *her* if *she* had panic attacks?"

"Of course not."

Jared sat back like he'd won an argument.

"It's complicated."

The wise young man was gone, and the teenager was back, rolling his eyes. "It's really not."

Nate's gaze crossed the room and settled on Kim, still in line and chatting easily with another woman. Maybe Jared was right. Being with her didn't feel complicated at all.

"You know you can always get meds for anxiety."

"No." Nate answered more sharply than he intended, and quickly softened his voice. "That's not an option for me."

Jared's eyes narrowed and his shoulders slumped a little. "Are you a recovering addict or something?" Suspicion colored his words.

"No. I'm not." Nate took a deep breath and said words he had never said out loud to another human being, ever. "My biological father… he had – *has* – a drug problem."

Jared stared at him for a long moment, then slowly nodded. "That sucks."

For a second, Nate felt a stab of guilt. He'd forgotten Jared's own parents were drug addicts. Or maybe he hadn't, and that was why he'd shared his own dirty little secret.

Kim reappeared, holding four little plastic cups. "They let me get your samples since these are non-alcoholic."

Nate stood and took two of the cups from her. "Thanks. I'd have come over to help if I knew you were going to do that."

She grinned. "It's fine. Would you believe I actually met someone who's seen my channel? She's super sweet and guess what."

"What?" He sipped the root beer. Jared was right, it was delicious.

"Her brother works for the Home Network and she's going to send him my links." Her eyes lit up even as she shrugged. "I mean, I don't expect anything to come of it, but still, it's pretty cool, right?"

"That's fantastic."

Jared agreed. "That's really cool. Maybe you'll get your own tv show."

She blushed. "Oh gosh, I'm sure that won't happen, but it's fun to imagine."

Nate put his arm around her. "You never know. Maybe I'll get back from filming and you'll be in Hollywood."

"That's not the kind of life I want."

Nate let the comment pass. Did that mean it was over if he got another big role and had to move? He scolded himself to not worry about an imaginary future when he had a real one to deal with. He was leaving Kim for longer than he'd known her, and getting through that was going to be tough enough without introducing crazy scenarios that amounted to little more than self-sabotage.

"Where'd you go?" Kim was looking up at him.

He shook his head. "I'm here. Just thinking about life. And whether I should go have a talk with that guy who keeps checking you out."

"What? Where?"

"He's over there, under the clock."

Kim discretely shifted to see. "There's no way a guy like that's checking me out."

Jared cleared his throat. "He totally is."

"You guys are ridiculous."

Nate squeezed her shoulders. "Nope, you're gorgeous and he's interested."

"Well, I'm not. He's not my type, anyway."

"What is your type?"

Kim giggled. "The guy over by the doorway. To the left."

Nate looked and laughed. The man had to be at least seventy-five. "I didn't realize you were into older men."

"I prefer to think of them as *mature*."

"A guy that age who's chasing a woman young enough to be his daughter isn't exactly mature."

Kim laughed. "Oh, please. That's every man's dream."

Nate thrust his chin in Jared's direction. "Some guys like older women."

Jared was checking out the bartender in her lowcut tank top.

Kim smacked his upper arm. "Jared. Get your eyes back in your head."

He blushed a bright red. "Can we go now?"

The room was half-empty, as tourgoers finished their samples and exited to the gift shop.

"Yup, let's go," Nate said.

They walked around the gift shop for a few minutes, where Kim bought a bottle of specialty barbeque sauce and Jared got a t-shirt to commemorate the tour. Back on the sidewalk, Nate took her hand while Jared ran ahead.

"This was a great idea," she said. "I wouldn't have thought Jared would enjoy a brewery tour so much."

"I'm glad he did. I'm glad you did, too. Except for lunch, it was a good day."

She squeezed his hand. "It was a good day, even with lunch. Your mom is delightful. We had a good talk."

"Good. I knew you'd like each other." He'd had no doubt about it.

"I think she'd like to see you again before you go. To make sure you're okay."

Nate opened her car door and closed it after she got in. When he got in his side, he said, "Yeah, I figured as much. I'll give her a call this evening."

"Be sure to tell her I made you. That'll get me extra mom points."

Nate laughed. "How do I get points with *your* mom?"

"We could have dinner with my parents before you leave, but it's short notice."

"Okay."

"Really?" She seemed surprised.

"Of course. I already met them, remember."

"Briefly, and there were more pressing things going on. And we weren't dating."

Dating. She'd said it out loud. As far as he was concerned, that made it official. "Is that going to make a difference?"

"My dad's a retired cop. There will be an interrogation."

"Yikes." He thought of Keith's intimidating handshake. An interrogation was to be expected.

"I wish your stepdad had been able to come to lunch."

"Me, too. Mom said his flight got canceled because of some storms. He should be home this evening."

"Does your mom mind how much he travels?"

"Sometimes yes, sometimes no. I think it only really bothers her when she has a trip and he has one and she has another one and they miss each other for weeks at a time."

"I wouldn't like that, either."

"No, but I think whoever retires first will go nuts being stuck at home all the time."

Jared said, "Is there a bathroom anywhere, like, soon?"

Nate glanced in the rearview mirror. "We should be coming up on a town in a couple minutes, can you wait?"

"Yeah."

Kim tsked. "That's why I told you to go before we left the brewery."

"Really not helpful," Jared said.

Nate pulled into a fast-food parking lot. Jared was out of the car and dashing into the building before he and Kim were out of the car.

"Might as well stretch our legs," Kim said.

"I'm going to get a soda. You want one?"

"Sure." Kim took his hand and they went inside. Around the corner, an employee with a booming voice was describing the last sexual experience he'd had – or more likely imagined he'd had – while the cashier glared at the manager on duty, who was texting instead of dealing with the issue.

"Sorry," the cashier mumbled as she handed over their change and cups.

"Don't apologize," Nate said rather loudly. "It's not your fault customers have to listen to this inappropriate conversation."

The manager's head snapped up and she apparently caught the gist of the employee's discussion. She disappeared around the corner and the voice abruptly stopped.

Carrying their cups to the soda fountain, Nate leaned

toward Kim's ear and said, "If we had ordered food, I would have kept my mouth shut. They'd probably spit in it."

Kim gestured to a thick line of grime around the base of the fountain. "If we had ordered food here, we'd probably get salmonella."

They filled their soda cups as Jared came out of the restroom. Kim handed him a cup. "Coke."

"Thanks."

They hurried back to the car. Jared hurled himself into the backseat and made a loud grunting noise. "That bathroom was *disgusting*. It would have been more sanitary to pull over along the road somewhere. Bleh. So gross."

"Yeah, I don't think we'll be eating there anytime soon."

"Or not soon or ever," Nate added.

When they arrived home, Nate dropped them off in front of their house. "Dinner?"

Kim grinned. "I have a lasagna ready to be put in the oven. It'll be ready in an hour."

"What can I bring?"

"Just your pretty self."

He laughed. "Okay. How about salad?"

"Perfect." She leaned over and gave him a kiss before getting out and joining Jared on the porch.

Chapter Forty-One

In the kitchen, Kim pulled the lasagna out of the fridge. "Can you turn the oven to 350°, please?"

"Sure."

Kim pulled the foil up and peered in at the lasagna, then replaced the foil. After putting the lasagna in the oven, she noticed Jared watching her. "What's up?"

He chewed his bottom lip for a moment, then took a deep breath. "Can Isobel come over?"

"For dinner? It's kind of short notice, but if it's okay with her parents, it's fine with me."

"Okay." He pulled his phone from his back pocket as he hurried from the room.

Kim watched him, wondering what was going on in his mind. With a shrug, she set a timer so she'd know when to put the garlic bread in the oven, then went into her office and decided to update her social media accounts and scroll through other people's drama.

Forty minutes later, the doorbell jangled, and she immediately looked at the timer. Footsteps clomped down the stairs and the front door opened.

A minute later, Jared poked into Kim's office. "Isobel's here. We're going outside, so let us know when dinner's ready."

"Fifteen minutes."

"Okay."

"Hi, Ms. Donahue."

"Oh for Pete's sake, Isobel, call me Kim."

The girl giggled and said, "Sorry. Hi, Kim."

"Hello, Isobel."

"Is Nate coming to dinner?" Kim couldn't miss the emphasis she put on his name.

Jared groaned. "Yes, he's coming. Now come on. We only have a few minutes to talk."

Isobel sighed and followed Jared through the kitchen and out the back door.

Sadie jumped up on Kim's desk.

"I have no idea what that's all about," Kim said.

"Meow."

"Yeah, maybe."

The doorbell rang again and Kim shut the laptop. "That's probably Nate."

"Meow," Sadie agreed.

Kim opened the door. Instead of Nate, her parents stood on the porch.

"Oh! Hey."

"We were in the neighborhood," her mother said.

"Really."

Keith rolled his eyes. "We just finished dinner and thought we'd stop by and see how Jared's doing."

Kim stepped back. "Come in. We're just getting ready to eat. Nate's coming over and Isobel is here."

"Full house," her dad said. "Guess we should have called and made an appointment."

"Oh, stop." Kim recognized that tone.

MaryAnn poked him with her elbow. "We hadn't talked to Jared in a few days."

"I don't know how much he'll talk tonight since Isobel's here."

"Girlfriend?" Keith asked.

"Friend. He's too young to have a girlfriend."

Keith snorted and MaryAnn nudged him again.

In Kim's office, the timer went off. "Might as well come in the kitchen. I have to put the garlic bread in."

She stopped in her office to grab the timer, then joined her parents in the kitchen.

"How's he been?"

"Good. He's had a few more sessions with Sawyer and it seems to be going well."

"I knew he'd be the one for Jared to talk to. He needs somebody who knows how to talk to kids."

Kim raised an eyebrow and finished putting the garlic bread on the baking sheet. "Yeah, it's been good for him."

"I'm sure it's hard for you."

She slid the bread into the oven and took her time placing it on the rack and pulling the foil off the lasagna. An uneasy feeling prickled at the back of her neck. She reset the timer.

Just then, the back door opened and Jared and Isobel came into the kitchen, and the doorbell rang.

"That'll be Nate," she said unnecessarily, glad for the distraction. She hurried to the door, unable to shake the feeling that something was up, and she wasn't going to like it.

She yanked the door open and nearly knocked the salad out of his hands as she launched herself into his arms. He balanced the salad bowl with one hand, hugging her tight with the other. He leaned back a little to look down at her.

"I don't know," she answered his unspoken question. "My

parents just got here and something's up, but I have no idea what." She gave him a quick kiss.

Nate put a finger under her chin. "Hey. It's going to be fine."

"Isobel's here, too."

He grinned at her. "My number one fan. Awesome."

She relaxed in his presence. "Number *two* fan."

Putting his hand on the small of her back, Nate followed her into the kitchen, where a new tension thickened the air.

Kim looked at her parents, who were exchanging a look between themselves, then at Jared, who had a shocked expression on his pale face. Isobel clutched his arm with both her hands.

"What is going on?"

Her parents exchanged another look and her father spoke. "This isn't the time." He shot a pointed look in Nate's direction.

"I can go." Nate set the salad on the counter.

"No." Kim reached out and grabbed his arm. "Somebody needs to tell me what's going on." She looked to Jared. "Now."

MaryAnn sighed. "We only asked if things were going well."

"That's not what you said." Jared's voice shook. He turned to Kim. "They asked me if I tried to kill myself again."

Kim's fingers dug into Nate's arm. "What? Why would you ask something like that?"

"We're just making sure he's okay. You're very… distracted lately." She shot a look at Nate.

"You can't be serious."

Keith scowled. "Don't take that tone with your mother. You don't know what it's like to raise a child, so we're here to help."

Frowning, Kim looked back and forth between her parents. "I've had Jared off and on his entire life." From the time he was an infant, Kim had been his guardian any time his mother couldn't take care of him, which amounted to just shy of half of his fourteen years.

"It would be best if he came to stay with us for a while."

Kim's mouth dropped open.

The timer went off for the lasagna, the shrill *beep beep beep* drilling into Kim's brain, but she couldn't make herself move to turn it off.

"What?"

Keith stood and she felt Nate tense beside her. "Your mother has been worried sick about him. You've obviously got bigger priorities and we're not going to let you neglect Jared so you can scratch whatever itch you've got since William left."

Isobel slunk over and turned off the timer, then immediately went back to Jared's side.

Blood pounded in Kim's head. She squeezed her eyes shut, willing this to be some strange, realistic nightmare. "You need to leave."

"Jared, let's go."

She stepped between her father and Jared. "He's not going anywhere."

"Until you're prepared to discuss this rationally, he's going to stay with us."

Kim smelled the garlic bread burning.

"Kimberly. He ran away and tried to hurt himself on your watch." Keith poked his finger at her face. "You're not his mother."

His words hurt more than if he'd slapped her. She shot back, "His *mother* became a drug addict on *your* watch, and now she's dead."

Someone gasped, either MaryAnn or Isobel. Kim deeply regretted the words even as they came out, but there was no way to take them back.

Jared yelled, "Stop it! Stop talking about me like I'm not even here."

"Let's go, son."

"I'm not your son, and I'm not leaving."

Keith's jaw clenched. He wasn't used to his authority being challenged.

Nate went over and turned the oven off, then put on an oven mitt and took the lasagna and inedible garlic bread out of the oven.

"We'll discuss this later. We won't stand by while you're put in danger."

Jared looked like he was fighting tears.

"You need to go." Kim's voice was low and calm.

"This isn't over." Keith stormed through the house and out the front door.

Tears ran down MaryAnn's face. She whispered, "How could you say that to us?"

"How could you try taking Jared from me?"

"We just want what's best for him."

Kim barked out a humorless laugh. "Does this look like the best thing for him?"

MaryAnn opened her mouth, then snapped it shut and followed her husband outside. When the car door slammed and they drove away, Kim sagged against the island for support. "What just happened?"

"They can't take me, can they?"

"No." She said the word firmly, with far more confidence than she felt.

"But Grandpa's a cop."

"Retired, and that doesn't matter. He can't just barge in here and make you leave." *Could he?*

His chin quivered.

"I have no idea where that all came from. I haven't even

talked to them for a few days." Kim looked up at Nate, hoping he had some magical answers.

He didn't, but he put his hand on her back and that made her feel a little stronger.

She wiped her hand over her face and stood straight. "I hope the lasagna is okay."

Jared and Isobel set the table in silence while Nate filled glasses with ice water. They all picked at their lasagna without speaking.

Nate finally broke the quiet. "The top's a little well-done, but it's good."

"Too bad about the garlic bread," Kim added.

Isobel and Jared poked at their food.

When they were all finished, Isobel and Jared went out to the porch while Nate helped clean up the kitchen and wash dishes.

After the dishes were put away, Kim wrapped her arms around Nate's middle and just breathed in his scent.

"That totally counts as dinner with your parents."

She gave a little laugh. "Totally."

"You okay?"

"I will be. I'm so confused. I don't know where this came from. I mean, I've had Jared off and on his entire life, and he's been with me every day since my sister died."

"Maybe they meant well and it just blew up into something else?"

"I'm finding it a little difficult to give them the benefit of the doubt at the moment." She squeezed her eyes shut and told herself not to cry. "Hold me tighter."

He did.

Chapter Forty-Two

What just happened? Nate kept a tight hold of Kim long after he would have let go. His hands splayed across her back, his cheek rested on the top of her head. He didn't think she was crying, but she still clutched his shirt, so he held on.

"I should talk to Jared," she mumbled into his chest.

"He's fine."

"I don't understand what they're thinking." She pulled back and looked up at him. Her tear-streaked face yanked at his heartstrings. "Why would they just come in here and announce they want to take Jared from me? Because I'm spending time with you? Even real moms get to date."

Jared's voice came from the doorway. "You're the realest mom I've got."

Nate let go as she pulled away and grabbed Jared in a tight hug. "I love you more than anything."

"We should do the adoption."

Kim pulled back, the shock evident on her face. "How did—"

"I heard you and Nate talking about it."

"Jared, I… I had no idea you heard any of that."

"If you adopt me, then they can't take me away."

Kim put her hands on the sides of his head. "They can't take you anyway. I'm your legal guardian, which legally is basically the same thing as a parent."

"I still want you to adopt me."

"Let's talk about it tomorrow after we've had a good night's sleep, okay?"

Jared's chin quivered. "If you don't want to…"

"Hey. Stop. There's some information *you* need, and it's too late to get into it for tonight."

Isobel leaned in the doorway. "He's afraid you'll get sick of the drama and give him away but if you adopt him you can't."

"Isobel!" Jared wiped his nose on his sleeve and glared at her.

She shrugged. "My parents are on their way. I'll wait outside."

"I'll wait with you," Nate said, wanting to give Kim and Jared some space.

Isobel turned and went through the living room and out the front door. Nate followed her and closed the door behind them. Isobel sat on the porch swing, so Nate took the chair across from her.

Isobel let out a long, sad breath. "I shouldn't have told."

"No, it's good you did. Kim worries about him and there are lots of things Jared won't tell her."

"He says she loves him more than his real mom did."

Nate leaned back and crossed his leg, putting his ankle on his other knee. "I don't know the whole story, and I never met Jared's birth mother, so I can't comment on that. What I do know is that Kim loves him like her own son, and she'd move heaven and earth to take care of him."

Isobel picked at the edge of her cell phone case. "His grand-parents always seem really nice. This whole thing," she waved her hands around to encompass the evening, "was so surreal. Like, literally weird."

"I agree." Nate wondered what happened that they suddenly decided Jared was better off with them. He had a feeling it had something to do with him, from the way her father had looked at him. Maybe it was better that he was leaving. Then again, maybe it would make things worse for Kim if he wasn't there to support her.

Tires crunching in front of the house pulled him from his reverie.

"That's my parents. Bye, Nate."

"Good night, Isobel."

She bounded from the porch to the car. The lady inside the car waved, so Nate waved back. After the car pulled away, he debated whether he should go back inside, or go home. Not wanting to interfere, he walked home.

In his own kitchen, he pulled his phone out to text Kim and let her know Isobel was safely on her way home, and that he'd come home.

> I'll come back over if you want.

He was putting his phone back in his pocket when it dinged with an incoming text. Smiling, he hoped she'd want him to come over. Instead, the smile dropped off his face, and he let out the longest string of curses he'd ever uttered in his entire life.

> Great news! Production moved up, you're flying tomorrow. Emailed new itinerary.

This was not great news. In fact, it was pretty much the

opposite of great news. Nate opened his laptop to check his email.

This was definitely the opposite of great news. His flight would be leaving at noon, which meant he'd have to leave the house by nine. Which meant he had to have everything packed tonight. And he had to talk to Kim.

He debated whether to call or text her, then decided to just go over. It couldn't wait.

His feet dragged as he crossed the wet grass. This was going to suck. On Kim's porch, he lifted his hand to knock, then lowered it and took a deep breath. It wasn't going to suck any less if he waited ten minutes, so he knocked.

A few minutes later, he heard footsteps, then Kim opened the door. "Hey. I got your text."

"That's not why I came over." He ran a hand through his hair.

"What is it?"

"Kim…" He looked over her head and saw Jared standing in the doorway to the kitchen. "Can I come in?"

"Of course." She stood aside and let him pass.

"I hate to even say this. They changed the production schedule."

"What does that mean?"

"It means I have to leave sooner than I expected." There was a gnawing in the pit of his stomach.

Kim whispered, "When?"

Nate squeezed his eyes shut, not wanting to see her reaction. Or Jared's. "Tomorrow."

His eyes were still closed as Kim wrapped her arms around him and snuggled into his chest. He murmured against her hair, "I'm sorry."

"Don't apologize."

"I feel horrible, the timing sucks."

"But we can still meet in Florida, right?" Jared asked.

Nate reached over and grasped his shoulder. "We'll figure something out." He was leaving that ball in Kim's court.

Kim nodded.

"We film in Jordan first, so I'll see if I can get the rest of the schedule and we can make some plans."

"When's your flight?"

"Noon."

"So you have to leave what, about nine?"

"Yes."

"Can we take you to the airport?"

"Yeah, can we?" Jared chimed in.

"That'd be great." It wasn't going to be great. It was going to suck. He'd rather say goodbye at home, but he couldn't tell her – or Jared – no.

Kim squeezed him tight, then let go. "I'm guessing you don't have anything packed yet."

"No."

She sighed heavily. "You should probably go do that."

"I should."

She stood on her tiptoes and kissed him, then stepped back. "Go pack. We'll see you tomorrow morning."

Reluctantly, he moved toward the door. "See you in the morning."

The door clicking shut behind him sounded so loud and final. He crossed the wet grass back to his own place, but it sure felt like he was walking away from home, not toward it.

Chapter Forty-Three

Kim stared at the door and fought the urge to cry. She didn't dare wonder what else could go wrong.

"Are you okay?" Jared put his hand on her arm. It was unusual for him to reach out, so she didn't want to call attention to his action.

Instead, she stayed still but turned her head in his direction. Honesty was the only response she could give him. "I'll be fine. Right now, it sucks so bad. I was counting on having more time with Nate, especially after the bullshit that went down this evening." She let out a huge sigh and ran a hand through her hair.

"Bullshit of epic proportions," Jared quipped.

It brought a smile to her face. "Language," she corrected mildly.

He grinned in response.

"We should probably get to bed."

"Nate's stuck packing all night."

"At least he'll be able to sleep on the plane."

Jared paused at the bottom of the stairs and looked out the window toward Nate's house. "I'm gonna miss him, too."

"I know."

"We're going to Florida, right?"

Kim patted his back. "We'll have to work out the details, but I think we will."

"Cool." Jared sprinted up the stairs and disappeared into his room.

Kim stared out the window a little bit longer, then went to her bedroom. She changed into her pajamas, then in a moment of inspiration, went back downstairs to her office. She pulled out a sheet of paper and sat down at her desk to write Nate a letter. Sadie helpfully sat her fuzzy butt on the page, meowing at the insult when Kim picked her up and set her down on the floor.

When she was satisfied, she neatly rewrote it, then folded it and put it in an envelope and slid it into her purse so she wouldn't forget it in the morning.

Unsurprisingly, sleep eluded her and she spent most of the night tossing and turning. When she did sleep, she dreamed of running down long roads, trying to find Jared. Somewhere around two o'clock, she got up and made a batch of cinnamon rolls. While they baked, she sat at the island and cried.

Sadie jumped onto the island and rubbed her head against Kim's. When the timer dinged, Kim wiped her eyes and put her weepiness aside. That was enough of that. She scratched Sadie's head and got up to take the rolls out of the oven. While they cooled, she dozed on the couch.

***

Morning found her grumpy and irritable. She stood in the shower, hoping the warm water would ease her attitude. She didn't want her last hour with Nate to be marred by a bad disposition brought on by a lack of sleep.

Carefully applying moisturizer to her face, she began to feel a little better. Coffee and cinnamon rolls would help even more. She dressed and stopped to knock on Jared's door. It was almost eight. He was already awake.

He scrunched up his nose. "Did you bake something?"

"Yeah. I couldn't sleep." She followed him downstairs and texted Nate.

> Good morning, if you're up I have cinnamon rolls.

A few seconds later, her phone dinged.

> Still packing, would you mind bringing one over?

She didn't bother responding. Instead, she told Jared to come over after he got dressed and put three rolls on a plate. She carried it to Nate's house.

The door opened before she could knock. Nate stood there in jeans that fit just right, and a faded green t-shirt. The man rendered her speechless.

He stepped aside and followed her to the kitchen. "If you don't mind checking the place every now and then, here's a key." He gestured to the counter. "Don't get too excited, the Picasso and Da Vinci are in storage."

"Darn. I was hoping to-"

Nate's mouth was on hers, one arm around her, one hand on the back of her head. Kim gasped and kissed him back as he backed her against the counter.

A knock at the front door elicited a soft curse from him. He pulled back, kissed her again, then went to answer the door while she caught her breath.

She heard Jared's voice with Nate's as they came back to the kitchen. Straightening her shirt, she turned and fussed with unwrapping the cinnamon rolls.

They ate the cinnamon rolls quickly.

"How much do you have left to pack?"

"Not much. Just have to double-check that I have my chargers and whatnot."

"We'll clean up the kitchen while you finish packing."

"Thanks."

Kim wiped the counters and table while Jared cleaned up the dishes from the cinnamon rolls. She checked her watch. "We should be leaving soon," she called.

"Yup, almost done." Nate wheeled his suitcase to the front door. "Oh crap. I didn't clean out the fridge."

"We can take care of it this afternoon. Trash goes tomorrow."

"I hate to ask you to do that."

"You didn't. And you don't have time to do it now." She nodded toward his suitcase. "Sure you have everything?"

"Yeah."

"I'll get the car." Kim hurried across the lawn and grabbed her keys and purse, then drove the short distance to Nate's driveway and popped the hatch of the SUV open. He loaded his suitcase and backpack and shut the hatch, then got into the passenger seat.

"Are you going to be okay, with all the crap going on with your parents?"

She managed a smile. "It'll be fine."

"I hate leaving right now. The timing sucks."

"It can't be helped. Do you have your boarding pass and everything?"

"You're changing the subject."

Kim glanced over at him. "I'll be fine. The situation will be fine. I'll keep you in the loop. There's nothing more to say about it at this point."

For the rest of the hour's drive to the airport, they kept the conversation on lighter topics. Kim pulled into the parking facility and they unloaded Nate's suitcase. "Only one suitcase and a backpack for a trip this long?"

Nate grinned and kissed the tip of her nose. "Guys don't have to carry makeup and fifty pairs of shoes."

"Funny guy."

Hand in hand, they walked to the counter for Nate to check his bag, then they stood in the lobby just outside the security checkpoint.

"I got an app so we can see your flight," Jared said, holding up his phone. "It shows delays and stuff and you can see where the plane's at in the air."

Nate looked pleased. "That's awesome. I'll text you the rest of my flights so you can keep track of me."

Jared took an awkward step toward Nate, then stepped back.

Nate reached over and pulled him into a tight hug. "I'm gonna miss you, buddy. Take good care of your aunt, and don't let the drama get to you, okay? Everything's going to work out just fine. Remember, you've got an alien warlord on your side."

Jared nodded vigorously. "Okay. Have a good trip." He stepped back and turned away.

Kim's chest tightened. "You better get going."

Nate reached for her. "I already miss you," he murmured next to her ear.

She squeezed him tight, the words sending warmth flowing through her. She listened to his heart beating, trying to memorize the rhythm, until he leaned down and kissed her, and the rest of the world melted away.

Chapter Forty-Four

Reluctantly, Nate pulled back and took Kim's face in his hands. He kissed her again, wanting the taste of her to stay with him. "I'll call you when I can."

She nodded, gave him a quick kiss, and stepped back. "Have a good trip. Be safe."

One more quick squeeze for Kim, then Nate patted Jared's shoulder. "I'll see you soon."

He appreciated Kim's grin when she said, "Hey, the sooner you leave, the sooner you can get back home."

He smiled back. "Got it. I'm going." He hiked his backpack onto his shoulder and wove through the security line. He wasn't sure why they made people go around and around when there wasn't much of a line. Stopping at the checkpoint, he took off his shoes and put his items in the designated bins, then stepped through the body scanner.

Looking back, he gathered his things and gave Kim and Jared a final wave, then went down the hallway, leaving them behind. More than once he considered turning around.

The minutes ticked by slowly until he boarded his plane, then landed in Chicago and had to run to catch his connecting flight. He managed to send one quick text before he had to turn his phone back to airplane mode and wasn't able to send or receive messages. He glared at the seat in front of him. You'd think with today's technology, and the cost of a ticket, every plane would have wifi. But nope.

"Annoying, isn't it?" a pretty redhead in the seat beside him said, holding up her own phone. She echoed what he'd just been thinking. "For the price of plane tickets, we should have internet."

"Yeah."

"I'm Alicia."

"Nate."

The intercom was a welcome interruption. Even with all his experience dealing with the public, Nate still had trouble politely disengaging from conversations.

When the captain finished speaking, he tried settling back into his tiny seat and catching a nap.

Alicia was undeterred by his closed eyes. "Where are you headed?"

"L.A."

"Me, too."

Nate bit off a sarcastic remark about how that's where the plane was heading and instead said nothing.

"Your family there?"

Glancing over at his chatty neighbor, he shook his head. "No."

"Heading to L.A. for work?"

"Yes."

"Me, too. Maybe we could have dinner or… something."

"I'm married." The white lie just popped out.

"So am I." She lifted her left hand. A gold band rested on her finger, topped with an obnoxiously large diamond ring.

This wasn't the first time he'd had pretty much the same

conversation, but it still rattled him. Why did people get married if they didn't want to be faithful? "Thanks, but no." He turned to stare out the window.

The plane thankfully began its descent into L.A. and the second he was able, Nate jumped up and grabbed his bag and made a beeline for the door. He was ready to breathe a sigh of relief in the terminal, but a perfectly manicured hand grabbed his arm.

Alicia pressed a card into his hand. "Just in case you change your mind, *Nate*." She said his name like it was a dirty word, gave him a wicked grin, then strode off.

He looked at the card, with the handwritten phone number scrawled across the back, and deposited it in the nearest trash can. He slung his bag over his shoulder, then followed the river of people to baggage claim, got his suitcase, and waited on the sidewalk for his ride.

One limo ride later, Nate checked into his hotel and texted Kim to let her know he'd made it safe and sound.

His next call was to Dennis.

"Excellent. There's a cast dinner tonight at nine to kick off the season. This opener's going to be the most epic reintroduction to a series ever."

Nate listened to him ramble excitedly and let Dennis's enthusiasm buoy his own. He was here, he might as well enjoy it.

Hours later, he stifled a yawn. He'd gotten used to being on east coast time and going to bed at a decent hour. It was almost one a.m., making it four for his body, already tired from traveling across the country earlier. The rooftop party was picture perfect, strings of white lights illuminating to just the right brightness.

The cast was still going strong, in good spirits, sharing stories with the newest additions to the crew, when Dennis stood on a sofa and clinked silverware against his glass.

"I'm glad to see everyone," he began. "The rumors are true. This is our final season, but it's going to be our best. Tomorrow, ten a.m. sharp, we're going to start going over the scripts. I think you'll all be pleased at the direction we're taking. But for tonight, enjoy yourselves." He raised his glass. "To *Daystar Rising!*"

"To *Daystar Rising!*" the crowd echoed his toast and drank.

Nate swallowed the last of his champagne and set the glass on the tray of a passing waiter. He'd talked to nearly everyone, answered the inevitable questions about his health, avoided a few questions about his stalker, even exchanged a few bland but cordial words with Miranda, and now it was time to get some sleep.

Making his way around the perimeter, he slid out the door. It clicked behind him and he breathed a sigh of relief as he trotted down the stairs and out of the building. Catching a cab, he kept a wary eye on the traffic and the handful of passersby.

By two thirty, he was safely in his hotel room, collapsed on the bed, wishing for a horrible fate to befall whoever the loudmouth in the hallway was.

Chapter Forty-Five

Kim felt a million times better as she left the office of the family attorney she'd scheduled an appointment with. As she'd suspected, her parents had no valid claim to Jared, and unless they made something up, even her dad's former occupation wouldn't help them in court. She'd paid a retainer, just in case, even though she was confident a reasonable conversation with her parents would clear things up.

Breathing a sigh of relief, she texted Tara, then Nate. Now that she was armed with information, she could devote some mental energy to getting to the bottom of why her parents had suddenly gone off the deep end.

She went through a fast-food drive-thru and took lunch home. "I'm home," she called as she closed and locked the front door, something she had never bothered doing when she was home. It was a little disconcerting to suddenly have to protect herself against people she trusted. Shouldn't it be the boogeyman she was afraid of?

"Okay," Jared answered. A few minutes later, he came down the stairs to join her at the kitchen table. He unwrapped his sandwich. "I don't want to see Sawyer anymore."

Kim sat back in her chair and wiped her fingers on her napkin. She couldn't let him stop therapy. "Jared."

"No, hear me out."

"I know it's weird, but I'm not sure I trust him after Grandma and Grandpa went all batshit crazy."

She let the language slide.

"Not that I think he told them anything, at least I hope he didn't. But I think I'd rather see somebody else."

It made a lot of sense. If Jared couldn't trust his counselor, it wouldn't do him much good. And at this point, he'd only seen Sawyer three times, so it wouldn't be a huge adjustment to see someone else. "This can't be an excuse to stop counseling."

"I know. But it's too coincidental."

Kim couldn't disagree. Sawyer seemed like the consummate professional, so she didn't think he'd violate Jared's privacy. Still, she wouldn't be comfortable with a counselor who saw her parents regularly, either.

"I found a place in Walker Lake. I'll text you the link."

Unable to keep the surprise off her face, Kim pushed her untouched fries away. "Okay. I'll call and cancel your next appointment with Sawyer and then take a look at this place." Walker Lake was only a twenty minute drive. Totally doable.

"Thanks."

They finished their lunch, then Kim threw away the trash.

After an uneventful week passed, she was thrilled when the phone rang and it was Nate.

"It's so good to hear from you. How's the desert?"

"Hot. Very, very hot. I have sand in places that should never have sand, and I'm not sure I'll ever get rid of it."

"Ew, sounds awful." She laughed as she curled up on the couch, cradling the phone to her ear.

"How are things with you?"

"Good. It's been quiet. Most of Jared's credits transferred, just a couple easy ones he has to make up, and he's doing well. I met with an attorney and Jared's caseworker about the guardianship, and thankfully it would take something extraordinary for the court to even consider moving Jared."

"That's great news."

His enthusiasm came through the phone loud and clear. It made Kim feel better, knowing he was in her corner, even if he was halfway around the world.

"I got the filming schedule. It's pretty much set in stone at this point, so I figured I'd let you know the dates I can be in Florida. I checked flights and I can get in around six a.m. on the 23rd and I'd leave around six p.m. on the 25th. I know it's not a lot of time, but we could either do the Disney thing like we'd talked about, or we could meet in Key West."

"That's great." Kim wrote the dates down on the back of a receipt she fished out of her purse. "I don't know which Jared will prefer."

"You don't have to decide right now. Just let me know in a day or two, okay?"

"I will. How's the show?"

He pulled in a huge breath. "Where to start? I can't wait to see the finished product. It's going to be epic. There's so much CGI that's being added in. We have to act with props. There's a huge scene I have where I'm battling a giant sand snake, only it's a big plastic tube I have to pretend to be terrified of."

"That actually sounds like a lot of fun."

His tone suggested he was having a great time. "It is. I wish I could have brought Jared over here to see how this works. I think he'd love it."

"I'm sure he would." She waited a beat, then asked, "How are you holding up? Have you been okay?"

"Yeah. It's actually better than I expected. We're pretty much stuck to ourselves here, so I think that helps. How's *your* show?"

"Great. I'm adding some interviews with local crafters. The first one is a lady that speed knits and I also lined up Fern from the antique store."

His warm laugh came through the speaker. "Speed knitting? That sounds like it could be a cutthroat Olympic event."

"You're not kidding. These ladies are serious about their yarn. Hopefully it comes across in the video. It'll be a challenge to have other people involved since I'm so used to doing it all myself." The best part of trying something new when you do it all yourself? It never has to see the light of day. But she had a good feeling about adding guests to her show.

"It'll be amazing. So great you'll wonder why it took you so long to start interviewing people."

"You're the best."

"I am."

"I kind of miss you."

"Only kind of?"

Kim smiled into the phone. "Kind of a lot."

Nate's voice dropped to match hers. "I miss you kind of a lot, too."

"Can't wait to see you in four weeks. Four short weeks."

"They'll fly like the wind."

He chuckled. "It'll be here before we know it."

"And then you'll be halfway to heading home. Or are they keeping you longer?"

"I'm pretty sure they're killing me off in the fourth episode. I haven't seen the script yet, but it's definitely gearing up to be a spectacular demise for Qaaxag."

"You sound excited."

"I am. I'm so glad to give him the sendoff he deserves. That the fans deserve."

"You don't think they'll be upset to get you back from the dead, only to see you get killed off right away?"

"If I'm doing my job, they won't be upset, they'll be devastated."

"Cocky bugger, aren't you?"

He laughed. "I suppose so."

"I'm glad to hear you sound so happy."

Jared's voice called out ahead of his pounding footsteps down the stairs. "Is that Nate?"

Chuckling, Kim said, "Jared wants to say hi," and held out the phone.

"Nate, hey! How's your trip?"

Kim watched his face light up with excitement as Nate filled him in. Her heart felt like it might burst from her chest. Nate had been gone for ten days, they'd be seeing each other in four weeks, then another four weeks or so, and he'd be home for good. This long-distance thing wasn't so bad after all.

Jared gave Nate a recap of school, and reluctantly said, "I guess I'll give you back to Aunt Kim. ... Yeah ... I will. ... That'd be awesome, thanks! ... Talk to you soon. Bye." He handed the phone back to Kim, then disappeared back up the stairs.

"Wow, he was excited to talk to you."

"Me, too. I miss that kid."

"He misses you, too."

"I promised to send him some selfies he can show Isobel."

Kim laughed. "She'll be over the moon."

"I guess I should go. It's almost midnight here."

"Oh, crap, I forgot about the time difference." Kim glanced up at the clock. It was just before eight. "Are you doing okay with the change?"

"It's not too bad."

"How about your dreads? Are they epic and awesome?"

He laughed. "Yes, and wait til you see my abs. I'll send you a picture."

Kim swallowed hard. Yeah, he meant his rubber costume abs, but her mind was headed straight for the real thing.

"You still there?"

She jolted, embarrassment heating her face. Glad he couldn't see her, she said, "Yeah, sorry, I got a little sidetracked thinking about your abs."

His deep laughter came across the line. "Maybe I won't send you a picture. I don't want you to be disappointed when you see my actual abs."

Lowering her voice, she said, "Maybe you should just send me a picture of the real thing instead."

"Dang." His voice dropped to the same level. "What will you send me back?"

Her heart fluttered. "Oh, wow, this conversation should not be happening."

"Too far?" He sounded amused.

She covered her burning face with her hand. "Way too far. Sorry. I shouldn't have started it."

"Why not?"

It was a good question. "Because I don't want to be over-heard." And because she'd only kissed the guy a couple of times, so long-distance dirty conversations were probably better saved for later in their relationship. "And because we probably shouldn't go further over the phone than we have in person."

He chuckled again. "Okay. So how exactly do I get to kiss you over the phone?"

"You don't. But you'll get to kiss me in Florida."

"I can't wait."

"Neither can I." She glanced up at the clock. "Oh, no, it's twelve thirty now. I didn't mean to keep you up."

"Not your fault. I don't want to hang up."

She snuggled deeper down into the corner of the sofa. "Me, either. I like hearing your voice."

"I miss you."

"I really like hearing your voice say that you miss me."

"I miss you."

She laughed softly. "I miss you, too."

"I can't wait to see you."

She could imagine hurling herself into his arms in Florida. "I can't wait to see you."

"I can't wait to kiss you."

"I'm putting the brakes on or we'll still be on the phone when it's time for you to go to work."

"I'll talk to you in a day or two, okay?"

"Can't wait. Sweet dreams, Nate."

"Sweet dreams, Kim."

After she hung up, she held her phone against her chest for a long while, replaying Nate's words in her mind.

She was still smiling when she crawled into bed a few hours later.

Chapter Forty-Six

Nate sat still while the makeup artist put the finishing touches on his face. His chest was already sweating under the thick layer of fake muscles. They'd had to modify a few of the fight scenes after his knee started acting up, which disappointed him more than anyone. The director hadn't seemed bothered at all, nor had his costar. But it niggled at Nate that he couldn't perform like he had before.

Shoving it from his mind, he gave the makeup artist a smile and left the trailer to get to the set.

"I bet you're thrilled, aren't you?" Miranda stalked up to him, her hands on her bare hips, her skimpy costume leaving little to the imagination.

"About?"

"Oh, please," she practically spat.

"Okay."

She held her arms out. "What, you don't see the blood? You didn't read the script? You aren't fully aware that I'm dead now?"

Looking at her, he did finally notice the blood and creepily realistic stab wounds across her middle. "I only read my own scenes."

She stood, glaring.

"Must have been a great battle scene. I'm sure the fans will be happy."

"Screw the fans. I was destined to rule the planet. It was in the prophecy."

Nate was glad the prosthetic cheeks made it easy to hide his smile. "You do know this isn't real, right?"

Miranda smirked and said, "Hope you don't have a panic attack while you're trying to act. She's out of jail, you know. Maybe lurking behind one of those dunes."

Letting out a chuckle, he shook his head. "You can do better than that."

Her face contorted, like she wanted to spit at him. "You have a tiny dick."

At that, he did laugh.

The director yelled, "Let's go, people!" so Nate walked to the set without wasting another word on her.

When they finished for the day, Nate couldn't wait to get the costume off. He was hot and miserable, with grains of sand lodged in the worst places. The costumer removed his fake parts, and he dashed back to his own trailer to shower.

Nate settled in with his laptop and connected to the internet. He searched and found exactly what he was looking for. A rental house with three bedrooms and beach access. Perfect. He knew they hadn't decided for sure whether they were doing Orlando or Key West, but this was too good to pass up. He briefly considered texting Kim, then decided to surprise her with a done deal. He entered his credit card information and half a minute later, the beachfront dream house was theirs for a few days.

Chapter Forty-Seven

"I'm sorry, who?" Kim asked the person on the phone. She tucked the phone between her shoulder and her ear while she stirred batter for a cake.

"Rory Anderson. I'm sorry, let me start at the beginning. My sister Lainey said she met you a few weeks ago at a winery?"

She made the connection. "Oh! The brewery."

"That's it. Anyway, she sent me links to your channel and I spent the last few days watching all your videos."

Kim's hand stopped in midair. "*All* of them?" A fat drop of cake batter dripped off the spatula and landed on the counter.

"All of them. I showed them to a few other people here at Home Network, and we're very impressed with your work."

She dropped the spatula into the bowl. "Wait, are you serious?"

"Of course. We've got a new web channel in the works, and we have some ideas for hosting that might interest you, and I'd bet you have some great ideas as well. We'd like to have you come out and give you a tour of the studio, meet some of the project heads, and see where we can go from there."

Kim blinked rapidly. "Um, wow. Sorry, this is kind of out of the blue. I wasn't expecting this."

"Lainey accuses me of getting ahead of myself, so it's completely on me. We'd like to get moving though, so we can launch the channel. We were hoping we might be able to get you out here for a few days before the end of the month. Say, the twenty-first? Our plan is to launch July first with a massive Christmas in July extravaganza."

"Um. That only leaves a month to have everything ready."

"Yes, but I've got a good feeling about you and how this could work."

"Going into the hard sell, huh?"

He chuckled. "I have to be able to give Lainey good news."

"My nephew will be traveling with me. I hope that's not an issue."

"Not at all. We'll take care of everything and I'll email you the details. What's your address?"

She told him her email address and he read it back to make sure he had it correct.

"This all sounds great."

"I'm really excited, Kim. This is going to be huge."

Her head was still spinning when she hung up.

Sadie's face was in the bowl, licking the cake batter. Kim absently shooed her away.

"What's up?" Jared's voice startled her. She jumped, then spun around, her hands out. "Home Network wants me to come to California and interview to host their new web channel." Saying it out loud felt strange. It had been a dream for years, and now, out of the blue, it was happening. She. Was interviewing. At the Home Network. Unreal.

His eyes went huge. "Whoa, that's crazy."

"They want us to come out on the twenty-first." She clamped her hand over her mouth. "Oh, no."

"What?"

"Nate wants to meet in Florida on the twenty-third."

"Oh. What are we going to do?"

"Good question." She sat on a stool and propped her elbows on the island. "I don't know. They're going to email me the arrangements. I wonder if we can go out the twenty-first and then maybe leave the twenty-third and go straight to Florida. That might be able to work."

"They'd pay for you to go out for one day?"

Her shoulders slumped. "Probably not."

Jared got a can of soda from the fridge. "What do you want to do?"

"Ugh. I want to see Nate *and* fly out to the Home Network, but it doesn't look like that's going to happen."

"Tough choice." The can hissed as he popped it open.

"Thanks. So helpful."

He rolled his shoulder. "What happens if you don't go?"

"They find somebody else."

"What happens if you don't see Nate?"

"Well, hopefully he doesn't find somebody else." Resting her head in her hands, she sighed.

"That would suck."

Kim lifted her eyes. "Really?"

Jared smirked. "Come on, you know he's going to be excited for you. Not like he's gonna dump you over this."

"Don't you have some homework to do?"

He took a long swig of his soda, then burped, long and loud.

"Gross."

Laughing, he went back upstairs.

She fished her phone out of her purse and called Tara. If anybody would have good advice, she would.

Tara answered. "Perfect timing. I'm just standing here washing dishes. What's up?"

Kim filled her in. "I want to see Nate, but I'd be foolish to miss this opportunity. Even if it doesn't pan out, it could lead to something else."

"That's a tough one. I mean, it's not, because you have to go meet the people from the Home Network, but it really sucks that it means you won't be able to see Nate until he's completely done with the show. Unless you can fly to Puerto Rico or something."

"Yeah." She huffed out a laugh with little humor.

"You *could*, you know."

Kim considered. Would it really be that much different than flying to Florida? Probably not. Of course, Nate might not want them hanging around where he was trying to work. On the other hand, maybe she and Jared could do touristy stuff while he was working, and they could meet up after he was done for the day.

"Are you taking Jared along?"

"Of course. I can't leave him here alone, and I apparently can't trust my parents not to hide him from me when I get home."

"Have you talked to them?"

Kim sighed again. "No. I have no idea what to say, and I don't want to get into a screaming match with my dad. There's no way I can back down on this one, and he doesn't do well with people standing up to him."

"It'll be ugly, but you have to get to the bottom of it."

A whoosh of running water punctuated Tara's words.

"I know. You're right. I just hate the idea of getting into it. I'm still so baffled by the whole situation and I hate not having any answers. I'm going into the whole confrontation unarmed. With no control." It was more than baffling. Her parents had never once questioned her ability to raise Jared.

"Maybe it won't be a confrontation."

"Yeah, right."

"I'm serious. You have more control than you think. Call to open a dialogue, and if it gets confrontational, say you're hanging up, then do it. Refuse to engage in a confrontation."

"Easier said than done."

Tara agreed. "Isn't everything?"

"Why does everything always happen at once?"

"The universe is cruel."

"Okay, enough of my drama. Tell me what's going on with you. Leave nothing out."

They talked – and laughed – for another hour before Tara groaned. "Movie's over, so I'm back on duty. Keep me posted."

Hanging up, Kim felt better, but still not quite ready to deal with her parents. And it was nearly one a.m. for Nate, so she couldn't call him.

She spent a few hours editing videos and sketching out ideas for more episodes, then went to bed and barely slept. The next day, she worked in her office, looked over Jared's homework, and counted the minutes until noon, when it would be seven p.m. for Nate.

> Can you talk?

She texted him.

Half a minute later, her screen lit up with an incoming video call.

"Hey, beautiful," he greeted her with a big smile.

"Hey yourself. Let me get situated." She poured a glass of tea and sat at the island, propping the phone so she didn't end up with a hand cramp. "Battle any tube snakes today?"

The sound of his easy laugh filled the kitchen. She wished she was hearing it in person. She also wished she could see his dreads in person. It was so weird seeing them on the screen. "No snakes today, but we did have a very real sandstorm. That was kind of freaky."

"Sounds terrifying."

"They said it was just a little one. Didn't last long, but it was pretty scary." He paused. "Looks like you have something on your mind?"

"Yeah. Good news and bad news situation."

"Uh oh. Tell me the bad news first."

"I can't. They go together, so the bad news won't make sense without the good news."

"Okay."

"It's nothing *bad*-bad." She took a deep breath. "I got a call from Rory Anderson. He's the brother of that woman I met at the brewery who told me her brother works for the Home Network."

"He does exist." Nate grinned.

"He does. Lainey – the sister – gave him some links and he watched all my videos. *All* of them. Said he was really impressed and passed the links along to other people at the network."

"I bet they were impressed, too."

"Apparently so." She'd practiced how to tell him the next part, but she still dreaded saying it.

"That's fantastic, Kim. I'm so proud."

"They want to bring me out to California to tour the studios and meet everyone. They're in the late planning stages for a web channel they want to launch July first and they want to interview me as host for the channel."

He clapped his hands and pumped a fist in the air. "Wow! That's great!"

Kim could hardly look at his grinning face. "Just one thing. They want me there on the twenty-first."

"Ah."

"That's the bad news." Her hands clenched in her lap where he couldn't see them.

He leaned back a little bit and ran a hand over his face. "Well, crap." Letting out a long breath, he gave her a smile. "I won't lie. I'm really disappointed about the timing. But this is an incredible opportunity, and I'm so proud of you."

"I'm sorry." She felt trapped between a rock and a hard place – she wanted to be happy and excited about the opportunity, but canceling plans to meet Nate threw a wet blanket over her enthusiasm.

"Stop."

"No, I mean it. I really want to see you, and the timing sucks."

"Hey. There's nothing you can do about it. It's not a big deal."

"It's a big deal."

"Okay," he conceded, "it's a big deal. But being invited out to interview with the Home Network is a bigger deal. I want you to celebrate, Kim. How many people get an opportunity like this? Don't feel bad about it just because it means adjusting plans to see me because that makes me feel awful. You should be excited, babe. You've wanted this forever. And hey, it just means waiting a few more weeks before we see each other. Nothing we can't handle."

Kim wished she could hug him for saying all the right words. "I know you're right."

"Of course I am." He held up his wrist and tapped his watch. "Aren't you hungry? You're missing lunch."

"I wanted to talk to you."

"I'm glad."

"I miss you. And I hate that I'm not going to see you." Tears stung the backs of her eyes.

"You *are* going to see me. Just not when we planned."

Blinking rapidly, she looked to the ceiling. "I know."

"It'll all work out. Kim. Look at me."

She looked at the screen.

"It'll all work out."

Nodding, she sniffled. "Okay. I just miss you."

"I miss you, too."

"Did you eat dinner yet?"

"Nope."

"You should go eat."

"So should you. Go get lunch and text me all about it."

"Okay." She wiped her nose and smiled at him. "Talk to you soon."

"Absolutely." He blew her a kiss.

Kim disconnected the call and let her shoulders slump forward. Indulging in a minute of self-pity, she slipped her phone into her pocket and got up to make lunch.

Chapter Forty-Eight

Nate tossed his phone onto the bed with a heavy sigh, grumbling to himself for securing a rental house without talking to Kim first. He tried shoving his own disappointment aside to focus on her great opportunity, but it just wasn't happening.

He couldn't wait for this whole thing to be over. He was tired of the sand, tired of the interpersonal politics, tired of the drama, tired of being away from home, and tired of people asking him for updates on his stalker, like she was an ex-girlfriend instead of a criminal.

It was too late to go out anywhere and too early to just crawl into bed and be done with this day. He could imagine how Kim felt giving him the news – he was so happy for her and proud of her, but he'd been living for the moment he got to see her in Florida, and now he had to wait another month. It sucked. When the knock came on the door of his trailer, he was still grumpy.

"Yeah?" He pulled the door open.

"Got a minute?" It was Dennis.

"Sure." Backing away from the narrow doorway, he took one step into the mini kitchen. "Coffee?"

"That'd be great." Dennis sat at the tiny table and accepted the mug Nate handed him.

Settling across the table with his own cup, Nate lifted an eyebrow. "What's up?"

"I wanted to talk to you about the contract."

"You're supposed to talk to Jerry about that stuff."

"Yeah, but if you aren't interested, there's no point in going to Jerry, right?"

Nate leaned back against the vinyl cushion and took a long sip of coffee. "Interested in what?"

"An extension." Dennis grinned. "For the rest of the season."

Nate knew he was supposed to be thrilled at the prospect. He was not. "I thought you were killing me off."

"Well, here's the thing. The writers have been going nuts making sure even the smallest loose ends are tied up before we wrap. With Miranda gone, there are only two other possibilities for who can fulfill the prophecy."

"No, just one. Dahlia."

"Wrong. There are two possibilities. Dahlia, and Qaaxag."

Nate shook his head, setting his dreads in motion. "How? He's an alien."

Dennis beamed like a kid on Christmas morning. "That's the beauty of it. If you go back to the actual wording of the prophecy, it doesn't specify the ultimate ruler's origin. Qaaxag's story actually fits. Perfectly."

"The viewers aren't going to buy it."

"I have four thousand online comments that say otherwise."

"Wait, you leaked the theory?"

"Pretty clever, huh?" Dennis wore a nasty grin. "And, of

course, if you aren't interested, we'll kill you off as planned and it'll be Dahlia."

Nate tried to digest the information. Qaaxag was supposed to save the planet, but he was never intended to rule it afterward. "Shouldn't this have all been decided long before we started shooting?"

Dennis laughed, loud. "There's something to be said for living on the edge."

"Yeah, that's why you had to buy stock in Rolaids."

"There's a big fat raise to sweeten the deal."

"I got a big fat raise to come back. How much are you talking?"

"Let's just say you won't feel bad using Benjamins to light your cigars."

Nate finished his coffee in one swig. "I don't smoke."

Dennis laughed again. "Okay, Mister Wild and Crazy, you'll be able to throw a fistful of Benjamins into a high yield investment account every time you fart."

"You sure know how to sweet talk," Nate laughed.

He grew serious. "The only thing is… I have to know soon."

"How soon?"

"Tonight."

"What the heck, Dennis? Tonight? You know Jerry has to go over the details before I agree to anything."

He shrugged and drained the rest of his coffee, then rose. "Let me know."

Nate watched Dennis leave the trailer, the loud click of the door snapping him fully alert. He pulled out his phone and dialed a number.

"Hey, what's up?"

"Sorry, Mom. I know you're at work, but I just got some news."

"Hang on, let me close my office door." There was some

rustling, then a click, then more rustling. "Okay, sweetheart, I'm all yours for the next thirty minutes."

Nate filled her in on the beach house, Kim's cancellation, Kim's trip to California, and finally his own offer to stay on *Daystar Rising* until the end. "And it's another boatload of money."

"You say that like it's a bad thing. Invest it, donate it, bury it in jars in the backyard."

"Naw, I know. It just feels like that's supposed to motivate me to stay on, but it really doesn't."

"Do you want to?"

"It makes sense."

"That wasn't the question."

"I guess I do. It'll make for a dramatic finish, which the fans will love."

Pattie sighed heavily.

"Okay, fine. Yes, I'd like to stay for the rest of the season, and then I'd like to be done and go home for good."

"There's your answer, then. You've got an end date. Might as well take the extra episodes, take the extra boatload of cash, and then you'll be free to take some time off and figure out what it is you want to do. Besides, didn't you say after filming is done in Puerto Rico, the rest of it will all be in the U.S.?"

"Yeah."

"There you go. Once you get done in Puerto Rico, it'll be just like being at home."

"Not quite."

"Close enough. It's a lot easier to travel in the states than internationally. Especially if you're traveling with a teenager, right? Or if you're traveling to see someone who would be traveling with said teenager. Wouldn't you agree?"

Nate smiled into the phone. "I'd agree."

"You'd be stupid not to."

"Always."

"Now call Kim and give her the news."

"I should let Dennis know first."

A most unladylike snort came through the phone. "Sweetheart, let him twist a bit longer. Besides, don't you have to talk to your agent before you finalize anything?"

"Yes. You're right. I'll call Jerry first. Then Kim. Then Dennis. Maybe. Or maybe I'll wait for him to call me in a panic when he needs my decision desperately." He liked that idea a lot. Let Dennis sweat for a while.

"Good boy. I'll see you when you get home. Love you."

"I love you, too. Miss you."

"Don't go getting all sappy on me, my makeup has to get me through a board meeting in five minutes."

"Okay. Talk to you soon, you old goat."

"Hey!" She laughed. "Don't push it."

Grinning, he ended the call and dialed Jerry, who already had the proposal from Dennis, and ultimately gave the thumbs up. Which Nate expected, since Jerry would get twelve percent of this new boatload of cash on the deal. Not that Nate was complaining. Jerry earned every penny.

After Jerry, he dialed one more number.

"Hey! I didn't expect to hear from you again today."

The happiness in her voice warmed his heart. "At least you sound glad."

"Of course I am. Did you just miss me that much?"

A pang hit him in the chest. "I *do* miss you that much. But I also have news."

Her tone went serious. "Good news or bad news?"

"Mostly good news."

"But partly bad news?"

"Maybe." At this point, he didn't know what news was bad or good, or which way was up or down.

"Okay, I'm sitting down. Hit me with it."

"Dennis came by." He took a deep breath.

"Dennis is the producer?"

"Yes."

"Okay."

He blurted it all out at once. "They want me to stay for the whole season. Apparently, Qaaxag is a candidate for fulfilling the prophecy, so they want to keep everyone guessing until the very end."

"That's awesome, Nate. You wanted the fans to have a satisfying end to the series, and it sounds like this will be amazing."

"I think it will. But it means I'll be gone for a few more months. The upside is that I'll be in the U.S., but still… I'm not sure what it means for us."

There was a long pause. "It doesn't have to mean anything, does it? It's exactly what we've been doing, only for a few more months, right? I mean, didn't you just give me this exact speech like an hour ago?"

"Right." He didn't feel as confident as she sounded. "I just don't like it."

Her soft, low laugh sent a tightening to his belly. "Good. I'd be worried if you did."

He bounced his fist on the table. "When you're done with the Home Network, I want to plan a visit. Set in stone. No changes from either of us."

"Absolutely."

His fingers tightened around the phone. He didn't want to wait. He wanted to be home. With her. Holding her, breathing in the scent of her shampoo, standing in her kitchen mixing up dough for cinnamon rolls, laughing with her when Jared catches them kissing…

"Nate?"

Her voice yanked him back to attention. "Sorry, what were you saying?"

"I asked if you're okay."

"Yeah. I'm good. Just homesick all of a sudden."

"It'll be over before we know it, and you'll be glad for having done it."

"I hope so."

"I know so." She lowered her voice. "Hey, who knows. Maybe I'll rethink my stance on phone sex."

That was the best news he'd heard all day.

Chapter Forty-Nine

The morning of the twenty-first found Kim arguing with an airline employee about the size of Jared's carry-on bag.

"It's smaller than the dimensions on the website."

The man sniffed, annoyed, and whipped a metal frame out from under the counter next to the boarding tunnel. "It won't fit in here. You'll have to have it checked." He grabbed the bag and attempted to demonstrate how it wouldn't fit. It did.

Kim said nothing and tried to keep her face from expressing precisely how stupid she thought he was.

Another employee came over. "Is there a problem?"

The man scowled. "No."

Kim shook her head. "He was just making sure our carry-on bag wasn't too big."

The woman looked back and forth between them, then gave a cheerful smile. "Okay, then."

Kim grabbed Jared's bag and sat down as far from the counter as possible.

Jared muttered, "What's that guy's problem?"

"No idea." It was Jared's first time on a plane. She didn't

need some jerk on a power trip making him more nervous than he already was.

"Maybe he's got a small penis."

Kim laughed before she could catch herself. "This is where I'm supposed to reprimand you for being crude."

He saluted. "I'll consider myself lectured."

"Thanks for saving me the trouble."

Luckily, the snotty man with the attitude problem was gone when it was time to board the plane.

"Do you want the window or the middle?"

Smirking, he said, "Window. Then *you* can be squished up against a stranger."

"Thanks, buddy. So thoughtful."

The flight was uneventful. Jared acted like a pro, even when they switched planes and had to run to make their connecting flight.

Waiting for their bags in LAX, Jared said, "That was kind of fun. We should do it again."

She laughed. "How about in four days?"

"Ha, ha. I meant like take another trip sometime. Maybe Puerto Rico."

"How random," she deadpanned.

"I know you miss him. We should go."

"After we see how this pans out, we're going to make plans to meet. I don't know when or where, but soon. And yes, I miss him like crazy. It's the only thing that I regret about this trip."

"When you're filthy rich and own the network, you won't regret anything."

"Thanks for the vote of confidence."

He grinned again. "I've seen your channel. It doesn't suck."

She narrowed her eyes. "High praise indeed."

He snickered, then pointed to the bags spitting onto the conveyor belt. "Is that ours?"

"Yes." She fought her way through the shoulder to shoulder crowd to the conveyor, then yanked their bags off.

Near the exit, a man in a suit held a sign with Kim's name on it. He offered to take their bags and led them to a limo. He opened the door and they climbed in the back.

"Whoa, they must really want to impress you."

"Yeah, it's kind of overkill, isn't it?" She snapped a picture. "Here, let's take a selfie to send Nate."

For once, Jared didn't fuss about taking a picture. He even gave a normal smile.

She sent it, then slipped her phone into her pocket.

After an hour of stop and go traffic, they came to a massive hotel. In the lobby, they were greeted by a chipper young lady in a smart suit. She introduced herself as Jasmyn-with-a-y and checked them in with a corporate credit card. "Okay, great! Let's get you up to your suite and you can drop off your things and take a quick second to freshen up and we'll head out and meet Rory at the restaurant since I'm sure you're both super hungry after all that flying, okay?"

Kim wondered if she ever took a breath. "Sounds great."

They rode the elevator in silence. Jasmyn stared at her phone while Jared stared at her butt. Kim tried to be subtle as she elbowed him. He got the message, casting his gaze to the floor, pink staining his cheeks.

When the door opened on their floor, Jasmyn speed-walked to their door, forcing Kim to practically run to keep up. Kim swiped the card to unlock the door and her jaw dropped. The suite was nothing short of spectacular. It opened into a spacious living room with massive windows. A kitchenette was to the left, and two doors on either side of the living room opened to large bedrooms.

"Holy crap," Jared said.

Jasmyn bobbed her head, sending her sleek blonde ponytail into motion. "Isn't it great? I'll head down to the lobby and wait for you guys. Be down in, say, twenty minutes?"

"Perfect, thank you," Kim said. After closing the door, she said, "Which room do you want?"

Jared checked out one room, then ran over to the other one. "They're about the same. I'll take this one."

"Great." She wheeled her suitcase to the other bedroom and did a double-take. A king-sized bed, covered in a luxurious white comforter and more pillows than six people would need, was situated in the middle of the room. Doors on either side of the headboard revealed a closet and a bathroom.

Kim muttered to the mirror, "Why would anyone need a walk-in closet in a hotel room?" She laid out her cosmetics, touched up her makeup and hair, then changed into a flowy sundress and comfortable heels.

Back in the living room, she took a picture of the view and sent it to Nate.

Ten minutes later, they were back in the elevator, riding down to meet Jasmyn-with-a-y.

"Where do you think they're taking us?" Jared asked.

"I have no idea."

"I bet it's someplace super expensive."

"I'd bet you're right. Although why they're pulling out all the stops, I don't know. Surely they have other candidates for the position."

Jared shrugged. "Maybe, maybe not."

The doors slid open and they stepped back into the opulent lobby. Jasmyn cocked her head to the side and gave them a perky wave and a perky smile. Perky, perky. Everything about this girl was perky. Including her figure. Following her out, Kim looked at the back of her neck to see if there was a charging port, then mentally scolded herself for being mean, even if it was in her own head.

"So," Jasmyn-with-a-y chirped, "the limo is already out front, so we'll head right to the restaurant. I'm sorry I won't be able to stay this evening, but I'll be here to get you bright and early tomorrow morning, mmkay?"

Before Kim could ask, Jared said, "What's 'bright and early' mean around here?"

"Nine o'clock," Jasmyn said, then gave him a perky smile. "Sharp."

Jared responded with a goofy grin, and Kim cleared her throat. "Perfect, thanks."

"I know you're on East Coast time, so that'll be like five o'clock for you. I'm, like, really sorry about that."

Kim didn't bother correcting her.

"Okay, here you go!" Jasmyn stopped at the limo door. "See you tomorrow!"

"Great!" Kim mimicked the perkiness. She just couldn't stop herself.

In the limo, Jared settled back into the seat and watched the scenery go by. "What happens if you get this job? Do we have to move to California?"

Kim noted the worry he was trying to cover. "Honestly? I'm trying not to think too far ahead. One step at a time. It's for a web channel, so it might be possible to work from home. If it goes that far and they want us to relocate…" she took a deep breath and let it out slowly. "I have no idea what we'll do."

"Would you and Nate have to break up?"

The limo came to a stop in front of a swanky building. She patted Jared's leg. "I don't want to get ahead of myself. No sense worrying about all the what-ifs. One step at a time."

Jared snickered. "How many clichés can you jam into one

conversation? Or will we cross that bridge when we come to it?"

"Alright, brat."

The door opened and they stepped out.

Jared grinned. "Let's lead this horse to water."

"Keep it up."

"I intend to."

A man in a dark blazer and expensive looking jeans approached. "Kim?"

She reached her hand out to shake his. "Rory, I presume?"

He gave her a dazzling smile, revealing thousands of dollars' worth of orthodontics and dental bleach. Money well spent. "I am. And you must be Jared."

They shook hands.

Rory gestured to the restaurant. "Seth's already inside."

Kim walked in, where an apparently recently Botoxed hostess led them to the table where Seth sat, tapping on his phone.

Rory cleared his throat. Seth looked up and got to his feet. "Kim." His voice was a rich, smooth baritone. He grasped her hand and held on just a little too tight, for just a little too long. The back of her neck prickled, but she pushed the uneasy feeling away.

"Nice to meet you."

He smiled and she thought of a wolf.

They sat and she finally looked around. The restaurant was modern, with a koi pond in the middle of the room and tanks with exotic fish dividing the dining room from the kitchen. The tables and chairs were black, sleek, and minimalist. She felt out of place and a little unsettled by Seth's constant glances.

A waitress handed them black folders and walked away. Kim would have liked to at least order a drink.

"Get whatever you like," Seth said. "I have a feeling you'll be worth the expense."

Her skin crawled.

Rory laughed. "We know you are. We've seen your work."

Kim tried to keep her eyes from bugging out of her head at the prices on the menu. Jared was unable to. "Holy crap," he whispered to her. "Thirty-two dollars for a burger?"

She patted his leg.

Seth smirked at Jared. "We don't mind paying for what we want here on the left coast."

They finally placed their order.

Kim finished with, "And ice water, please." She was parched.

Seth touched the waitress's arm. She didn't seem to have any reaction to the gesture at all. "No water. We'll have the Screaming Eagle Cabernet Sauvignon."

"I'll still have the water. Thank you." She wasn't much of a wine drinker as it was, and she certainly wasn't going to drink alcohol without any water, even if she wasn't ridiculously thirsty.

Seth's eyebrows twitched, but he leaned back without further comment.

Jared ordered a burger – no fries – and a water.

Rory gave him a smile. "You don't have to worry about the price, buddy. If you want fries and a soda, knock yourself out."

In the end, Jared ordered a soda but couldn't bring himself to get the twelve-dollar fries.

"So," Rory began, "as I mentioned, we're really impressed with your work. Your channel is really successful, and we think you'd be a great fit with the Home Network."

Seth interrupted. "We don't have to jump right to business."

"That's why she's here," Rory answered. "She'd probably like some of the big picture details up-front. Right, Kim?"

"Yes, please." She was eternally grateful Rory was here. He was warm and friendly, with zero creepy vibes. She could absolutely see working with him. Seth… not so much. Hopefully he was one of those people who would fade into the background and she wouldn't have to deal with him again.

Rory continued. "We were particularly impressed with the brand-new episodes that included guests. I know it's not something you do regularly for your channel, but it did give us a good idea of how you'd interact with the guests we'd be lining up. You were very natural, and did a great job of keeping them on task and moving the project along. Now we did notice those episodes were a little bit longer, so it's probably something you'll need more practice with, but overall, it was great."

Kim warmed at the praise. "Thanks. I'm always afraid of offending someone by keeping them moving, especially since it's just my channel, it's not like I have bosses to answer to or anything."

Their food came. Their tiny food. Tiny expensive food. Kim eyed the chicken breast she'd ordered. No way that was from a full-grown chicken. A full-grown cockatiel, maybe. Whatever. She'd order room service when they got back to the hotel.

Seth poured her too much wine. She took a polite sip, then set the glass back down and drank more water. No way she was drinking a bunch of wine on an empty stomach, and the sad excuse for a meal in front of her wouldn't absorb any of it at all. No wonder everyone out here was skinny. And never smiled. She was having a hard time smiling, too, after traveling all day and then being starved.

Rory talked a little more about their vision for the web channel as they ate. Seth didn't say much, just sat there and stared at her chest. Kim nearly choked on her water as her tired brain joked *he's probably never seen a set of real boobs before.*

She covered up her amusement with a cough.

Jared leaned over. "Can I go look at the fish for a minute?"

"Sure." The wall of tanks wasn't too far away, and there were no customers at the tables that he would be bothering.

Rory set his napkin on the table. "I'm going to the men's room. I'll be back."

Kim nodded and picked up her water glass, as though it would be some kind of buffer between her and Seth.

He took a long sip of his wine, watching her over the rim of his glass, then set it down. "Kim." He leaned forward, putting his forearms on the table.

She leaned back in her chair, putting her empty hand in her lap and sipping her water just to have something to do with her other hand.

"When Rory showed me your videos, I have to say, I wasn't impressed at first. But the more I watched, the more interested I became. You've got a good presence in front of the camera, even with the caliber of equipment you must have."

Gee, thanks.

"I'm still not a hundred percent sold on you being the host for the entire channel. It's a big job, and whoever gets the job has to be intelligent, knowledgeable about everything their guests will be bringing to the table, and… friendly." He leaned forward a little more. "We know you're intelligent." His voice dropped. "And knowledgeable. I'm curious, though, about how friendly you are."

Kim swallowed hard and set her water glass down.

His hand shot over and his fingers brushed hers. "You see, Kim, the friendlier you are, the further you'll go."

Farther. At least she managed to only correct his grammar inside her head. She said nothing out loud.

"I'm sure you understand what I'm trying to get across.

Stop by my office tomorrow during your studio tour. We'll find something for the kid to do so you and I can talk."

Her skin crawled so much it felt like there were spiders in the back of her dress. Apparently, she was doing a decent job of keeping her feelings off her face because Seth was still leering.

"They have neon green fish in there. I bet they glow in the dark. Come look." Jared's voice startled her.

She managed to smile up at him. "I'll look when we're heading out."

He dropped back into his chair just as Rory returned to the table.

Kim wondered if he knew what Seth was up to and had given him some privacy, or if he actually had to use the restroom. If he knew, it was disappointing. He didn't seem to notice any lingering tension as he handed the server a credit card, then signed the slip when she came back.

"It's been a long day for you guys, so we'll have the limo take you back to your hotel." He handed Kim a business card. "If you need anything, give me a call, day or night."

She studied his face for any underlying proposition but found none. Had Seth spoken the same exact words… gross. More crawling skin. But Rory seemed sincere enough. She supposed time would tell.

On the way out of the restaurant, Rory held the door, and as she walked past, he lightly put his hand on the middle of her back. Again, she couldn't find any underlying creepiness. He probably shouldn't touch her, but it seemed more of a gentlemanly thing to do, coming from him.

At the limo, Seth held out his hand to shake hers. "I look forward to meeting with you tomorrow, Kim."

Reluctantly, she shook his hand.

Rory raised an eyebrow. "I didn't think you were sitting in on the executive meeting tomorrow, Seth."

Relief flooded Kim. So Rory wasn't aware. Good. She didn't feel quite so much like a naïve backwoods hick.

Seth shrugged. "I just have a few questions, since I'm on the hiring committee. It won't take long."

A confused look crossed Rory's face. "Okay. Well. Anyway, you guys get some rest and Jasmyn will be by to get you in the morning. Was she helpful?"

"She was great," Kim said, then wondered if Jasmyn-with-a-y had had to sleep with Seth to get her job. "Very helpful."

"Good." He gestured to the open limo door. "We'll see you in the morning."

When they were inside, Rory gave them a warm smile and closed the door.

Only after they pulled away from the curb and were moving down the street did Kim relax.

"What's wrong?" Jared was studying her face.

She forced a smile for a moment, then let it drop.

"Did that creepy Seth guy say something to you?"

Perceptive kid. "Yeah."

Scowling, Jared shook his head. "He looks like one of those pervy creepers they catch in sting operations."

She had to laugh. "I don't know about all that, but yeah, he made me uncomfortable."

Jared narrowed his eyes. "A feeling, or did he do something? When I came back from the fish tank, you looked upset."

"Okay, Dr. Phil, he said something, but of course it could be construed as perfectly innocent."

"What did he say?"

"That the 'friendlier' I am," she made air quotes around the word, "the farther I'll get with this network."

He made a face. "That's gross. What are you going to do?"

"I guess I'll go on the tour tomorrow and see how it goes. I am *not* going to his office alone, and if it means someone else gets the job, so be it."

"Isn't that illegal?"

"Sure, if you can prove it."

Jared turned and looked out the window, disappointment evident on his face. "We should have just gone to Florida."

She reached over and squeezed his hand. "Hopefully it's just one creepy guy and it doesn't ruin our trip."

She knew he wasn't convinced, but he didn't argue. They rode to the hotel in silence. Back inside, in the elevator, Kim's stomach rumbled. "I'm ordering room service."

"Yes, please." Jared sounded desperate. "That burger wasn't enough to feed a mouse. And I'm not sure it was real meat."

In their suite, she found the room service menu, placed their order, then changed into yoga pants and a t-shirt. Food, then sleep.

As they were eating, Jared said, "What are you going to tell Nate?"

"Just the basics. I'm not going to get him upset."

"You're not telling him?"

"I'm not telling him every little detail, but yes, I'm telling him the guy was a creep." She yawned. "I'm not going to hide anything from him, but it's not fair to make him want to come punch the guy when he can't do anything about it, know what I mean?"

"Yeah. As long as you're honest, though."

She stared at him for a long moment. "What's up? Why are you so adamant about me talking to Nate about this?"

He blinked rapidly. "My mom lied to my dad a lot. About guys. Not just her, him, too. They had so many secrets. Maybe if they hadn't both lied so much and hid so much..." Wiping his eyes, he took a shaky breath. "I want you and Nate to be okay."

Kim appreciated his honesty to her core. Even more, she appreciated that he felt safe enough to talk to her about this. "Nate and I have our issues, mostly this long-distance thing, but we've been open and honest with each other about everything. That's not going to change, okay? And I promise I'm going to tell him about Seth."

Jared nodded. "I'm going to bed. Do you care if I have the TV on?"

"As long as I don't hear it." Kim stood up and pulled him into a hug. "I love you. And I'm glad you're here with me."

"Love you too."

She turned off the lights and went into her bedroom and debated how much to tell Nate, then tried to calculate the new time difference between them. Her tired brain refused to cooperate, so she simply went to sleep.

Chapter Fifty

Nate was glad to leave Jordan. It was a beautiful country, but he was tired of the rogue grains of sand under his prosthetic chest. He checked into his hotel in Puerto Rico and dropped his bag on the floor, then glumly stared out the window at the picture-perfect view. He didn't want to be in gorgeous Puerto Rico. He wanted to be in gorgeous Key West, with Kim beside him, sipping a fruity drink and making out like teenagers after sending Jared off to bed. Or even better, gorgeous Hickory Hollow. Home.

Yanking the curtain shut with a sigh, he grumbled, "Can't always get what you want."

The Rolling Stones melody popped up and firmly dug into his brain, the line playing over and over and over until he was not only grumpy, he was downright pissed and wanted to claw the song out of his head.

He pulled on a pair of shorts and a t-shirt and went out for a run along the beach. The resort area they were in was entirely reserved for the show, which was nice. No worries about fans or tourists.

After his run, he went back to his room and showered, then met Dennis for lunch.

"You glad you're staying on?"

Nate took a huge bite of his sandwich and nodded. "Yeah. I think it's the right call."

"I got some more news for you." Dennis looked like the cat that swallowed the canary. He leaned in and lowered his voice. "This is top secret. You can't tell *anybody*."

Swallowing, he looked over at Dennis. He didn't want any more news. "You want me to pinky swear? What?"

"There's going to be a spinoff."

"That rumor has been going around for a year."

"Yeah, but it was just a rumor. Now it's not a rumor. It's a fact."

"Okay." Nate was certain he didn't like where this was going.

"Casting will be done immediately after *Daystar Rising* wraps. It's going to be a prequel, and here's the thing. One of the main characters is Qaaxag's grandfather in his prime."

The sandwich soured in his belly. "And?"

"And since Qaaxag is the spitting image of his grandfather, it makes a lot of sense for you to play him. And you already know the language. It's a done deal as soon as you say yes."

Nate pushed the empty plate away and took a long drink. He wasn't much of a day drinker, but right now he could use something a little stronger than tea. "I'm not saying yes right now. If they're not even casting yet, let's just get through the end of this and go from there." He hoped Dennis wouldn't push.

"Sure, sure. I'll send everything over to Jerry anyway."

"Yeah. Do that." Nate was anxious to be done with *Daystar Rising*. Even after filming wrapped, there would be events and cons and late-night television appearances, interviews and awards shows... the mere thought was exhausting.

"It'll be great for you, too. Your per-episode rate will make this look like peanuts. You can buy a mansion in Malibu and still vacation in that little hick town you're so fond of."

Nate forced a laugh and hoped it didn't sound too fake. "Sounds great. We'll talk about it later."

Dennis stood and clapped his shoulder as he walked past. "Enjoy your day off."

It always came down to money. Dennis couldn't understand that it didn't motivate Nate anymore. He already had more money than he could spend in four lifetimes. He'd paid off his mom's house, bought her and Ron cars, invested heavily into his retirement plan, bought some real estate, donated a small fortune to various causes... it was almost obscene how much money he had. It could do things to a person. Change them. He made sure to always be conscious of that fact.

Chapter Fifty-One

"I don't know, maybe I was imagining it." Kim was sure she hadn't, but the words came out anyway.

Tara's huff of impatience underscored the ridiculousness of her words.

"Okay, I know." She pulled her clothes out of the suitcase and put the phone on speaker as she brushed her hair.

"Even if you're exaggerating, which I know you're not, and even if he's completely innocent and just comes across as a creep, you have to listen to your gut. Do not, under any circumstances, meet with him alone."

"I won't."

"Sadie says hi."

Kim laughed. "Does she?"

"Okay, she's still mad and only comes out from under the bed to eat and use the litterbox, but she's doing fine. How's Jared?"

"Good. Great. He actually picked up a vibe from Seth, too."

"There you have it then. Don't second guess your instincts. God gave them to us for a reason."

"Yes, ma'am."

"Women have been conditioned for far too long to ignore their gut feelings."

"I know."

"I'm only lecturing because I love you and I don't want anything to happen to you."

Kim smiled against the phone. "I know. And I love you, too. I'll be careful. I can't imagine we'll be anywhere sketchy, and I'm not going to his office, even if that means they put me on a plane back home."

"Good. How's Nate?"

"I haven't talked to him for a couple of days. We've texted but haven't been able to line up our schedules enough for a call."

"That sucks."

"The whole long-distance thing sucks."

"Is he worth it?"

A smile spread across her face. "Definitely."

Someone squalled in the background. "Never fails. My butt hits the comfy chair and everything goes to crap." Tara sighed. "I suppose I should go make sure no one's being murdered."

"Good luck. I'll keep you posted on the Seth situation."

After they ended the call, Kim put on her makeup and got dressed in one of her favorite businessy outfits, a medium-slate-gray suit with subtle pinstripes with a white shirt. Black heels, not too high, and she was done.

Jared was already in the living room, dressed in nice dark jeans and a polo shirt.

Kim did a double-take. "You look great."

Shrugging, Jared flipped his head, sending his hair out of his face for a second.

"Yeah, well, don't expect it all the time," He grumbled, but Kim could tell he was pleased.

"You got it."

They rode the elevator down to the hotel restaurant and had breakfast. When they were finished, they waited in the lobby for Jasmyn-with-a-y.

She arrived, perky as ever, chattering as she led them to the waiting limo.

Kim could barely concentrate on what she was saying. Instead, her mind decided to play through a million scenarios, ranging from awful encounters with Seth all the way to a job offer on the spot, with a sweet seven-figure salary.

When the limo pulled into the studio parking lot, she was entertaining thoughts of Seth being fired in a blaze of glory as she outed him in front of a warehouse full of people.

Reality was far less dramatic. Rory met them as they entered the building, then introduced her to everyone they came across. The names and faces blended together.

"Here's the set we use for the holiday card extravaganza." Rory led them into three-quarters of a room, set up with long tables and chairs in a classroom style. The fourth wall was missing, allowing cameras and crew to film the card classes. A large, pristine, white counter at the front of the room was where the host stood and demonstrated the steps.

Another set was made up like a cozy dining room, another like a homey living room, and of course, there were several kitchens in different styles.

"So everyone works from here?"

"For all the live studio shows, yes. For the web channel, the bulk of the shows will be done on location and remoted in."

"And the hosting?"

"We're still trying to figure out the logistics. And we want input. It could be a matter of relocating you, or it could be a matter of us coming out and setting up a studio in your home you'd use. We'd control the cameras and the feed from here."

"Wow."

Rory grinned. "Isn't technology great?"

She liked the idea of working from home but didn't love the idea of having cameras everywhere that were operated by someone else. "It is. How would that work, hosting remotely? Since I wouldn't be with the guests or anything?"

"Basically, you'd get information about the upcoming show and we'd shoot the intro. It'd be a lot more scripted than if you were on location. There would be a fair amount of travel to the guests' locations, too."

"Oh. That makes sense." The idea of being scripted made sense, but she loved talking on the fly.

"You'd still have your own show, of course, but we'd tweak the format, have it follow the same format as the other shows so it's all cohesive."

"Yeah, of course." Kim was rethinking the entire situation. "I wouldn't be able to do my own channel anymore, right? I'd be on the Home Network exclusively."

"Yes. Of course, we're hoping your current viewers will migrate over and subscribe to us."

"Wait, subscribe?" This was the first she was hearing about a subscription.

"It's free to the viewer, but they do have to create an account and then subscribe to the individual shows they want to see. Unless they're premium shows. There's a subscription fee for those, of course. Most likely your show would start out on the free level, then bump up to premium depending on viewership."

"Oh." That sounded really slimy. Get people interested, then start making them pay to watch. Wasn't that what advertising was for?

"I know. It's a whole different process than what you're used to. And we're more than willing to listen to your suggestions."

"But you're paying a ton to marketing and social media experts, so my suggestions would be filed appropriately." She softened her words with a smile.

He wasn't put off. "Kim, I understand your hesitation, I really do. We're asking you to be a little fish in a big pond, and right now, you're a big fish in a little pond."

"It's not that little."

"Depends on how you look at it. I'm talking about the niche you've carved out of a giant market. That niche is a small pond right now, but it's growing. The upside is that you're growing with it, doing a great job of staying ahead of the trends and even setting some of the trends. You've got a great eye."

"Thanks. I get what you're saying, and you're right, it's a huge change."

"The upside for you would be that a lot of the administrative work you're doing on your own would be on us, so you'd have more time to produce content."

"What about creative control?"

"You'd have some, of course. We have a calendar of topics you'd have to adhere to, but within that, you'd have a lot of leeway."

"Great." The more he told her about the position, the more the excitement wore off. She'd known working for the network would mean some creative compromises, but it would also give her some stability she was currently lacking.

Unless the network cancels the show or fires you.

"What kind of employment contract will be in place? Or is this strictly at-will?"

"I'll have to check with the HR people, but I'm pretty sure it's at-will. We wouldn't want to lock you into something."

"To be clear, you want me to close down my channel, migrate my viewers, and help brand the channel without any sort of guarantee or safety net?"

Rory held up a hand. "Like I said, I'm not the one to talk about the contracts. I'm just making assumptions. I could be way off base. Can we save those questions for later? I'm not shutting you down at all, I just don't want to give you any misinformation."

She didn't feel like he was being deceptive or shady, so she backed down a bit. "I'm not trying to be difficult. I need to know what I'm getting into."

"Of course." He gave her a sidelong look. "Nobody is trying to cheat you. I'm really sorry if it sounded that way."

Once again, she felt he was being genuine. "Not at all. But the only person here looking out for my best interests is me."

"Understood."

They left the warehouse-sized room where the sets were and went down a hallway with several doors. Rory pointed them out as they passed. "Greenroom for guests, break room for employees, prop storage, equipment storage…"

Jared spoke up. "This place is huge."

Rory nodded at him. "We thought so, too, when we moved in. Until we built the sets and got all the stuff moved in. We could use another five thousand square feet."

"What happens if you run out of room?"

"Smaller sets, more shows done on location, more shows done remotely. We're not at that point yet, but we always keep an ear out for places that might be coming up for lease."

Kim zoned out as Jared and Rory talked about the building. She was tired, and getting hungry. Her stomach didn't care about the time difference.

They turned another corner and Kim sucked in a breath. Seth strode toward them. Kim waited a beat, thinking maybe her creepy feeling from the night before was off base or exaggerated. He smiled and reached out to shake her hand.

It wasn't.

His finger brushed the underside of her wrist, then trailed to her palm.

She yanked her hand back and briefly entertained the idea of slapping him across the face. She couldn't remember the last time she'd disliked someone so intensely.

Jared subtly inched closer to her.

"Do you have a few minutes?" Seth asked her.

"Um…"

Rory jumped in. "Not now. We were just heading out to lunch."

Kim and Jared exchanged a glance.

"Oh." Seth's demeanor shifted ever so slightly. "See me when you get back." He turned and walked away, his shoes clicking on the tile as he went.

Rory ushered us down the opposite hallway and out a heavy door. The bright sunlight hurt Kim's eyes as she squinted against it.

"Is there something I should know?" Rory asked.

Kim looked at him. "What do you mean?"

"I'm sensing some kind of tension around Seth."

Jared blurted, "He's a creep."

Rory's expression didn't change.

Kim said, "You don't look surprised."

"We should get lunch." Rory took a few steps away, giving his attention to his phone.

Jared looked up at her, his expression worried. "Sorry. I shouldn't have said that."

Kim smiled at the earnest expression on Jared's face. "It's fine. It's the truth."

"Yeah, but I don't want to mess up your chances with this job."

"No, really, it's fine. If being honest is something they can't handle, that's a problem."

He didn't look convinced.

A minute later, Jasmyn-with-a-y bounced through the door and met them, just as the limo rolled up. She had a manila folder. "Here you are, Mr. Anderson."

"Thanks." Rory took the folder, then opened the door to the limo and let them all in.

At the restaurant, a much more low-key, less pretentious place this time, Rory placed the folder on the table. After they'd ordered, he gave her another smile and slid the folder across the table. "Some details I think you'll be interested in."

Before she could open the folder, the waitress set their drinks down. She took a sip of water and opened the folder. Glancing over to Rory's smiling face, she returned his smile, then kept her expression neutral as her eyes scanned the pages.

Chapter Fifty-Two

Nate finished his room service dinner and, avoiding everyone, found a spot on the beach to watch the sun go down. Leaning back in one of the resort's beach chairs, he tried to relax. One by one, stars popped out as the sun slid into the water, pulling the light with it. A breeze kicked up, ruffling his shirt.

The phone he'd almost left in his room vibrated in his pocket. With an annoyed huff, he pulled it out. His annoyance vanished.

"Hey!"

"Hey yourself. How's Puerto Rico?" Kim's voice was exactly what he needed to hear right now.

"Warm. The weather's perfect. Everybody's here, so we're going to start shooting tomorrow instead of waiting until the twenty-sixth."

"That's great. Does it mean you'll get home a few days earlier?"

"Yes. I'll be home in two weeks, then heading out west. Only for a day or two, though."

"Better than nothing. I miss your face."

He smiled into the phone. "How's Jared? How's California?"

"Jared is fantastic. He's loving this ridiculous suite we have. Right now he's poring over the room service menu."

"I'll text him after we hang up. Or call him, do you think he'd like that?"

"He would *love* that."

Nate heard her voice hitch. Apparently he'd said the right thing. Yay, him. "And California?"

"It's pretty. Everything and everyone is pretty. I almost feel like I'm in that old episode of the Twilight Zone where the couple wakes up in a town and everything's a façade." She sighed. "That sounds awful. It's not awful here. It's nice. The weather is spectacular. Everything's convenient."

He could picture her squinting toward the sky as she tried to come up with positive things to say. "And the network?"

"It's been disappointing."

He hadn't expected to hear that. "Oh, no. Why?"

"I've dreamed of having a show on the Home Network forever. For *ever*. And this whole thing just seemed so perfect. Serendipity. Meeting Lainey at the brewery tour, her brother liking my channel, the timing being perfect for their web channel launch... I had such high hopes. Like I'd already decided this was the way to go and all I had to do was get the details." She sighed again.

Something splashed out in the water. Nate watched the waves overtake the ripples on the surface. "And?"

"And then I got here. Everything looks great. They set us up in this incredible suite, drive us around in a stretch limo, take us for expensive food... but when we started talking about the details, they want a lot more creative control than I'm willing to give up. As in, *all* of it. They pick the topics, the guests, the projects, everything. The hosting stuff would be totally scripted, and even my show would have a scripted intro and signoff and have to follow a loose script. On top of that, I can't showcase any products unless they're on an approved list of sponsors. In fact, I can't even *use* any tools and products on the show unless they've been approved."

He wasn't surprised. "Sorry, babe."

"I get they want continuity and cohesiveness, but it's too much. Then we've got Seth the Creep, who would be overseeing the channel, and on top of that, I saw what my budget and salary would be."

"Wait, who's Seth?"

"Ugh. He's a creep. Of course he hasn't said or done anything that would sound bad, but he gave me this really icky vibe. Like when he shook my hand he held on too long and he told me friendly people go father in this business, but the *way* he said it was just gross."

Unfortunately, Nate was all too familiar with the type. "Yeah, I know a lot of guys like that."

"He wanted me to come to his office for a private meeting, but that's not happening."

"Definitely don't." He sat up straight, knowing exactly what 'come to my office' meant.

"I know."

"What about the salary and budget?" He'd assumed that would be the biggest plus to the position.

She made an annoyed noise. "It's less than what I bring in now through ad revenue and affiliate links and sponsors. A *lot* less."

Nate felt his eyebrows lift. "Really? That surprises me. I would have thought they'd have offered you significantly more than what you're bringing in on your own. Especially with their massive corporate sponsorships."

"That's exactly what I thought, especially since they've got to be dumping thousands of dollars into this interview I'm on. But apparently not. I'm not sure if they're intentionally lowballing me with a number and expecting me to negotiate or what."

"If you want, you can send me the numbers and contracts and I can have Jerry look over them. He owes me plenty of favors."

"I'm not sure there's a lot of point."

"It's up to you."

"I'm pretty sure I'm going to turn them down."

"If you're not totally sure, though, talking to Jerry might be beneficial. I'm not trying to be pushy or obnoxious, but Jerry's one of the best agents in the industry."

"Okay." She still sounded reluctant. "Hang on."

He heard a series of clicks.

A moment later, she said, "There, I emailed it to you."

"Great. I'll call Jerry as soon as we get off the phone."

"Okay."

"Kim? You okay?"

A long sigh filled the phone. "I'm fine. I just had this vision in my head of how this trip was going to go. Don't get me wrong, everyone's been so nice and we're definitely getting the red carpet treatment. I should have had lower expectations, I guess."

"I don't think expecting an income similar to what you're currently making is unrealistic."

"You're right."

"Whoa, say that again."

"Ha, ha, very funny."

He was happy to hear the teasing note in her voice.

"I feel better because I talked to you, but worse because now I miss you even more."

He kept his tone light. "Of course you do. I'm irresistible."

"You mispronounced incorrigible."

Joking. That was even better. He chuckled. "I'll talk to you again soon. And I'll let you know what Jerry has to say."

After they finished and Nate hung up, he logged into his email, forwarded Kim's contract to Jerry, and dialed his number.

"What's up, Golden Boy?"

Nate smiled into the phone. "I just emailed you a contract to glance over. As a favor to me."

"A favor?"

"My girlfriend-" that sounded weird. Good, but weird- "has an offer from the Home Network to host their new web channel. She's not impressed with their contract and I said I'd have you give it a quick look."

Jerry grumbled a little. "You know regular people pay two hundred dollars an hour for me to look over their contracts, right?"

"Regular people don't net you a small fortune in commission."

Laughing, Jerry said, "Got me there. Now let's see... Hmm... yeah, yeah, that's pretty standard... blah blah blah... oh. Wait. Hmm. Well, Nate, if I were your girlfriend's agent, I'd tell her not to sign it. It's mostly boilerplate, but there are a few clauses that I don't like. I'll flag them and email it back so she can take a look. And if she was my client, I'd tell them to either double that pathetic salary or pound sand."

"Perfect. That's what I was thinking, but you're the expert. You can put your time on my tab."

"Speaking of being the expert, I got a message from Dennis." Jerry's voice was hesitant.

"Yeah."

"Something about a *Daystar* spinoff. What's the plan there?"

Nate sighed. "I told him I don't want to talk about it until we're done filming. I played the moody artiste card and said I couldn't bear to think about another role while I'm still playing this one."

A barked laugh filled his ear. "Did that actually work?"

"For now."

"You interested?"

"Not really."

"But you don't want to tell him that until you have to."

"See? I don't just keep you around because you're gorgeous." Jerry was many things, but gorgeous was definitely not one of them.

"Yeah, you do. My brains are just a bonus."

"Don't forget your sparkling personality."

"It's a given."

"Thanks, Jer."

"No problem."

Nate hung up and texted Kim.

> Jerry says salary is a total lowball, some issues in contract. Will email you his notes.

A few minutes later, his phone dinged with an incoming thumbs up emoji.

Followed by a heart.

Shaking his head, he thought maybe he was too old to be this excited about a stupid little heart on his phone. Too mature to respond in kind.

Until he found himself sending a green heart back. And a blue one. Because why not.

Ten minutes later, he was laughing out loud as he and Kim traded emojis, and he knew she was laughing, too.

Chapter Fifty-Three

Kim was still grinning when she turned off the light and pulled the cover up to her chin. One more day in California, then she and Jared would be on a plane heading home. She couldn't wait.

She slept well, waking rested and anxious to get the day over with.

Tara texted her a picture of Sadie curled up in bed with one of the kids. She was happy knowing Sadie was well taken care of, but it made her even more homesick.

Apparently Jared wasn't loving California any more than she was.

"UGH. I thought we were leaving today. We're stuck here a whole other day?"

"Yep. Suck it up, buttercup."

"Bleh. Can't we just get on a plane and go home before they try picking us up?"

She reached over and ruffled his hair. "We'll be home before you know it."

He side-eyed her.

"Okay, fine. But in twenty-four hours, we'll be getting on a plane."

He grinned. "Twenty-three hours and fifty-six minutes."

"But who's counting."

They had breakfast in the hotel, then Jasmyn-with-a-y was meeting them to do some touristy things, like visit Rodeo Drive. Kim thought she should be taking some videos while she was there, but it seemed wrong to be snagging footage for her own channel while she was there on the network's dime.

Punctual and perky as ever, Jasmyn arrived, looking stunning in a white pantsuit that no one should look good in.

"The contracts are back at Rory's office. He knew you'd probably have some tweaks or changes or questions. We'll do the tour, do a little shopping, then head back this way where we'll meet Rory for lunch and then back to the studio to go over the contracts. Sound good?"

"Sounds great."

It wasn't all that great. She had zero interest in the celebrities' mansions, even less interest in shopping for overpriced clothes that were completely impractical for Pennsylvania's weather, and she was tired of the lunches that wouldn't satisfy a bird. It was like being in a different country. Or on a different planet.

The day dragged on, but eventually, they got back to the studio. Jasmyn took Jared to visit a neighboring set. Kim and Rory sat in a small conference room with huge windows that looked out over the city.

"What do you think of California?" he asked.

"It's different. Definitely not home."

He chuckled. "I left Maryland and came out here almost thirty years ago. I go back for holidays and family stuff, but I can't imagine being back east full time."

"It's good that you're at home here."

"What did you think about the contracts?"

She'd read Jerry's email and made notes on the contract. "There were a few things I didn't..." She trailed off. "Look. Rory, I really appreciate you bringing me out here, I do. It's been a really nice trip, and everyone has been great. But the salary offer is so much less than what I'm making now-"

"It is?" Surprise colored his words.

"Significantly."

"We can negotiate the salary, Kim. But I'm guessing that even if you name the number, this isn't going to go my way, is it?"

She let out a long breath. "I'm sorry. I can't tell you how much I appreciate this opportunity."

He gave her a bright smile and reached over to shake her hand. "I'm disappointed, but I respect that you know what you want."

"I'm disappointed, too. Working for the Home Network has been a dream of mine for years. It feels so weird to turn it down."

"Well. Don't lose my number. If you change your mind down the line, please do *not* hesitate to give me a call. And if it's okay with you, I'll keep you in mind for future projects that might be a better fit."

"Thanks."

He stood and led her out of the room. "Jasmyn should be back with Jared any time. Great looking kid, by the way. Think he'd be interested in doing any modeling?"

"I doubt it."

They went to a large, comfortable employee break room. Rory glanced at his phone. "I'll be back in a minute, I have to take this, okay?"

"Sure." Kim sat on a white couch — *white!* — and checked her own phone, then sent Nate a text.

"Well, hello."

The hair on the back of her neck stood up before she looked up. "Seth."

"Having a nice time?"

"Sure."

From this vantage point, she could see that his nostrils were really narrow. They reminded her of the slits snakes breathe through. A forked tongue wouldn't have surprised her much.

"I'm disappointed you didn't make an effort to see me, Kim."

She hated the way he said her name. "I haven't exactly made my own schedule."

"It's a shame. I would have liked to hire you. But since we didn't spend any time together..."

Kim stood. "Save it. I'm not listening to your gross innuendos."

His eyebrows rose, sort of. She hadn't noticed how stiff his forehead was. Did men out here Botox, too? "I have no idea what you mean. Clearly I've made the right decision in not hiring you."

Before she could respond, Rory came back into the room. "Bad news, Seth. Kim declined our offer."

Seth smirked. "I was just telling her she wouldn't be a good fit anyway. It's for the best."

Rory looked confused and opened his mouth to speak just as Jasmyn and Jared came into the room. Perky Jasmyn with her gorgeous smile said, "This evening the plans are all up to you. Dinner wherever you want, and then we can check out any local hotspots you'd like."

Kim looked at Jared, who was chewing the inside of his lip.

"Actually, if no one minds, I think we'd like to just go back to the hotel, get room service, and relax."

Jasmyn blinked a few times. Clearly they were not the typical guests. "Are you sure? We have plenty of room in the budget."

"I'm sure."

"Is there anything else I can do for you?" She seemed slightly panicked.

"Not at all. You've been wonderful." Kim threw her a bone. "I'm sure it's just the time difference. Jet lag."

"Ooooh, right." She perked back up and gestured to the doorway. "Then we'll get you back to your hotel. Have your accommodations been to your liking? Anything you would suggest for improvement?" She peppered them with questions as they walked to the exit.

"Nothing at all. It's been wonderful."

Crossing the parking lot the waiting limo, Kim wished the driver could just take them to the airport now.

"If you change your mind and want to go anywhere, please call me. We have use of this car until midnight."

Midnight? Gah. Kim felt old. Midnight was for New Year's Eve and little else. "Thanks."

"Tomorrow, the car will pick you up at seven to get you to the airport. I hope that's not too early."

"Nope, that's perfect."

Jasmyn rode with them to the hotel, chattering with Jared while Kim stared out the window.

After dinner and an evening spent packing and watching old reruns, Kim settled into bed. The ridiculously high thread-count Egyptian cotton sheets were nice. The massive pillows were great – she'd be buying some king-sized pillows when she got home. The comforter probably cost more than her first car. But she couldn't wait to get back home to her own bed, where Sadie would curl up beside her head and purr.

• • •

Morning found her jittery. She donned yoga pants and a t-shirt she'd "borrowed" from Nate. Hair up in a ponytail, no makeup, fresh novel in her carry-on, sandals on her feet, and she was ready to go.

She and Jared double checked they hadn't left anything behind, checked out of their room, got breakfast in the hotel, and practically leaped into the limo.

A few hours later, they were airborne after only a ten minute delay. Kim watched Jared as he watched out the window, then lost herself in the novel until they landed back in Pennsylvania.

It was good to be home.

Chapter Fifty-Four

The days stretched into forever, as far as Nate was concerned. It had taken two weeks, but he was finally on a plane, landing in Florida for a layover before heading home to Pennsylvania. He'd insisted on flying home before going to California, and he was so close he could taste it.

His leg jittered with anticipation until he boarded the plane. From there, he stared out the window, willing the plane to move, move, move, as if he could get it to take off with sheer will. Drumming his fingers on his leg, the plane finally started to roll, then, after another eternity, lifted into the sky, heading north, heading for home.

Heading for Kim.

And for Jared. He missed that boy almost as much as he missed his girl.

The miles sped by under the belly of the plane, but not fast enough. When they finally landed, Nate actually considered abandoning his carry-on bag just to get off the plane. Instead, he waited patiently while his seatmates filed out, helped pull their bags out of the overhead compartment, and then tried not to run from the gate.

People seemed to be deliberate obstacles in his path, pulling their bags, talking and spreading out across the hallway, their laughter drowning out the sounds of the cash registers clicking and beeping in the tiny stores and fast-food joints lining the way.

Oncoming traffic slowed, so he dashed out around the group in front of him and jogged toward the lobby.

He spied the top of Jared's head over the flow of people, his eyes frantically searching for Kim.

There she was.

Beside Jared, she gripped his arm to steady herself as she teetered on her tiptoes, searching the crowd for him.

He'd only half-raised his arm when she spotted him, her "Oh!" loud and clear through the noise of everyone else. As soon as he cleared the secure area, she ran to him. He dropped his bag on the floor and held out his arms.

Kim launched herself at him, and he caught her, squeezing her tight against him, never wanting to let her go.

A moment later, he had no idea how long, Jared came alongside them, and he reached out to pull him in. The kid might be a tough teenager, but he hugged Nate just as hard.

He pulled back a little bit, wanting to see Kim's face. "Hi."

Tears glistened in her eyes. "Hi," she whispered back.

Jared stepped back and cleared his throat. "We, um, should get your suitcase?"

Nate nodded, not trusting himself to speak. He bent and scooped his backpack off the floor, slung it over his shoulder, and only let go of Kim long enough to follow her down the escalator to the baggage claim area.

Waiting for his suitcase to ride the conveyor around the carousel, he had one arm around Kim, one around Jared, and leaned his head down to rest on top of Kim's head. He breathed in her fruity shampoo.

"There it is." He reluctantly let go to grab his suitcase. "Okay, shall we?"

Kim nodded. "We're up in the parking garage, so we have to go over here."

He followed her, one hand on his suitcase, one on her back. "How's school? Did you get everything turned in?"

"Yeah, I'm officially done for the summer. Well, except for the reading list."

"That's great. Are you going to do the same schooling for next year?"

"I hope so. It was a lot better. More interesting, too, because I got to pick different things to study."

"Awesome."

Kim agreed. "It was a much better end to the year than it would have been."

"You'll have to send Tara flowers," Nate joked.

"That's brilliant. I'm going to do that."

They exited to the parking garage. Kim hit a button on her keychain to open the hatch of her SUV. Nate put his suitcase in and closed it, then got in the passenger seat.

On the drive home, Kim kept reaching over and touching his hand. "Are you hungry? Did you want to stop somewhere and get something?"

"No, I just want to get home." It was already getting dark, and he didn't want to take the time to sit down somewhere and eat.

"I made cinnamon rolls."

Jared piped in from the back seat. "And a cake, and a giant thing of lasagna and a big salad and a pudding dessert."

Nate laughed. "Nerves?"

"What gave it away?" She grinned at him, then turned her attention back to the road.

He loved that she kept reaching over to touch him, and he hated that he'd be leaving again in thirty-six hours.

Chapter Fifty-Five

After they'd eaten, Jared weaseled out of dish duty under the guise of giving them some time alone.

Kim put the last of the dirty silverware in the dishwasher and turned around. Her heart skipped a beat as Nate, without a word, backed her into the counter and kissed her. Melting into him, her arms found their way around his back.

Too soon, he pulled back. "What time should I come over in the morning?"

"Seven? Is that too early? We can go get breakfast at Sonny's."

His smile went straight to her heart. And her belly. He kissed her again.

"I'll be over at six thirty."

"Okay."

He kissed her again.

"I'm gonna go."

"Okay."

He didn't make a move to leave. Instead, he kissed her again.

"Any minute now."

She laughed softly against his mouth.

"Am I leaving yet?"

"Nope."

He kissed her again. "Now?"

"I don't think so."

He ran his hands down her arms. "I think I figured out the problem."

"What?"

"You're not letting go."

She kissed him again. "Oops."

His fingers laced with hers, behind his back. "I'm practically a hostage."

"Huh-uh. You're free to go anytime."

He kissed her again. "I don't want to."

"Stockholm?"

It was his turn to laugh. "Could be." He put his arms back around her and held her tight as he kissed her.

Finally, she pushed him away. "Go now or you won't get any sleep."

He raised an eyebrow, grinned, then took a step back. "Six thirty."

"On the dot."

Nate eventually left, and she watched him cross the lawn to his own house. She practically ran up the stairs and yanked her pajamas on, anxious to get to sleep. The sooner she went to sleep, the sooner she'd wake up, the sooner it would be seven o'clock and she'd have Nate next to her. For the whole day.

She'd just dozed off around ten thirty when a loud knock on the front door jolted her awake. Laying still for a moment, trying to determine if the sound was real or part of a vivid dream, it came again.

Grabbing her phone, not that it would offer much protection, she hurried to the hallway, where Jared stood, his hair poking out in every direction, his eyes wide with fear.

"Stay up here."

"Yeah, right." He followed her down the stairs.

Kim flipped on the porch light and took advantage of the blinding light to peek out the window and see who was disturbing them.

"Who is it?" Jared stage whispered from behind her shoulder.

Her heart dropped. "My parents."

"What? What do they want?" His voice was tinged with fear and anger.

She said, "You can go upstairs if you want," knowing he wouldn't.

Slipping on her shoes, she braced her foot against the door as she pulled it open just enough to talk. "What is going on?"

Her mother's already-red face crumpled. It looked like she'd been crying for a while. "I'm so sorry," she sobbed, her hands gripping the edge of the screen door.

Kim looked to her father, who wasn't crying, but looked just as upset as her mother. His voice was raspy. "Can we… may we come in?"

"No." She reached one arm behind herself, placing a protective hand on Jared's arm.

"We came to… we're so sorry." His voice broke.

Kim's knees shook. She couldn't remember ever seeing her parents so upset. "Jared, stay inside." Regardless, protecting Jared was her first priority. She slid through the door and motioned to the bench on the front porch.

Light across the way caught her eye. Nate's bedroom window was illuminated. The noise had probably woken him up. She wasn't sure if he was looking, but she gave a little wave anyway to let him know she was okay.

Her parents sat on the bench, Keith's arm around Mary-Ann's shoulders. He cleared his throat. "Kimberly. I know we can't make up for... for what we did. We only... we were trying to do what... what was best for Jared."

She crossed her arms. "You're going to need to do better than that."

He cleared his throat again. "I screwed up, Kimmy. Everything I found was wrong." A tear escaped his eye and rolled down his cheek.

Kim hugged her arms together, freaked out. She'd seen her father cry exactly one time in her entire life, and that was when her sister died. This had to be bad. Very, very bad. "I don't understand."

MaryAnn sobbed again and pressed her face into Keith's shoulder. "We ran a background check on your new friend. We found all sorts of things."

Keith picked up where she left off. "Stalking, drugs, theft..."

Using one of her father's favorite interrogation techniques, Kim waited, silent.

He pulled in a long breath and let it out slowly. "I should have gone deeper before we came over. But I felt like we had to act." His chin trembled. "When I did – dig deeper – I found out he was the victim, and that the drug charges and stealing belonged to his father."

Kim stood, furious and shaking. She screamed, "You're a cop! You know all about doing your due diligence! How many times have you told me to line up all the facts before jumping to conclusions? To never take things at face value? But this? One lousy google search and you come into my home and make demands and accusations and try to disrupt Jared's life?

I'm not some criminal, I'm your daughter, and you didn't even afford me the same courtesy you'd extend to a murder suspect."

He hung his head in shame. "I know."

"You need to leave." The words burned in her throat.

"Can we come over tomorrow? I need to talk about this."

"What *you* need isn't my concern. You can't come over tomorrow, we're spending the day with Nate. Whose history is both perfectly fine and none of your business. I'll call you. Maybe this weekend. *Maybe*."

"Okay."

She'd never seen her father look so small.

"I'm sorry," he whispered.

MaryAnn's wet eyes pleaded with Kim, but she surely knew from experience that the best thing they could do would be to give Kim some space, so she said nothing.

Kim went inside and watched her parents leave.

Jared wrapped his arms around her waist and lay his head on her shoulder.

"Let's get some sleep." She followed him upstairs, then tucked him into bed. "You okay?"

His eyes shone with tears. "I don't know. It's so weird."

Kim brushed his hair off his forehead and placed a kiss there. "I know. We'll talk in the morning."

As she pulled the door shut, Jared said, "Aunt Kim?"

"Yeah?"

"I love you."

"I love you, too."

Chapter Fifty-Six

By morning, Nate had gone through every emotion known to man. He'd heard the pounding on Kim's door the night before and had watched out the window until her parents left and Kim's lights were back out. Exhaustion from traveling all day was the only reason he got any sleep.

In the booth at Sonny's, they waited for their breakfast. Nate put his arm around her and kissed her temple. He felt like he was an inch tall, leaving them again when they could use his support. Instead, he paid for breakfast and drove them home so he could do laundry and pack. Again.

The rest of the day sped past at breakneck speed, and before he knew it, morning had come again and Kim was driving him to the airport.

"Déjà vu," she said as he checked his bag at the ticket counter.

He gave her a half-smile. "At least this time we have a firm end date. And I'll be able to come home in about three weeks for a few days, then we're halfway there."

They walked to security, where Jared hugged him, then stepped back to give them a moment.

Nate kissed her and hated pulling away. "I'll talk to you tonight. And I'll see you soon."

"Be safe." She rose up on her tiptoes and kissed him, then hugged him tight. "Go save the world and fulfill the prophecy."

"You got it."

One more kiss, then he was alone, stuck in another metal tube, hurtling across the country.

In California, Dennis met him at the hotel. "Let's grab dinner and chat."

"Sure."

They went to the hotel restaurant and Dennis went straight to the point. "Are you gonna do the spinoff or not?"

"You said I didn't have to decide right now." This was the last conversation Nate wanted to have.

"Well, things changed. I need an answer."

Nate let out a long breath.

"And before you give me an answer, you should know that these last episodes could be affected."

Nate cocked an eyebrow. "How so?"

Dennis drained his wine, trying to build anticipation. "If you don't want to be a team player, we can use these last few episodes to set up other people who are more cooperative."

"You'll kill off Qaaxag again, and Dahlia fulfills the prophecy."

"Yes." Dennis said the word firmly, like it was a threat.

It was the perfect out. "Do it."

"What?" Dennis sat back abruptly, clearly not expecting Nate to call his bluff.

"Kill him off." Saying it out loud warmed his soul. It was time to lay Qaaxag to rest.

"You can't be serious. You don't really want us to kill you off."

"Not me, Dennis. Qaaxag. A fictional character. Remember, I was almost killed off for real. I know the difference."

"Come on, Nate, work with me here." He clearly had not expected Nate's reaction.

"I'm here, Dennis. Doing my job. Fulfilling my contractual obligation. If you want to get rid of me, you have to pay out the rest of my contract." He'd have to remember to thank Jerry for that little clause.

"You're not thinking clearly, Nate. Most actors would kill for a role like this."

"I'm grateful for the role, but I'm not bending over to thank you for it."

Dennis's eyes hardened. "I can make sure you never get another role."

"Promise?" Nate stood up and walked out of the restaurant, abandoning his untouched meal. For the first time in three months, he felt free.

Ten days later, Qaaxag suffered a spectacular on-screen death. It was the best performance of Nate's life, the kind he'd still talk about when he was in his eighties. Two hours after his makeup was off, he was in a cab, on his way to the airport.

Twelve hours after that, he was exhausted, but adrenaline and happiness kept him awake.

"How much coffee have you had?" his mother asked from the driver's seat.

"A lot. Not enough. Is there a Dunkin' Donuts somewhere so I can get more?"

"No." She patted his hand. "I'm glad you're home. I think you made the right call."

The car slid to a stop in front of Kim's house.

Pattie grinned. "So you don't have to run across the yard like a weirdo."

He leaned over, kissed her cheek, then jumped out of the car. "Love you, Mom. Thanks for the ride. I'll call you tomorrow."

She waved a hand at him, then drove next door to his house.

Nate jogged up to Kim's porch and rapped on the door.

It opened and a second later, Jared nearly knocked him over with a bear hug.

"Who is it?" Kim came from the direction of the kitchen. "Jared, who- Nate!"

She threw her arms around him, her face smooshed into his chest, her floral scent filling his senses. She smelled like home. "What are you doing here? How long are you here?"

"I'm home for good."

Epilogue

Eighteen months later

Kim's sweaty hands shook as she stood between Jared and Nate. She smoothed the front of her dress.

The judge, intimidating in his black robes, tented his fingers. "Young man, are you sure this is what you want?"

"Yes, sir." Jared's voice was a squeak.

"Mr. and Mrs. Sanders, are you sure you want to take on the commitment of raising an almost-sixteen-year-old?" His mouth curled into a smile.

"Yes, sir," they answered in unison.

He picked up a pen, and with a flourish signed the papers that made Jared her son.

Their son.

Kim let out a nervous laugh. Nate's hand trembled on her back.

Keith and MaryAnn sat in the row behind them, beside Pattie and Ron. Isobel and her parents sat in the next row, beside Tara and her crew.

The judge banged his gavel and the room erupted with cheers and laugher and tears and hugs.

When the noise died down, the judge stepped down from the bench and hugged and shook hands with everyone and posed for pictures.

"Best part of my job," Kim overheard him say to Nate.

A moment later, Keith and MaryAnn came over and hugged her. After a long conversation, Kim had forgiven her parents. Their most basic intention was good – to protect Jared. Kim had spelled out some boundaries, something she expected her father to balk at, but Keith easily respected her strength and authority as Jared's guardian. It had taken him a bit longer, but Jared forgave them, too.

As for Nate, he was the best husband in the world. And the best business partner. And the best looking man on the planet, of course.

He used his fame from *Daystar Rising* to help launch their own little web network. Kim hosted her own show and directed two others, while Nate produced them all.

Isobel was finally able to be in Nate's presence without turning beet red, and at some point noticed Jared was a boy. They weren't allowed to officially date, not until they were both sixteen, but they spent a lot of time with each other's families.

Leaving the courthouse, Kim and Nate were the last ones out, holding hands as they followed the group outside.

Jared waited by the car, tugging on the locked door. "Come on, Mom and Dad," he yelled to them.

Kim came to a dead stop and burst into tears. And laughed.

Jared jogged over to make sure she was okay.

There she stood, on the sidewalk of the courthouse, crying and laughing and feeling completely ridiculous but unable to stop. She hugged Jared tight, and Nate wrapped his arms around both of them.

She tried to memorize every detail. The tears and hiccups and laughter and feel of Jared's scratchy suit jacket against her cheek and Nate's strong arms around them both.

Her husband.

Her *son*.

Her family.

It was the single best moment of her life.

Even better than marrying Nate a year earlier. Of course, she'd never say that out loud, even though she knew Nate would absolutely agree.

———

Enjoyed this trip to Hickory Hollow? Keep those warm fuzzy feelings going and dive straight into Book 4 in the Hickory Hollow series, Luck of the Draw.

When Sarah Winchester meets her partner for the town's annual scavenger hunt, her goal is to win the grand prize – not his untouchable heart. The Hickory Hollow Ladies' Society, however, has other plans for Sarah...

Hickory Hollow. Get comfy, stay a while!

You don't want to miss news of upcoming books, events, and behind-the-scenes sneak peeks! Sign up for my newsletter today at carriejacobs.com!